ZANE PR

YOU'RE THE ONE I WANT

Come back 1.50

Dear Reader:

Welcome to the world of Shane Allison, whose debut novel, *You're The One I Want*, will surely create fans for the talented author. His engaging style of writing and storyteller skills will keep readers on task turning pages to the end.

Meet Bree and Tangela, two best friends, who are competing for the same man although Bree is unaware of Tangela's yearnings for her doctor husband, Kashawn. His twin brother, Deanthony, arrives back in town and has his sights set on his brother's wife, Bree. This mix of feening for another one's lover and the attempt to destroy a marriage makes for scandalous drama.

Throw in others such as the twins' Mama Liz and a stripper, Katiesha, who is used as a pawn to make the love triangles even more twisted, and you have a tale of deception and suspense.

As always, thanks for supporting myself and the Strebor Books family. We strive to bring you the most cutting-edge, out-of-the-box material on the market. You can find me on Facebook @AuthorZane or you can email me at zane@eroticanoir.com.

Blessings,

Zane

Publisher
Strebor Books
www.simonandschuster.com

ZANE PRESENTS

YOU'RE THE ONE I WANT

SHANE ALLISON

SBI

STREBOR BOOKS

NEW YORK LONDON TORONTO SYDNEY

Strebor Books
P.O. Box 6505
Largo, MD 20792
http://www.streborbooks.com

© 2016 by Shane Allison

ISBN 978-1-59309-638-0
ISBN 978-1-4767-9826-4 (ebook)
LCCN 2015957699

First Strebor Books trade paperback edition July 2016

Cover design: www.mariondesigns.com
Cover photograph: © Keith Saunders/Keith Saunders Photos

10 9 8 7 6 5 4 3 2 1

Manufactured in the United States of America

For information regarding special discounts for bulk purchases, please contact Simon & Schuster Special Sales at 1-866-506-1949

The Simon & Schuster Speakers Bureau can bring authors to your live event. For more information or to book an event, contact the Simon & Schuster Speakers Bureau at 1-866-248-3049 or visit our website at www.simonspeakers.com.

1

BREE

What the fuck is he doing here?

I thought I was going to lose my shit when I saw Deanthony walk through the door of Mama Liz's house. Deanthony's skin glowed under the living room lights. He was wearing a red durag, a black tank top, and black, baggy jean shorts. A trace of red from his boxers was showing from the waistband. I'm not going to lie, he looked good, but still, what the hell was he doing here? It took everything in me to keep from dropping the cup of punch that Tangela had spiked with vodka when nobody was looking. Suddenly, my heart was pounding like a drum in my chest. I gawked at Deanthony like the devil himself had walked in Mama Liz's house, and as far as I was concerned, the devil was exactly who Deanthony was, a demon spawn. Tangela startled me when she crept up behind me, grazing my arm.

"Girl, did you see who just walked up in here?"

Deanthony looked dead at me as he shook hands, gave dap and half-hugs to friends and family. You would think he was some famous athlete or some shit, the way everybody gathered around him.

"I didn't think he was going to come."

"He looks good," Tangela said. "Damn good."

"You're not helping," I said, annoyed by Tangela stating the obvious.

I watched Kashawn from the kitchen window where he and Tyrique stood on the deck, nursing on beers.

"Hey, baby, you came," Mama Liz shouted, damn near knocking me down to get to her son. She wiped her hands dry from dish water on the apron that was draped around her, and gave Deanthony a big, mama bear hug.

"Hey, Mama. Of course I came. It's only my brother's birthday."

"You look so skinny. What, you don't eat up there in Hollywood Land?"

"I can't believe he's got the balls to show his face here, yet I don't know why I'm surprised."

"You want me to get rid of him?" Tangela asked.

"No, forget it. It's all good. I don't know why I was stupid enough to think that he wouldn't have the guts to show up for Kashawn's birthday party."

Everyone but me was happier than flies on shit to see Deanthony, especially since he didn't come around that much. You would think he had just returned from some space mission from Mars the way everyone was hovered around him like he was some golden child they needed to protect. I noticed Yvonne, Kashawn, and Deanthony's cousin staring at me from across the room. I knew right then and there that she must have had something to do with getting Deanthony to show up at the party, just so she could see my reaction. That nosey bitch needed to get herself some business.

"You're going to be all right, girl?" Tangela asked.

"Shit, girl, you know me. Calm, cool, and collected." I could tell by the look Tangela gave me, she didn't believe a word that tumbled past my lips.

I made my way out to the deck where Kashawn, Tyrique, and friends were talking, drinking, and playing spades. I ran to Kashawn's side like there was some evil thing hungry on my red-bottom, fuchsia Christian Louboutins.

I leaned in and whispered, "Deanthony's here."

Kashawn gawked at me as if I'd just told him I had six weeks to live. "He just arrived. He's in the living room with your mama."

"Where my brother at?" Deanthony hollered.

Always gotta be the ham, I thought.

He stood in the doorway that divided the deck from the house. The rest of the birthday party guests gathered around him like he was Tallahassee royalty.

Kashawn started toward him. I was scared shitless, not sure what Deanthony was going to say or do. My nerves settled when Kashawn greeted Deanthony with a grizzly bear hug of warmth and affection after three years of being away from the family. I couldn't help but wonder what brought Deanthony back to Tallahassee other than to ring in his thirtieth birthday.

"Man, where the hell have you been?"

"Bro, you know how I do. Still out here on this grind."

I nervously sipped spiked fruit punch from my red Dixie cup.

"What's up, Bree?" Deanthony asked, looking at me as if nothing happened.

He wrapped an arm around my waist, hugging me. I could feel his hand on my ass and prayed to God that Kashawn hadn't noticed the advance he made.

"You look good, girl, damn!" he said, shouting loud enough for the whole neighborhood to hear.

My plan was simple: avoid his ass like an STD. I could feel pearls of sweat dripping from the roof of my armpits. I knew damn well that Deanthony didn't have the balls to put what we did on blast at the fish fry birthday party here in front of all his friends and family. I learned the hard way not to put anything past Deanthony's sneaky ass. He might have had Mama Liz, Kashawn, and everybody else fooled, but I knew firsthand what a sinister bastard he could be, especially when he wanted something he couldn't have.

"All right, y'all come on and get it. The food's ready!" Uncle Ray-Ray, Kashawn and Deanthony's uncle, yelled while forking mullet, bream, hushpuppies, and fried oysters in an aluminum pan. The smell of fresh fried fish infiltrated the hot June air. Uncle Ray-Ray was known around Tallahassee for serving up the best of everything when it came down to food. The best fish, the best barbecue, the best banana pudding, the best pork chops, the best chittlins, not to mention being the go-to guy for installing stereo systems.

Everyone started to line up along the table, grabbing paper plates. Tyrique's big ass was the first in line, of course, forking what had to be five pieces of bream and mullet on his plate, followed by a mess of cole slaw and cheese grits. No matter where he was— restaurant, party, fish fry—Tyrique always ate like every meal was his last. I grinned, watching his wife, Ebonya, nudge him, scolding him to save some fish for everyone else. Tyrique had always been kind of this big, dumb jock, teddy bear of a man. Kashawn got him on as an orderly at Tallahassee Memorial Hospital.

"Baby, you hungry? You want me to fix you a plate?" I asked.

"Um, yeah, baby, would you please? You know what I like."

"You still eat them fried oysters like that?" Deanthony asked.

"Hell yeah, with some hot sauce. That ain't nothin' but good eatin'.'"

Kashawn grabbed another beer from the wash basin filled with ice and an assortment of beer and Chek sodas. Deanthony would nonchalantly look off in my direction, smiling, knowing something only he and I knew. If the truth ever came to light, it would kill Kashawn.

After seeing Deanthony, I had lost my appetite. The smell of fish and fried oysters was making me nauseous as I plated the seafood on a paper plate for Kashawn. Shit, I wish I could blame it on fish.

Seeing Deanthony was the real reason behind my queasy stomach. Kashawn and Deanthony sat at one of the patio tables, drinking beer.

"There you go."

"You're not going to eat anything, baby?" Kashawn asked, roping his arm around my waist, resting his hand on my booty.

I looked over at Deanthony and said, "I'm not really hungry." With laughter in those big penny-brown eyes of his, he took another swig from a Corona. "I left my cigarettes in the car. I'll be back."

"You all right?" Kashawn asked.

"Yeah, baby, I'm fine. Stomach bothering me, that's all."

"It's that cheap Winn-Dixie liquor Tangela put in the punch that's got you sick. I told you about drinking that stuff."

"Yeah, I guess." I gave Kashawn a kiss on the forehead. "I'm going to the car to relax."

"Okay. Feel better."

"Thank you, baby."

I ignored Deanthony as I walked off, easing my way through the crowd of guests armed with plates of food.

Tangela made her way over to me, sensing that I was in need of her best friend forever benefits. "Girl, what happened?"

"Come outside. I need a cigarette, bad."

Tangela's black Mustang was parked behind a row of cars in Mama Liz's pine-needle-strewn driveway.

"I got something better than cigs," she said, pulling a plastic sandwich bag of weed out of the glove box.

"Damn, bitch, you ride around with this in your car?"

"No, I just brought it today in case my best friend had to sneak out of her man's birthday party to get away from his brother whom she fucked around with." Tangela laughed, but I didn't find what she said the least bit funny.

"Whatever, bitch. Light that shit up."

Tangela was a slightly plumper version of me with apple butter-brown skin, hazel eyes that made her look like a vampire, and a weave that flowed luxuriously down her back. The low-cut red blouse she wore barely held in her round, cantaloupe breasts she loved showing off every chance she got. Tangela lit the end of the joint and took a couple of puffs and passed it to me.

"Hold on, let me crack the windows," she said. "Mama Liz isn't going to run out here cursing and screaming for smoking weed in her yard, is she?"

"Hell, she would probably join in. Kashawn told me she smokes weed herself. Medicinal marijuana, he said. Something about her bad knees or some shit."

"Yeah, whatever," Tangela said, taking her joint back. "So I saw you over there with Kashawn and Deanthony. I'm surprised you still keeping it together with him being here."

"Shit, barely. If I didn't get away from him, I was going to lose it."

"I thought he was on the grind in L.A., trying to do that acting thing?"

"That's what Kashawn told me. Deanthony said he had too much going on to come home. You saw that I was as surprised as anyone to see him bust up in here like that." When Tangela passed the blunt back to me, I took a long drag, letting the weed infiltrate my lungs.

"Damn, ma, slow down. That's about all I have until I get back to the house."

"Girl, you would think that out of respect for my marriage, he would have stayed away. That's what I get for taking the word of a high-yellow, Denzel Washington wannabe brother like him. Did you see Yvonne looking at me when Deanthony walked in? That busy bitch wanted to see my reaction and I fell right into that shit. I know she's the one who convinced him to come home."

"Bree, come on, now. Yvonne is family."

"Family, hell. She's had it out for me since the day I said, 'I do.'"

"Why would she mess with you like that, though?"

"Because ever since I told the family that I used to strip at Risqué, she hasn't liked me. I can't stand how she prances around here like she shits potpourri."

"She's so damn uppity since she got sanctified," Tangela added.

"And Akaisha at Radiance Salon, who went to Rickard's High School with her, told me she used to spread those hippo thighs for every dick that swung in her face."

Tangela bucked with laughter as she took a toke from the weed. "Damn, girl, you wrong for that."

"I'm just telling you what I heard. I'm sick of her giving me the stink eye every time she sees me. Matter of fact, I'm going to go in here right now and tell her to back the fuck off. I don't care whose first, second, or third cousin she is."

Tangela grabbed my arm as I opened the car door. "The last thing you need to do is go up in there, making a scene at Kashawn's birthday party of all places. Forget her. Leave it alone."

I sat there, feeling the effects from the weed. "Yeah, you right. Forget that heifer. I'm too high anyway."

"What she needs is some dick," Tangela said. "Some big Mandingo to fuck her cross-eyed." Tangela had me laughing my ass off when she said that.

As the two of us continued getting high, Mama Liz peeked her head out of the screen door.

"Oh shit."

"What are y'all doing out here? Come on inside. We're about to cut the cake."

"Okay, Mama Liz, we coming."

She stared at us, puzzled, like she was trying to make out what we were doing. "I mean it. Come on now."

"Are you going back in?" Tangela asked.

"I'm too fucked up and I don't want to go back in there smelling like weed."

"You wanna get out of here?"

"Yeah. Kashawn will understand. I told him that I don't feel good no way. I don't think I can go through the rest of the afternoon having to make idle chatter with Deanthony in there."

Tangela drove me home where we mellowed out to Beyoncé's "Sasha Fierce" CD.

"Damn, ma, you did your thing on the remodeling."

"You like it? You know I love that Afrocentric shit. Kashawn gave me his credit card and told me to have fun. You know, with his long hours at the hospital, he doesn't always have time. I damn near furnished the whole house in a day."

"I like these tables and the sectional. All this must have set y'all back a couple of stacks."

"Girl, you know I don't look at the price tag. If I like it, I get it."

"That painting of you is cute."

"It's all right. The artist is from Atlanta. I think he made me look too old. I want this artist Fullalove to do it."

"Who?"

"Fullalove. He paints these portraits of athletes and rappers. I'm going to New York in November so he can paint me. It'll be a nice Christmas gift for Kashawn." I walked over to the bar in front of the kitchen. "Hey, you want a drink?"

"Yeah, I'll have whatever you're having."

Tangela continued looking around in awe at all the new furniture like she was in a museum while I poured two glasses of Chardonnay.

"So girl, what are you going to do about Deanthony?" she asked as I handed her a glass of wine.

"No clue. I guess this is what they mean by making your bed and lying in it."

"You don't think he will say anything to Kashawn, do you? Came back to clear his conscience?"

"Deanthony doesn't have a conscience. Family or no family, he doesn't care who he hurts. Just like he showed up at the party without any thought for me. The best thing he can do is stay the hell away from me and Kashawn."

"Well, baby girl, you know I got you if you need anything. He'll have to go through me first if he's thinking about messing shit up with you and Kashawn."

"Thanks, Tange, but I don't think he'll be a problem. I plan on staying away from him." I was about to take another swig from my drink when my cell phone rang. I pulled it out of my clutch. I studied the number on the screen. "Oh, this brother's got brass fucking balls, girl."

"Who is it?"

I showed Tangela Deanthony's number on my phone.

"Don't answer it."

Against Tangela's advice, I pressed the green icon on my phone. "Why are you calling me?"

"I told you, didn't I? I told you I was coming back for you."

"Stay the hell away from me, Deanthony."

"Or what?"

"Or I'll make you wish you had." I pressed END CALL before he could utter another syllable.

"What did he say?"

"He ain't here for the cake. I gotta do something, 'cause if I don't, I'm going to lose Kashawn."

2

BREE

Three years seemed like a lifetime ago the night I was unfaithful to Kashawn. It was one of the worst thunderstorms ever that year in August. I was headed home from Cheeks and my legs were killing me after dancing my ass off all night. All I wanted to do was soak in a warm bubble bath, a treat Kashawn often had waiting for me. On my way home in the rain, I caught a flat. It was the front-left tire on the driver's side. The one I had been on Kashawn's bubble butt about changing for months.

"I told him a million times to take the tire off, that I didn't want to be driving down some dark road and I mess around and catch a flat."

I was coming from my girl's Latasha's baby shower. I couldn't really enjoy myself with him blowing up my cell every five minutes.

"What are you doing?"

"The same thing I was doing when you called me ten minutes ago. I'm still at Latasha's."

The only way I was going to have any semblance of fun was if I switched off my phone. When I switched it back on as I was leaving the shower, there were, like, eleven messages in my voicemail. All of them were from Kashawn. If I didn't call him back, I knew he would show up at Latasha's.

"What is it?"

"What were you doing? I tried calling you."

"No shit. I turned my phone off."

"I just wanted to make sure that you were all right."

Checking up on a bitch is more like it.

"I'm fine. You want me to grab you something to eat on my way home?"

"No, I just had a steak. What time will you be home?"

"The baby shower should be over around eight, so I will leave right after."

"Hey, Kashawn!" Latasha's crazy behind yelled in the background.

"Who is that?"

"You don't know Latasha's voice by now?"

"What is this, like, her fifth child? I bet she can't tell you where the baby daddies are if she had a search party."

I snickered into my phone. "Boy, hush. I'll be home in an hour."

"Tell the Human Mattress I said, 'hey.'"

"Bye, fool."

It was pouring down rain and I wasn't about to ruin my new pumps, stepping out there in all that, not to mention the weave I had just spent $300 dollars of good, hard-earned, booty-shaking money on. When I called Kashawn, his phone went straight to voicemail. So he could spend half the night blowing up my phone, but when I called him, his black ass couldn't be bothered. I called again and got the same thing: voicemail. This was him trying to be funny, but I didn't find anything remotely funny being broke down on a flat on the side of the road in pouring rain. I thought about calling Latasha to come and get me, but I didn't want to drag her out in bad weather.

I called Tangela, but as her phone rang, I remembered that she was in Atlantic City with her boy toy of the month. The rain pelted hard against the windshield of my black Range Rover, a gift on my thirty-second birthday from my *dependable* husband. I sat there listening to the rain, contemplating who I could call to get me out of this mess. Deanthony made sense because he had a tow truck back when he worked for Advance Towing. I scrolled through a list of numbers until I got to his and dialed. He picked up, thankfully, after two rings.

"Deanthony, hey, it's Bree."

"What's up, sweetness?"

"Don't start. I'm not in the mood. I caught a flat way out here on Lake Jackson. Can you come pick me up?"

"Where did you say you were at?"

"Lake Jackson. I'm on the side of the road in front of The Vitamin Shoppe."

"Where's Kashawn?"

"He's not picking up the phone. This rain is coming down hard and I'm scared somebody's going to hit me way out here."

"Okay, I'm not that far from you. It shouldn't take me that long to get out there."

"Whatever, just hurry up."

The last person I wanted to call was Deanthony, but since Kashawn had pissed me off for not answering his phone, I didn't have a choice. Three months before that night, Deanthony and I had started fucking around. Kashawn was feeling the stress of working sixteen-hour days at the hospital and I was frustrated from feeling abandoned. A day didn't go by when we weren't fussing about something. Money, getting the cars serviced, starting a family, even sex, the last thing I thought we would ever fight over. I secretly had a crush on Deanthony, attracted to that tough fucker exterior over Kashawn's four-eyed, bookish nerdiness. Kashawn could have gotten Deanthony a job at the hospital, but Deanthony opted out to do grunt, blue-collar work for some tow truck company.

Kashawn and I'd had one of our knock-out drag-outs that night. Instead of going over to Tangela's to vent, I made a detour to Deanthony's. He embodied *fine*, wearing a white tank top that was smudged with grease. The navy Advance Towing jumpsuit he wore hung around his waist, exposing a sliver of ass crack. Deanthony looked like one of those oiled-up models from a skin calendar. He resembled Kashawn slightly. They could have been twins, but the only thing that told them apart was the scar he got from a bar brawl he was in—the fight he wouldn't go into detail for some reason.

"That's the difference between me and my brother. I handle stress a hell of a lot better than him."

I was pissed that he was bad-mouthing his brother, my husband. "Why are you always bumping your gums about Kashawn? You put him down in the dirt every chance you get."

"He thinks he's king shit now that he's some doctor. Medical school changed him, and I wish I could say it was for the better."

"You could have gone to medical school. You're just as smart, and you had the same opportunities, so don't give me any shit about him acting any kind of way. The both of y'all grew up in the same household."

Deanthony took a swig from a bottle of Jack Daniel's. "You sound like my mama."

"Well, I hate to admit it, but maybe she's right. Kashawn offered you a j-o-b at the hospital, but you said you were doing your own thing."

"Well, it wasn't like I had a choice. Daddy saw to that."

"What are you talking about?"

"My *loving* brother didn't tell you? Daddy had his lawyer put a clause in our trusts that the only way that I could get my part of the trust, was if I went to college. He didn't want us to squander the money."

"That's not how Kashawn tells it, Deanthony."

"Bet he doesn't."

I felt a bit sorry for Deanthony and all this sibling rivalry mess that was going on between him and Kashawn. "Give me that. You've had enough to drink. Have you eaten?"

As I set the bottle of JD on the end table next to him, he gently grabbed my wrist and pulled me on top of him. I could feel the thickness of his dick pressing against my right booty cheek.

"Fuck dinner. I want dessert."

Deanthony pushed a hand down into my top, pulling my left breast free. He looked up at me as he started to tickle my nipple with the tip of his tongue. I don't know why, but I didn't stop him. The harder he sucked, the more turned on I became. My pussy was sopping wet. Before I knew anything, my top was bunched around my stomach. I was on my back on Deanthony's leather sofa, getting my pussy eaten by my husband's brother. In my moment of weakness, I didn't think about Kashawn or the damage I was doing to our marriage, not when Deanthony was busy tongue-fucking me. Deanthony was lapping at my juices like they were milk chocolate. Kashawn had cunnilingus skills of his own, but, damn, if eating pussy was a sport, Deanthony would be making millions. He wanted to fuck me that night, but I protested, scared that maybe Kashawn would smell another man's dick on my coochie. But he hadn't so much as tickled me in months, being too tired from the hospital to fuck.

"You can finger-fuck me, but that's it."

"That's what's up," Deanthony said as he slid a finger inside me. He sucked my nipples past his juicy lips as he fingered my pussy. I came three times that night. "Since you're not going to let me fuck, you might as well suck this dick, baby girl."

Deanthony pulled his dick out of the dirty jumpsuit. My jaw dropped at the sight of his dick size, seeing that he and Kashawn weren't identical in the places where it mattered. When it came down to sucking dick, I was a pro. As soon as I threw my lips to his appendage, he found out just how good.

"Fuck yeah, that's right, no hands."

When I felt his hand at the back of my head, I pushed it away. I paid too much for my hair and he wasn't a man worthy of putting his grimy fingers through my locks. I made Deanthony nut all over his carpet. He wanted me to swallow, but I wasn't down with that bullshit. I wish I could say that that was the first and only night we messed around.

It quickly became a once-a-week thing, meeting at the El Camino Motel on Woodville Highway, parking our cars across the street at some old abandoned junkyard so no one would spot them. I wasn't taking any chances of getting caught or seen, always wearing a black trench, shades, and a black cap. I eventually let Deanthony fuck me with that burrito-thick dick of his, being that he was literally begging for my goody. I thought this man was going to rip a bitch in two the first time I let him smash. I liked that Kashawn was nothing like Deanthony. The affair ended about as quickly as it began when my deception caught up with me. We met up every other Thursday night, 6 p.m. as usual. We were ass-naked, about to do the do, when we heard a knock at the door.

"Chill. It's just room service with the champagne."

When Deanthony answered the door, it wasn't some college student wearing a dorky uniform with a tray of chilled champagne.

Yvonne, his busybody of a cousin, took one look at me and said, "Once a ho, always a ho. And you—how could you do this to your brother?"

Yvonne hauled off, Deanthony tailing behind her, begging her not to tell Kashawn about what she saw. I, on the other hand, set a world record in the time it took me to get dressed and get out of there. Now whenever I pass by that hotel, I think about the worst night of my life.

As soon as I got off the phone with Deanthony, Kashawn called. I started not to answer, but there had been enough phone tag that night.

"I'm stuck on the side of the road out here on Lake Jackson with a damn flat from that tire I pleaded with you to change."

"I'll come and get you."

"Forget it. Deanthony's on his way. He should be here in five minutes."

"Well, thank him for me when he gets there."

"All right, I'll see you when you get home."

If I ever get home.

Two minutes after I'd ended the call with Kashawn, Deanthony pulled up behind me. I was officially pissed off with Kashawn. I wanted to break my leopard-print red bottoms off in his ass when I got home. The rain had finally eased up. I rolled down the window when Deanthony approached.

"Yeah, I see where it's flat right here in the front."

Deanthony looked so good, it was enough to make a bitch say *daaaaaaayuuum!* I hadn't seen too much of him since that night at the motel.

"So can you change it off?" I asked as rain water peppered my face.

"If you have a spare, yeah."

"I think so. There should be one under the car."

"Let me check."

"Are you going to be able to change it with me sitting in here?" I yelled.

"I'm not going to be able to change it at all, Bree. There's no spare."

"What? It should be a spare back there."

"It's not under the car where it should be."

It was then that I remembered Kashawn taking the spare a few days earlier. "Kashawn took the damn tire from under there, but he didn't put it back. I'm going to kill your brother when I get home."

"I'll take you and the SUV back to the house."

I was getting soaked. My $300 weave was spent. "Okay, hold on. Let me grab an umbrella."

Deanthony opened the car door, took my hand, and helped me to the tow truck.

My pumps were being done in by all the mud. "Kashawn's butt is grass when I get to the house."

The passenger-side door of the truck squeaked when Deanthony opened it. It looked nasty and I was scared to get in the rust bucket on wheels. I slid in, praying that I wouldn't slip and break my ass while trying to climb in the contraption. The truck reeked of motor oil and buffalo wing sauce, a scent strengthened from the Styrofoam that sat propped on top of the drink coaster. I held a finger under my nose to drown out the smell. I couldn't stand the smell of buffalo wing sauce, not since that time I puked them up one drunken night at The Varsity with Tangela.

I tilted the visor down to take a look at the damage that had been done. My makeup was runny and my weave was frizzed. Deanthony started laughing. "What's so funny?"

"You. You look like a wet cat."

"That's cute. You know, with the crazy night I've had, I'm glad I could amuse you."

"My bad, but I've just never seen you look—"

"Look like what? A hot mess?"

Deanthony sat chuckling with his hand over his mouth in an attempt to keep from laughing.

"So are you going to take me home or sit here laughing at me?"

"Okay, okay. My bad. I've missed you, that's all."

"Don't do this, Deanthony."

"Why won't you return my phone calls?"

"You know why," I said, smearing Passion Plum lipstick across my bottom lip.

"Yvonne isn't going to say anything. She promised."

"You sure about that? 'Cause ever since then, she looks at me like she wants to rip my throat out every time she sees me."

"Don't trip about my nosey cousin. I'll take care of her."

"It's not just that. I'm married to Kashawn. I can't risk him finding out about us."

"Let's get out of here."

"I'm ready to go, but you keep talking my ear off."

"I mean out of Tallahassee. I know some guys who are working in the movie business in L.A., Bree. You should come with me."

"You didn't hear a word I just said, did you? I can't."

"What the hell does Kashawn have that I don't?"

"It's not that, but—"

"Do you love him?"

"What?"

"Answer the question. Do you love him?"

"Yes. Yes, I love Kashawn."

"Oh, I get it. He's the brains and the money, and I got the body and the dick size."

"Stop it."

As Deanthony rambled on, my cell rang. I looked at Deanthony like he was a disobedient child.

"Hey."

"Did he get there yet?" Kashawn asked.

"Yeah, I'm on my way home now."

"What's up, bro!" Deanthony yelled.

"Did he change the tire?"

"No, because you forgot to put the spare back under the car."

"Damn, baby, my bad. I must have forgotten."

"Just forget it. We'll talk about it when I get home," I said. I hung up and stared at Deanthony.

He started up the tow truck and I was on my way. "He can never satisfy you like I can. Kashawn can't make you come seven times in a night."

"Look, I'm not going to lie. You got some skills that surpass even the most die-hard of pussy-eating connoisseurs, but I can't do this. It's not going to happen."

"Oh, no?" Deanthony placed his hand on my thigh and started working his hand up my dress.

"Stop."

"You don't want me to stop."

As he steered the truck with his left hand, he tore away at my black nylon with his right. I shivered as he sneaked a finger behind the wall of my silk, purple panties. When I felt his finger inside me, Deanthony was in full damn control. He was making my pussy purr.

"You still want me to stop?"

"Shut up and drive."

Deanthony fucked me until I couldn't take it anymore. He eased his finger out of me and sucked it clean of my juices. I was happy to finally make it home. Kashawn came outside as Deanthony pulled in front of the house.

"Are you okay?" Kashawn asked.

"Yeah, just a little *wet*, that's all."

"Hey, man, thanks for rescuing my girl."

His girl? Was he serious?

"I was in the area anyway. Besides, Bree is family," Deanthony said.

Deanthony looked at me, knowing now that I would come back, that I would have many moments of weakness.

TANGELA

The day Bree told me that she and Deanthony messed around, I wanted to drop to the floor and do the worm. And, of course, she would run to me. I'm only her best friend, the bitch she tells everything to. She called me, sounding all crazy and melodramatic as usual when she gets high-strung, saying that she needed to talk to me. I figured it was something bad the way she was going on, and I assumed it had something to do with Deanthony.

"What happened?"

"I don't want to tell you over the phone. I'm coming over."

Bree hung the phone up before I could tell her that I had a man over. But that's Bree: selfish as hell where everything has to be about her, and fuck everybody else. I honestly was nowhere near in the mood to hear about the cluster-fuck shit storm she had gotten herself into this time, nor did I care to lend her my shoulder to cry on. I had to take a rain check on the heart-pounding, toe-curling fucking this guy I'd met at Club Rehab, Trevor, was about to put down on me. With the way my pussy was screaming for some attention, this had better be good.

I was settled in for tonight with my silk white robe on, and naked as a jaybird underneath. Trevor was none too happy when I told him that I would have to take a rain check on fucking, that my friend was in distress and on her way over. I hated having to kick a fine-ass man like him out of my bed, and with a hard-on at that.

I gave him a wet-hot French kiss as a consolation prize, so I could play fake best friend to Bree.

Honestly, I was curious to find out what all the drama was about. It took Bree all of ten minutes to get to my house. I didn't even wait for her to ring the doorbell. I opened the door and Bree walked in like she was a woman on a mission. The way she looked, I thought she was going to tell me that she had killed somebody.

"So what's going on?"

Bree started to pace my living room floor, something she always did when she was stressed about something. "Girl, I fucked up bad this time. Kashawn is never going to forgive me."

I was tired and not in the mood. "Are you going to tell me what's up, or are you going to make me play guessing games?"

"I cheated on Kashawn."

As soon as I heard the word *cheated*, I pepped right up. "Say again?"

"Kashawn is going to leave me."

"Who did you have an affair with?"

Bree plopped her behind down on my chocolate leather sofa. "It was Deanthony."

"Oh damn, seriously?"

"I don't know what to do."

"I'll tell you what you do, girl, don't tell him."

"I have to tell him, Tangela. He's my husband. I don't want to keep something like this away from him. I don't want him finding out from someone else."

I was quick to correct Bree. "What if he kicks you out without a dime to your name? What then?"

"I can hear Mama Liz now: 'I told you she was no good.'" Bree got up and began pacing the floor again. "Tange, what the hell am I going to do?"

"Look, ma, if you want to keep your marriage together, don't tell him shit. It was a mistake, a slip. You need to just go home to your man and forget it ever happened."

"It's going to eat me up inside not to tell him."

"B, don't throw away what you two have built because of some dick." Bree looked at me, knowing good and well that I was right. I could tell that she was taking in the advice I was trying to hammer into her cheating head. Leave it to her to fuck up a good thing.

"Yeah, I guess you're right."

"It was *simply* a moment of weakness."

"I don't think I can forgive myself if Kashawn ever finds out."

"He won't find anything out if you don't tell him."

Bree sighed, her hand resting against her forehead. "I guess."

"Look, girl, if you still feel torn up about it after a few weeks, come clean, but give yourself time to think about it. If I were you, I would take that shit to my grave. You know how crazy Kashawn is about you."

"I don't want to start our marriage out with lies and keeping secrets."

"Do you think Deanthony will say anything?"

"He promised me that he wouldn't."

"Are you sure you can trust him? I wouldn't put shit past that man."

"He told me he wouldn't say anything."

Bree had just made my fucking up her marriage way too easy. The gears in my pretty head were already turning, trying to figure out how I could use this news to my benefit. I had to find out how Deanthony felt: if he actually loved Bree, or if he just wanted her for some booty. Either way, he was officially a pivotal chess piece in my plan. As I happily watched Bree stew in the pot of her own fuck-up, I relished in the fact that Christmas had come early for me that year.

DEANTHONY

I was about to settle into some porn when I noticed a black Mustang pull in front of the house. "Fuck is that?"

I was butt-ass naked on Ma's sofa with a box of Kleenex and a bottle of cocoa butter lotion. Ma and Uncle Ray-Ray were out running errands. With the way him and Ma dragged around, I knew they wouldn't be back for hours. It was the first time I've been able to have some alone time sense I'd left Cali. I quickly took the towel I was sitting on and wrapped it around my waist. My dick was bone-hard, poking against the tent of Ma's good white towel. I peeked from behind a sliver of curtain to see who had pulled up in the driveway. It was Tangela.

"But nothing beats the real thing," I said, smiling, licking my lips like I was L.L. Cool J.

I tucked the tissue and lotion under the cushions of the flower-printed sofa like they were dirty magazines and pushed the porn movie I was about to watch into a school of DVDs that were shelved on the black entertainment center. My dick was so hard, it hurt. Tangela rang the doorbell. I never considered her really my type, but pussy was pussy, and my dick didn't give a damn what cooch it was in. I went to my room and splashed some cologne on, not too much, but just enough. I gargled with some mint-flavored Listerine to wash out the oniony taste that was on my pallet after the two fried bologna sandwiches I'd had for lunch. I checked myself one final time in the bathroom mirror. You would think Ciara or somebody was at the door the way I was tripping.

I was beating my meat twice a day fantasizing about Bree's sweet pussy hugging my dick, her warm mouth on my piece. I answered before Tangela could ring the bell again.

"Hey, what's up?"

Tangela looked at me and sauntered in like she was a woman on a mission. She was wearing a red top that was cut low, showing just enough cleavage. Tangela has these huge titties, the kind I like to motorboat. Her nipples were pressing against the fabric of her blouse like two perky chocolate-dipped cherries. *Damn!*

"We need to talk." She was all matter of fact-like with her shit, looking like pure sex on legs in her platform, scarlet-red, six-inch pumps that screamed, *Fuck Me!*

"You want a drink first? You walking up in here like Steven Seagal after you."

"Nah, I'm good. This won't take long."

I caught her glancing at the bulge behind the towel and then quickly back up to my face. *Yeah, I see you looking. You know you want a bite of this banana*, I thought.

"Are you sure? I got some beers in the refrigerator."

"I know," Tangela blurted out.

"Know what?" I figured she was here because Bree had told her we'd fucked, but I played it off like I had no idea what she was talking about.

"Don't play dumb, Deanthony. You know what's up. Bree told me y'all had sex."

I wasn't surprised that she had confided in Tangela about what had happened. I sat back on the sofa, in the same spot where I had my dick in my hands minutes before Tangela graced me with her fine-ass presence. I nonchalantly pressed Big Byron down, but my big bull of a dick refused to heel.

"Okay, so you know about me and Bree. So what?" I wasn't in the mood to hear some holier-than-thou lecture. I get enough of that from Ma.

"Bree told me that you're not going to say anything to Kashawn."

"Why would I? That shit wasn't planned. It just happened."

Tangela hooked one hand on her hip. "So you, what, tripped and fell on her pussy?"

I laughed as I got up and walked toward the kitchen. "I'm getting a beer. I'll grab you one, too. You look like you could use one."

I could smell Tangela's perfume drifting through the air of the house, her sweet scent permeating through the living room. I plucked two Michelobs out of Ma's booger-green vintage refrigerator and twisted off the tops to the longnecks and handed one to Tangela.

"Cheers," I said, clanking my bottle against hers before I took a swig.

"So do you love her or did y'all just fuck because you were horny?"

"Why do you care where or who I run my dick up in?"

"Oh, make no mistake, I don't care who you fuck, D, trust."

"Then why all the questions?"

"I'm just trying to find out where your head is at, and I don't mean the one on the end of your dick. You don't think I see how you look at Bree when she's around? You practically have to be hosed down."

I reclined against the edge of the kitchen counter, my eyes glued to Tangela's breasts. She had no idea what she was doing to me and Big Byron. "Sounds like to me you're jealous."

Tangela sucked her teeth and rolled her eyes. "Of you and Bree? Boy, please." She laughed before she took a swig of beer.

I took my beer and ran the cold bottle across my chest, teasing the hell out of Tangela. "I care about Bree. I care about whether she's happy or not," I told her.

"Humph. If that was the case, you wouldn't have slept with a married woman, and not just *any* married woman, but the lady who's married to your brother."

I was bored with Tangela's goody-two-shoes attitude, acting like she wipes her ass with diamonds. I knew just the thing that would shut her up. Big Byron.

"So you think she's happy with my button-down, straight-laced, Oxford shirt-wearing-ass brother?"

"Did she tell you that she's not happy with Kashawn? Because... if not, that leaves *us* something to work with." Tangela started to saunter seductively toward me, undoing a couple of the buttons on her blouse.

"I don't follow."

She held the tip of the bottle to her red, dick-sucking lips, allowing beer to seep between them. Big Byron twitched as Tangela wrapped her lips around the spout of the beer bottle.

"Damn, ma, take it to the head, take it to the head."

I'm not going to lie. I wished it was my dick she had her lips wrapped around. *Yeah, you know exactly whatchu doin'*, I thought. She finished off most of the beer, not letting a single drop drip from her lips. Tangela ran her hands along my chest. Her fingers were like a delicate feather across my nips.

"Answer the question. Do you love Bree?"

The truth is, I was in love with Bree. I had been in love with her the first night I laid eyes on her. And I hated that she was with my pencil-dick of a brother and not me.

Tangela kept on until she got down to the towel and yanked it from around my waist, causing Big Byron to bounce free like a birthday surprise.

"I will say this: I would rather she was with me than Kashawn." Tangela held me in her stare as she gently eased her hand around my nine-inch thickness. I settled into her advances as she started to jack me off.

"So what if I told you that I had a plan where we could both get what we wanted?"

"How you figure that?"

Tangela placed her beer on the kitchen counter behind me. "I have a plan that could split the two of them up for good."

I looked at Tangela like she had lost her mind. She sent every nerve in me rattling as she ran her hand along my shaft. "Damn, girl," I whispered under my minty, fresh breath.

My heart began to thump faster when she eased down to her knees on Ma's kitchen floor. I looked down at her and she glanced up at me with those big, light-brown eyes as she teased the meaty tip of Big Byron with her long, wide tongue. In the time it took me to blink, Tangela threw her sin-red lips around my snake and started to milk it. She sucked me slow, just how I like it. Baby girl had some true, deep, dick-sucking skills that only came in a close second to Bree. This shit was on and popping. When I sank my fingers into her jungle of hair weave, I could feel the tracks as I pushed her head down on Big Byron.

"Deep throat that dick, bitch."

Tangela did what she knew would make a brother feel good, taking Big Byron to the base, holding him in her throat before she slid up to the juicy perineum. If she kept this up, I was going to drown her in jizz. Her blow job work was up there with the best of them, even a few fags I let suck my dick back in Cali. I wanted to fuck, though. I wanted to lay this pipe in her pussy deep.

"I wanna fuck," I told her as I eased Big Byron out of her mouth. My dick was smeared with lipstick, drenched with spit.

Tangela pulled up her skirt and peeled off the black panties like they were a second skin. "I know there's no love lost between you and your brother, so I know you don't have a problem fucking his world up."

Tangela was on point about that. I didn't give two rat shits about Kashawn. Just because we were twins don't mean we gotta like each other.

"Woman, has anyone ever told you, you talk too much?"

I hoisted Tangela up on the dining room table, sending Ma's crystal vase I gave her for Mother's Day last year, crashing to the floor. We paused for a minute at what I had just done.

"Fuck it; I'll buy her another one." I was horny as hell and the only thing that was on my dirty mind was knocking Tangela's back out.

I yanked her skirt up over her booty on the table with Tangela's pussy splayed out like it was the main course. Juices trickled from her pussy that was as soft as satin when I pried her hot-pink lips apart. Tangela moaned when I pushed a finger in. I unplugged my digit so I could taste her.

Mmm…that's what I'm talkin' about.

She purred like a kitten the minute my tongue hit her sweet spot. I like to fuck, but I *love* eating pussy. I'm like Fat Albert at an all-you-can-eat soul food buffet when it comes to cunnilingus. I drove Tangela crazy as I teased her, sucking softly on the lips of her pussy.

But I couldn't forget about my boy, Big Byron, who was thumping between my firm muscle thighs for some added attention. I eased up from between Tangela's robust thighs, her juices sloppy across my mouth like ice cream, and smeared myself atop of her. Thanks to Tangela, Big Byron slid in like a well-oiled piston. I pulled at her blouse until the buttons popped free, bouncing on the table and floor. I fucked Tangela slow and easy, my dick fitting like the perfect puzzle piece.

"Fuck me," Tangela yelped. "Fuck me like you fuck her."

I assumed she was talking about Bree. I always knew Tangela was freak-nasty like that. I pulled at her bra until breasts were exposed like a tawdry secret. I teased her perky knobs with my tongue as I fucked her, sending pulses of *sextricity* through her body.

Tangela's pussy lips hugged Big Byron as I fucked fast and deep. Her pussy was like a black hole: infinite. She rested her big, thick gams on my temple shoulders. "Get it. Get this pussy, get it!"

She and I had the dining room table rocking. So much so, I thought it would collapse under our weight, but like me, it held steady. I kept a look out for any signs of Ma and Uncle Ray-Ray. The scent of sex spirited through the kitchen.

"Fuck me like you fuck Bree."

Tangela kept on until I imagined she was Bree, smiling up at me. I fucked harder as I thought she should be with me instead of Shawn. He thinks he's such king shit, walking his happy, Howdy Doody ass around here like he's better than me just because he's a doctor and lives in a big house.

"Does he fuck you like this, huh? Does he beat that pussy up like I do?"

Who wants to live way out in Ox Bottom Manor with a bunch of cornball white folks anyway? I bet they gave him the real red carpet treatment. I'm surprised those white breads haven't burned a cross in his yard yet.

That's what I can't stand about niggas like Kashawn. They get some coin, and the first thing they do is move out in neighborhoods like Ox Bottom Manor, Killearn Estates, and Plantation Estates. I mean, what muthafucka wants to live in a neighborhood called Plantation Estates? That's all kinds of fucked up.

I had to put the thought out of my brain. Big Byron was starting to soften. I focused my attention back onto Bree, I mean, Tangela, who was giving me her best orgasm face.

"Don't stop," she pleaded. "I'm going to come!"

I, too, was close to popping a nut that had been stewing up in me all afternoon. I picked up more speed, fucking hard and crazy, stretching Tangela's sugar walls with each thrust.

"I'm coming, I'm coming!" she yelled. Her dirty words echoed through the house. I felt Big Byron skirt. Her pussy milked what felt like buckets of semen out of my dick. As I rested my head between the cleft of Tangela's breasts, she said, "So how about it? You want to get in on this plan with me to break Bree and your brother up?"

I lapped at Tangela's nipple, glanced at her, and said with a sinister grin, "I'm down for whatever."

5

TANGELA

Bree doesn't deserve a man like Kashawn. Leave it to her to fuck up a good thing by fucking your man's brother of all people. If it wasn't for Kashawn, she would still be shaking her ashy-ass at Risqué for rent money. Typical Bree, ungrateful bitch. It was me. I was the one who got Deanthony to come to the birthday party. I knew she would go bat-shit crazy when she saw him walk through the door. The look on her face was worth the price of admission. There was no way in hell I was going to spend the afternoon watching her hang all over Kashawn.

It's all enough to make me throw up. Look at this house. The living room is bigger than my low-income hovel. He's given her everything and what does she do? Piss it away for a big dick. I should be married to Kashawn. Technically, I saw him first. He was so cute, sitting off by himself, nursing a beer at Club Rehab. Bree was shaking her skanky ass on the dance floor with some loser as usual while I sat around being a magnet for trolls. Even then, it didn't take much to get Bree between the sheets. A wink and a drink and, boom, she was going home with some loser who reeked of aftershave and K-Mart cologne. It's a wonder she doesn't walk around with a mattress strapped to her back. I had these pretty hazel eyes on Kashawn all night and was about to go over and introduce myself when Bree pussy-blocked me. Before I could make a move, she was practically shaking her beach ball-sized titties in his face. The fucked-up thing was that he actually fell for that shit. I went home alone that night, wondering what it is about Bree men couldn't resist.

Back in high school, she was a mess, a walking broomstick who had no ass and titties the size of muffins. The jocks were all over her as soon as she started to bloom around the tenth grade. She went from broomstick to Ms. *Jet* magazine of the month in two seconds flat. Girls in high school didn't much like her when she was a skinny, bookish bitch, but when she started stealing boyfriends and it was rumored that she was fucking half the basketball team, they wanted to burn her at the stake. She can't fix her mouth to talk about Yvonne. I stood by her and got in any bitch's face who talked smack about Bree. That's until she made moves on Brent Martin, this cute boy who was in my World History class. When Bree found out how badly I was crushing on Brent, she sank her claws in and wouldn't let up until the brother was just another conquest to write about in her Hello Kitty diary. I played it off like I didn't care that she had fucked the most beautiful boy in school, but I was pissed and vowed to watch my back around Bree. I've been covering my ass ever since.

That night at the bar, she came up to me and said, "Don't wait up."

"Fuck you, bitch," I said under my breath as I finished off my Vodka Cranberry.

Bree and I were roommates at the time. We were going to school to study Cosmetology at Tallahassee Community College, but Bree discovered that she could make quick, easy money stripping, so she dropped out of the program and started shaking her ass for coins full time. It was just as well, being that I was pretty much carrying her through the whole program. She would have flunked out anyway. It was a miracle she graduated high school, seeing as how she couldn't keep her legs closed.

I sat in the car outside of *our* apartment that night while she finished fucking Kashawn into the floor. The deal we made whenever a man was over was, if the bedroom light was off, sex was being ensued. If the light was on, everything was cool. Of course, that bullshit rule only applied to Bree. I lost count of how many times she'd walked in on me and a man fucking, and then she would play it off like she didn't mean to bust in on me sucking dick. Weeks and months had passed, and she and Kashawn had become hot and heavy. Usually Bree was about hitting it and quitting it, so I didn't get what was so special about Kashawn until we were sitting down to breakfast and she told me he was some fancy doctor.

"Oh, so you're looking at a pay day. You don't actually love the man."

"I do love him, and the fact that he's a doctor is a nice bonus." She laughed.

It took everything in me to keep from slapping Bree's gold-digging ass into next Tuesday. It's hard enough as it is to get a black man with all of these white bitches snatching them up like they were candy from a piñata. Bree gets a good man and all she can see are dollar signs. Hood bitches like her give real sisters like me a bad name.

Kashawn was always at the apartment fixing stuff, cooking, cleaning, and deep-dicking Bree between it all. Her bedroom light stayed off and I was privy to her moaning and groaning like a porn star. I was officially through when she broke the news of their engagement.

Bree came to breakfast that day, giddy as a schoolgirl. I didn't think anything of it. She always acted that way after the pipe Kashawn was laying down between her legs.

"Notice anything different about me this morning?"

"You got your teeth whitened?"

Bree shrugged. "No, girl, guess." She rested her hand on her face to get me to notice the bling that was on her finger.

I put on one of my Emmy Award-winning performances and played it off like I was happy for her. "Oh, my God, girl, did he propose last night?"

"On bended knee and everything."

"Congratulations, Bree. Oh, my God."

"Thanks, girl. It looks like we have a wedding to plan, maid-of-honor."

"For real, you serious?"

"I can't think of anyone else but my bestie to stand by my side at my wedding."

The thought of Bree walking down the aisle in some virgin-white wedding dress tickled the hell out of me and she was dead set on wearing just that like she was the poster girl for virtue. The only thing funnier would have been her wobbling down the aisle several months knocked up.

"We haven't set a date yet, but you know I've always wanted a spring wedding."

"So I guess this means you will be moving out."

"Yeah. Kashawn and I are going to go look for a bigger place on Saturday."

"So are you going to quit dancing at Risqué?"

"Yeah. Blue-Black won't like it, but I don't give a fuck."

"He's going to hate losing his cash cow," I said, throwing in a dig.

"He's got plenty of girls to take my place. He won't miss me. He's always telling me that I'm a pain in his dick anyway, so…"

"Damn, B, it's going to feel funny not having you around. I'm going to miss our late-night talks."

"Well, I'm not gone yet, and our late-night talks aren't going to stop just because we don't stay together anymore."

"I guess," I said.

I was laying the shit on thick. The truth was, I was happy to see them go. The walls were paper thin and I liked not having to listen to Bree and Kashawn moaning and groaning like they were auditioning to be in some porn film.

The wedding was held at their house, this huge mansion in Killearn Estates, a well-to-do side of town. The backyard was the size of a golf course. Some of the girls from Risqué were bridesmaids. Classless cunts in expensive dresses. White and lavender were everywhere. Not the colors I would have chosen, but the look was cute. Kashawn spared no expense for Bree. Mama Liz didn't like her at first, being that she was a dancer, and hasn't gotten over it, I don't think. Yvonne wouldn't let up, either, mean-mugging Bree at every turn. Real or not, I teared up when they exchanged their vows. I stood staring at how handsome Kashawn was, thinking that it should have been me standing where Bree was, in a Vera Wang gown in front of 300 guests.

All this because she shook her titties in his face, I thought.

That wedded bliss shit lasted all of three months before Bree tired of playing housewife and started club-hopping with me. It wasn't long before she started wagging her ass to every dick that swung across her face.

It kills me what she's doing to Kashawn. She didn't deserve him that night at the club, and she damn sure doesn't deserve to have the man's hand in marriage. It was time Kashawn knew it.

6

KASHAWN

The party was winding down into the evening. People were starting to clear out, thanking Ma and Uncle Ray-Ray for all the good food. Deanthony and I were sitting at one of the patio tables cluttered with red Dixie cups and paper plates with fish bones and soiled, crumpled-up napkins. I was picking food out of my teeth with my index finger when Tyrique came up behind me and slapped me hard on the shoulder.

"We still going fishing on Saturday, right?"

"After all the fish, oysters and hushpuppies you consumed, you still want to go fishing?" I asked.

"Yeah. Ray-Ray says they're really biting this year. I want to go out and catch me a bucket of bream. Your uncle said he would clean 'em and fry 'em up for me."

"Okay, come by the house around six a.m. I got this new bait I want to try anyway."

"Don't flake out now like you always do," Tyrique warned.

"D, you want to come with us?" I grinned.

"Naw, fishing ain't never been my thing."

"Right, not since you fell over in Lost Lake that time and almost drowned," I said.

Tyrique and I bust out laughing.

"Now he won't go near water," I said.

"You know I would rather eat the fish," Deanthony said. "I don't have time to be sitting in a boat trying to catch them."

"I feel you on that, bro," Tyrique said, he and Deanthony coming together in a knuckle bump.

"I'll leave all that up to y'all, the pros."

"Listen, y'all, I gotta get outta here," Tyrique said. "Ebonya will have my ass if I don't get home."

"How are she and the baby doing?" I asked.

"She's due next month, so she's feeling anxious."

"That's cool, T. Congrats, man," Deanthony said.

"'Shawn, don't play now. Don't forget, man. Saturday morning, six o'clock. Don't let me have to wake your ass up."

"Man, just come on by. I gotcha."

I fished another Corona out of the wash basin of ice and screwed off the top.

"Please tell me that you have not ended up like that pussy-whipped brother," Deanthony said.

"Who? Tyrique? Why does he have to be pussy-whipped?"

"'I gotta get home to my wife or she'll have my ass.' Trust. Tyrique is pussy-whipped."

"Why you don't have nobody? You need to slow your own roll. You aren't eighteen anymore. Go make an honest woman out of somebody, have a few kids."

"The last thing I want is some shorty and some crumb snatcher spending all my money. Nothing against what you and Bree got."

"We're going to try and have a kid next year."

"You would make a great daddy," Deanthony said. "Unlike me, you have the patience for fatherhood."

"So how is Hollywood treating you? How's the acting going?"

"Slowly but surely. I've been an extra in a few action films and I'm shopping this script I just finished around to a few producers, so I have some stuff in the works."

"That's good. I'm glad you're doing well for yourself out there."

"Yeah, my agent is trying to get me this gig on *Banshee*, this hot new show on Cinemax."

I didn't believe one word that was coming out of Deanthony's mouth. He was just posing as usual, trying to make himself sound like he was somebody important. I indulged my baby brother anyway.

"I'm glad that things are going well for you."

"I'm happy, 'Shawn. Happier than I've been in a long time."

"Well, me, Ma, and Unc was anything but happy when you packed up and left without saying so much as boo."

"Kashawn, come on, man. Don't start. I explained why I had to leave, that I needed to find my own way."

"For months we didn't know if you were dead or alive," I said. "I was the only one here who could settle Ma down. I had to clean up your mess as usual. She was worried sick, all of us were, and you couldn't so much as pick up the damn phone to let us know that you were all right."

"Don't start that mess," Ma said, clearing cups and paper plates from the patio table. "He's home now and that is all that matters."

"No, it's cool, Ma. D was just telling me how good he was doing in Hollywood. He's going to be on this new TV show."

"Congratulations, baby," Ma said, snaking her arm around Deanthony's shoulders. "Is it *Tyler Perry's House of Payne?* I love that Mr. Brown. He is too crazy." Ma grinned. Ma was the kind who was quick to forgive. It was too bad I didn't inherit that same trait.

"No, Ma, it's a new show on Cinemax called *Banshee*."

"Oh, don't think I've ever heard of that one, baby." Ma turned to Uncle Ray-Ray and asked, "Do we have Cinemax, Ray?"

"Yes, but you don't ever watch nothing on that channel. After *Wheel of Fortune*, she's dead to the world."

"Oh hush up. Deanthony, baby, you let me know when it's on,

and I'll watch you in it. I'm so proud of my boys, I don't know what to do."

"Why don't you explain why you abandoned your family and never looked back? What gives, little brother?"

"I told you, man," Deanthony said.

"I told you, boy, not to start that mess in my house. Deanthony doesn't owe you, me, none of us an explanation. He is his own man," Ma said.

"No, Ma. He owes everyone at this table an explanation for why he was gone for so long, why he took off without so much as a postcard for three years."

"You need to drop it," Deanthony warned.

"Only Deanthony can be gone this long, then blow back into town and everyone can conveniently act like nothing happened, but I didn't drink the Kool-Aid."

Uncle Ray-Ray came over to join us at the table from cleaning the grill. Deanthony's voice went up a few octaves, sounding like he was about to do something.

"You want to know why I fucking left."

"Watch your language in my house, boy," Ma scolded.

"Maybe I got tired of living in your shadow, of being the black sheep."

"What the hell are you talking about?"

"Daddy had to be in control of the purse strings. Instead of letting us decide what we wanted to do with all that money. I figured you would follow in his footsteps, 'Shawn. After all, you're just like him. Mr. Could-Do-No-Wrong, Mr. Tallahassee All-American."

"You know that ain't true," Ma said.

"You've always played favorites," Deanthony said.

"Why didn't you say anything? Why didn't you just come and talk to me instead of running off?" I asked. "And I don't care what

Daddy put in the will. You're my brother. I wanted you to enroll in medical school with me."

"You don't get it, 'Shawn. I got sick of doing what you wanted, of living in your shadow. Why can't you get that? I wanted to go in another direction for once. What was so great about him anyway? The man wasn't even our real daddy."

"Hush. That's enough," Ma said. Ma cut a look at Deanthony like the scab of her deepest, darkest secret had been picked open.

"What the hell are you talking about?"

"Tell him, Ma," Deanthony said. "No time like the present."

"I said hush."

"Mama, what is he talking about?" I asked. She looked at me with a kind of puppy-dog sympathy. "Ma, tell me. What's going on?"

"It's true. Edrick wasn't your real daddy."

"What? Ma, what is he…" I looked at Deanthony and lunged across the table at him, tackling him to the ground. "Fuck you, you're lying." Deanthony blocked my first punch, throwing me off of him.

"Stop it!" Ma yelled. "Y'all are brothers!" Ma ran off toward the house, sobbing.

I felt Uncle Ray-Ray tug me by my collar off of Deanthony like I was a sack of potatoes. "You two, break this shit up. What the hell is wrong with you, boy? He's your brother and it's your birthday."

"No, he started it," Deanthony said. "I'm gonna finish this shit." Deanthony attempted to lunge at me, only to be yanked back by Uncle Ray-Ray.

"Go and see how your mama is doing, D!" Uncle Ray-Ray shouted.

Deanthony walked off. "Fuck with the bull, boy, you get the horns," Deanthony warned.

"I said git."

"Tell me he's lying, Uncle. Tell me he's full of shit."

"Sit down, 'Shawn."

"No, fuck that. I want to know what he meant by that."

"It's true. Edrick wasn't y'all's daddy. He adopted y'all when your real daddy made it clear he didn't want to be a father to you boys, so my brother adopted you when you were just babies."

Uncle Ray-Ray's conformation was like a punch in the stomach. I paced the backyard, reeling from the news I had been given. I looked at Deanthony consoling our mother.

"So who the hell is my real father?"

"Doesn't matter. He didn't want to be a father to you boys."

Anger had a firm hold on me and worthlessness was seeping in like a poison. "My whole life is a damn lie."

"Your mama loves and cares for you and Deanthony, and, as far as I'm concerned, you're my family, blood or not."

I picked up one of the patio chairs and flung it into the pool. I kicked the grill over, sending hot ashes and charcoal into the water.

"Kashawn, calm your behind down," Uncle Ray-Ray said.

Ma stood on the porch, sobbing as Deanthony watched in silence.

"Why, Ma? Why did I have to wait all of thirty fucking years to hear that I was the son of a man who didn't want me?" I shouted. I took my anger out on an oak tree that grew in the corner of the backyard. I punched it until my knuckles bled. Ma held onto Deanthony like he was her protector from the bastard child of the family. "I gotta get out of here. I can't be here right now."

"Kashawn, you've been drinking. Let's sit and talk about this."

"No, fuck this. I'm done."

"Please, baby, don't leave," Ma said.

"I can't even look at you right now, Ma. You carried on a lie for this long. What else are you lying about?"

I left her standing in the middle of the backyard, crying, but no one was more hurt than me. That house of lies was the last damn place I wanted to be.

7

DEANTHONY

M a placed the platter of half-eaten birthday cake on the kitchen counter, while Uncle Ray-Ray started washing aluminum pans and silverware. Neither one of them uttered a word.

"I'm sorry, Ma."

She looked at me with contempt in her blood-shot, teary eyes, as if she wanted to rip my tongue out of my head. "Is that why you came back here, to stir up trouble?"

"Me? What about Kashawn? I came here to see my family. He's the one who started in with me. I'm sorry I told him. It's just that he's always comin' off like he's holier than thou."

"How do you know how he acts? You've been gone for three years."

"Jesus, not you, too."

"It was not your call, boy, to tell Kashawn nothin'."

"Come on, Ma, you were never going to tell him. You should have—"

Before another word came out of my mouth, Ma slapped me across the face.

"Don't you ever…ever tell me what I should and should not do in my own house, boy. You understand me?"

"Just like old times."

"If that's an apology, you can get out of my face right now."

I looked at Uncle Ray-Ray who didn't say a word like Ma slapping me was what I deserved. "Believe it or not, I didn't come back here to start anything, but you know how Kashawn is always pushing buttons. I came back here because I missed my family, like I said."

"Well, this is one hell of a homecoming."

There was nothing else I could say. Ma was pissed. I thought about going to Kashawn to apologize, but fuck that. I thought about it, realizing that I had nothing to feel sorry for. The truth was finally out. No matter how it came out or who told it, it was out. If it's one thing I have learned, a lie can never last. He started that shit. I was sick of Bree playing Barbie to his phony-ass Ken. He was a bigger fool than I have always thought him to be if he thought he could please a woman like Bree. I stormed out of the door.

"Where are you going?" Ma asked.

"I need to get some air if that's okay with you."

8

UNCLE RAY-RAY

Kashawn and Deanthony reminded me so much of me and Edrick. We were always fighting about something. Toys, cars, girls. If it was there to fight over, we fought over it. I couldn't help but look at them and think of my daughter, Joelle. She would be a few years younger than them if she had lived. Twenty-six years old to be exact. A day didn't go by that I didn't think about her and Danita. I can only hope they're looking down from heaven, proud of the man their daddy and husband has become.

"Get some help, Ray, or I'm taking Joelle and going back to Atlanta," was the last thing Danita had said to me a week before I lost her and my baby.

I had spoken to her the night of the accident, telling her that I had decided to seek help for my drinking. I'd told her, "I don't want to lose you and Joelle. You two are my whole world and I'm willing to do anything within my power to get clean, and be the man, the husband and the father to our baby, that you want me to be."

The truth was, she, along with the rest of my family, had heard it all before, my tossing around promises as if they were poker chips. Edrick and Danita were the only two in my life who hadn't turned their backs on me while everyone else got sick and tired of cleaning up my messes, which I didn't blame them for, considering I had doused gasoline on the bridges I'd built with them and set them aflame.

Knowing what booze did to Daddy, I swore to myself that I would never end up a drunk like him, but a drunk is exactly what I became when I got laid off my job at Tallahassee Transit three years after Joelle's third birthday. Frustrated that I could no longer provide for her and Danita, I couldn't deal with Danita being the only provider for our family. It got so that I was drinking rubbing alcohol, anything that would numb the inadequacy of not feeling like a man who could provide for his wife and daughter. After two interventions and two rehabs to follow, I would come out, only to end up falling on my ass from stumbling off the proverbial wagon no matter what I did, and how much Danita and Edrick sought to get help for me.

On the day I told Danita that I was going to get straight, I prepared a special dinner for us. Fed up with my drinking, she took Joelle and moved in with her sister, Lavondra. Danita had reservations about having dinner, but after thirty minutes of pleading with her to break bread with me, she finally gave in. I had cleaned and scrubbed the house from top to bottom to a high shine, something I had never done. I prepared Danita's favorite: barbecue chicken with dirty rice and red mashed potatoes with the skin on. She used to love how I made barbecue chicken. The trick was broiling it in my famous homemade, special sauce. I wasn't so good at baking, so I bought a pound cake from Publix and placed it on a cake platter to make it look like I'd spent all day in the kitchen. I wanted to make a good impression, show Danita that I was putting my best foot forward in getting her and Joelle back.

I made sure that everything was perfect. When I noticed myself in the living room mirror, wearing Danita's cherry-printed apron, I chuckled. The entire house smelled like barbecue chicken. My stomach was doing cartwheels, somersaults, and hand stands, I was so hungry. All I had to eat that day was half a bagel for breakfast.

The time of our dinner was seven o'clock. I was anxious to see Danita, to throw my arms around her, and kiss my baby daughter. I had missed them terribly and had a whole lot of making up to do.

Seven had come and gone. I was starting to worry, so I called Lavondra to find out what was going on. I had this feeling that she had convinced Danita not to join me for dinner. She never liked me and often attempted to wedge her big ass in between our marriage. Lavondra had an opinion about everything and was always in Danita's ear telling her I was a no-good drunk and that she should leave me. She was always talking to someone about leaving somebody, which was understandable being that she could only keep a man around for all of five minutes before they hit the road running. As much as Lavondra tried, Danita never left me, but stuck it out, cleaning up my messes, putting up with my drunken tantrums, and mopping throw-up off the bathroom floor.

I dialed Lavondra's number and it rang three times before she answered the phone.

"Hello?"

"Lavondra, hey, long time, no hear from."

"Hey, Raymond," she said in a less than enthusiastic tone.

"I was wondering if Danita is there."

She sighed heavy on the phone like I was the last black man she wanted to talk to, but I didn't give a damn. I didn't call to talk to her anyway.

"Danita left here about an hour ago. I thought she would be at the house by now," Lavondra said.

Hearing that an hour had elapsed since she had left Lavondra's made my heart drop. "No, she's not here. Did she take Joelle with her, or is Joelle there with you?"

"She took the baby with her. Joelle is so cute and she's getting so big. She's a spitting image of her mama."

That was Lavondra's way of throwing a dig. Everyone thinks that Joelle looks like me.

"Yeah, she's growing like a weed," I said with a tone of frustration. "Okay, listen, if you hear from her, please call me and let me know."

"Okay, I sure will. I'm sure there's nothing to worry about. She probably just stopped off to the store to get some stuff for the baby."

I wasn't sure what was going on. I was getting one of my bad feelings. "You're right. I'm sure everything is fine," I said as I studied the cookie jar clock that hung above the kitchen sink.

"If I hear from Danita, I will let you know." It was nice hearing Lavondra be cordial to me for once instead of being a high-riding bitch.

I hung up. "Come on, 'Nita, baby, where are you?" I said to myself. It was killing me not knowing of her whereabouts.

It was a little after eight when I went to go look for her. I didn't have a clue as to where to start, but it was a hell of a lot better than sitting around, staring at that damn clock like a madman.

Before I left, I blew out the candles and put the barbecue chicken in the oven to keep warm. I grabbed my coat and my keys to the truck. As soon as I opened the door, two police officers pulled up alongside my pickup. Both of them were white. One was fat with a potbelly and dark hair, and the other was much younger with blond hair like he was fresh out of the police academy. I knew with the sullen, sad expression on their mugs, that something was wrong, that something had happened.

"Sir, are you Mr. Raymond Parker?"

"What's wrong? Is it my wife?"

"Mr. Parker, sir, I'm sorry to tell you this, but your wife was in a car accident."

Their words were like a crowbar to my head. I felt a part of me dying with her, the part of me that loved Danita to my soul.

"My baby...what about my baby, Joelle? Was she in the car?"

The two cops looked at one another like it was news they didn't want to give me.

"I'm sorry."

It felt like my life source had been taken away from me. "Danita, noooooooo!" I hollered. I broke down in a heap of tears. The cops had later informed me that they had been struck by a hit-and-run driver.

"We apprehended him and he's being held without bond at the Leon County Jail."

All I could think about was that I had lost the two most important people in my life who were my everything. As far as I was concerned, a big part of me had died with them that night.

Edrick had gone with me downtown to the morgue to identify Danita and Joelle. When it came time to see my baby girl, I couldn't bring myself to do it. I didn't want my last image of her to be of her lying on some cold metal slab.

The day of the funeral, it felt like I was in a daze. Edrick kept me together as much as a little brother could, being that I had picked up the bottle again in a need to numb the pain I was feeling. I drank until I blacked out, wishing that with enough liquor, I could numb the memory of losing my wife and daughter. When booze wasn't enough, I started using crack. No matter how much drinking I did, or how much crack I smoked, none of it was enough. I eventually became addicted and pawned everything I had, including Danita's jewelry, to get money so I could get high. I blew through money as if it was candy, eventually losing my house and truck to the bank.

Edrick took me in when he saw how bad off I was. He made me promise to get some help, and that if he saw me doing drugs in his house or if I stole from him, he would kick me out.

"I swear. I'm going to get clean this time, Ed," I told him.

"Yeah, I've heard that before."

I got clean for a good week before I started to do crack again. I often laid a guilt trip on Edrick if I couldn't get what I wanted. I was careful about doing drugs in front of him, heeding his threats of kicking me out.

Edrick would always tell me how I had hit rock bottom. He was just like Mama, while I took after Daddy, who spent much of our childhood running the streets. The streets were surely what killed him when he was shot by a pimp named Butter. Everybody called him Butter because of his yellow teeth. Daddy got into it with him after some mess with one of his hos. Butter took out his gun and shot Daddy clean through the heart. He knew that no one would say a word, being that the rule on the street was snitches get stitches.

Edrick and I were sleeping when these two cops came to the house and gave Mama the news that Daddy was dead. I remember her screaming so loud, she woke the whole neighborhood up. Her hollering echoed through the house. Edrick cried while the rage I felt because of Daddy's murder burned in me like hot lava. Revenge was what I wanted. I took Daddy's pistol from a shoebox he kept in the attic. He didn't know I knew that's where he kept it. I tucked Daddy's gun in my waist, put on an old ski mask so nobody could make me out, and stole Mr. Perkin's bike to ride up to the bar on Basin Street where I knew Butter hung out. He didn't even see me coming when I rode up alongside his Thunderbird that was blacker than the devil's asshole. I pulled out the gun and shot Butter point blank in the head. Blood and brains splattered everywhere.

I never told anyone what I had done. I didn't tell Edrick until much later in life when we were in our twenties. I told him what I did and we never discussed it again after that.

Edrick finally got fed up when I started pawning his things in the house to get money for drugs.

"I'm done with you. Get the fuck out, Ray. I told you what I would do if you stole from me. I love you, but you have to go. You can't stay here. I will do what I can for you, but I can't do this shit anymore."

"You just going to throw me out like that? I'm your family. We're brothers. What was all that shit you were saying about family over everything?"

Edrick wasn't going to be a passenger on another one of my guilt trips. He really was done. "You have until the end of the week to find somewhere else to stay."

I left with nothing but the clothes on my back and a small bottle of Jack Daniel's in my back jeans pocket.

"If you're not out, I'm calling the cops."

"I can't believe you're doing this. I'm your goddamn blood."

Edrick didn't have anything else to say.

The day that I left, Edrick was at work, working part time fixing cars at Carter's Garage on South Adams Street.

It took me six years to get my shit together and when I finally did, it was too late to make amends to my baby brother. I found out from Yvonne that Edrick had died. Edrick, Danita, and my baby, Joelle, were gone. But instead of picking up the bottle this time, I vowed to spend the rest of my life making it up to Ed by being there for Liz and the boys.

Family over everything, baby brother.

9

DEANTHONY

Fuck this! I knew I shouldn't have come back here. Ain't nothin' changed, all that favoritism shit just like when we were kids. Kashawn got the pat on the back for being Mr. Perfect, while I got scolded and beaten with a belt. Her prodigal son. Everything that has gone down tonight only reminded me why I got out of Dodge in the first place. I thought I was going to throw up the honey bun and beef jerky, watching Bree hang all over Kashawn's nerdy-ass like a fake fur coat. Yeah, uh-huh, a real match made in heaven. I almost can't believe how good she looks still. Big titties, firm ass you could sit a glass of wine on, with juicy, dick-sucking lips.

That was the first thing I noticed about Bree when Kashawn brought her to the dinner Ma had thrown for them. My mouth dropped to the living room floor when I laid eyes on her. Kashawn couldn't stop talking about her, but I didn't pay much attention, seeing as how his taste in honeys has always been for shit. The first thing I thought was, *how in the hell did you snag a sweet potato like her?* I knew she was way too much woman for Kashawn, considering his track record of fingering ugly, simple-looking librarian bitches. When he told me that she danced at Risqué, it made sense. Bree was out for a pay day. Dollar signs were all she knew.

I stared at her across the dinner table the whole night. Ma went all out too, making some of my and Kashawn's favorites: baked chicken, mashed potatoes, black-eyed peas, and Dutch apple cheesecake for dessert. Bree's titties were practically spilling out of the low-cut blouse she wore to dinner that night. I could look at Ma and tell that she disapproved, but baby girl had my dick on swole. I kept tugging at it under the table. I thought I had nutted in my pants until I went to the bathroom to rub out a quickie before Ma served the apple cheesecake. I thought about Bree with every stroke, wondering what she looked like naked. She'd have her knees in her ears, fucking with me.

Ma kept going on about how pretty Bree was, and Bree ate that shit up. Ma always could lay it on thick.

"Well, would you settle for a daughter-in-law?" Kashawn said. "I asked Bree to marry me."

"And I said yes!" Bree modeled the blinged-out ring for everybody to see.

Ma was fawning all over her like she was the Queen of damn Sheba.

"Congratulations, bro," I said, giving him a fake, half-assed hug.

Fuck 'em and leave 'em blowing up my cell for more is my motto. I grinned a little bit, thinking about the two of them having sex. Bree instructing him on the finer points of eating pussy. I wanted to fuck her silly that night, smear her apple bottom-ass across the dinner table of baked chicken and black-eyed peas, deep-dick her right there in front of Ma, Uncle Ray-Ray, and my lucky brother. I wanted to smother my mug between those cantaloupe titties, lick giblet gravy from her cooch until she sprung a leak like they all do once I've tamed that kitty cat. I was drooling at the dinner table like some horned-up mutt. That night I caught her in Kashawn's old room, messing around with some of his old toys that he had long left behind.

"Daddy got him that train track for his sixth birthday."

Bree jumped, startled by my presence.

"My bad, baby girl. I didn't mean to scare you." I finally got her cute ass alone.

"No, it's my fault. I shouldn't be in here being nosey anyway."

Her teeth were so pretty and white when she smiled. I doubted they were falsies. She was too young to have them. I didn't notice any track marks on her arms, so she didn't seem like she was on smack or nothing.

"Forget about it. I don't think Ma cares anyway."

"It's nice that his mom's reserved all of this stuff for y'all," Bree said, admiring the collection of old toys Kashawn had accumulated.

"All the stuff I had I sold, lost or tore up."

"Yeah, he's never been about throwing anything away. I'm not surprised that he still has all this stuff."

Bree smelled good as fuck. I wanted to lick her like a chocolate-dipped cone. "Were you all close growing up?" She looked at me cautiously, like a frightened rabbit that was waiting to hop off if I made any sudden moves.

"We were about as close as brothers could ever be," I lied. The truth was that we were as different as night and day.

"What were you all like growing up?"

"Kashawn kept his face in a textbook while I ran the streets trying to make a dollar, if not prowling for pussy. Kashawn worked with Daddy at the office, but not me. That shit was for suckers."

Bree looked at me, unimpressed by my frankness.

"We had a normal childhood, I guess you could say. We fought and argued, typical brotherly shit."

"Your mom looked like she didn't play."

"Oh, she didn't and she doesn't. If we got out of line, she was quick to get the belt."

Bree took my hand and sat it on my knee when I started to caress her hand with my index finger like I was some child who couldn't keep his hands to himself. "So Kashawn tells me you're a rapper."

"A little. Acting is more my bag. I guess you could say I'm more of a Tray Pain than Case Briggs."

"Ugh, don't mention that brother's name."

"Who? Tray Pain?"

"No. Case Briggs. That shit he did to my girl was fucked."

"Well, you know why she went back to him, don't you?"

"No, why don't you enlighten me," Bree said, rolling her eyes, like she knew I was going to say something she wasn't going to like.

"She couldn't resist those long strokes she was getting from that dick."

"Damn, is that all you brothr's think about, fucking?"

"What else is there?"

"How about love?"

"Can't have love without fucking," I said. I started to run my hand up along her thigh. She pushed my hand away. Bree wasn't fooling me with that hard-to-get shit. I knew she liked it. "So you still strip down at Risqué?"

"Kashawn told you?"

"He doesn't keep nothing from his family, baby girl."

"I quit the life when Kashawn proposed. He saved me, to be honest. You gotta watch your ass in that line of work. There's always somebody out here trying to take advantage. They flatter you, talk all pretty, promising you the world when all they want to do is fuck."

"So what makes you think my brother's so different?"

"I wasn't sure how Kashawn would take it once I told him I danced. I knew I would risk losing him, but knew if I wanted a future with him, I had to be straight with your brother from jump."

I was already half past bored hearing her run her mouth when I could think of one or two things she could be doing with it instead.

"Kashawn treats me with respect, you feel me? He's the first man that has ever done that. That's shit I can't even get from my damn no-account daddy."

"It seems like you and I have more in common than you and my brother."

"I doubt that," she said as she leaned into me. "I've seen countless men like you roll in and out of Risqué. Y'all act all big baller with a wad of cash, but don't amount to much."

"So you've known me all of twenty minutes and you think you know what's up? You think you the only bird who's tried to get in Kashawn's pockets? Get in line."

"Think what you want, Deanthony, but I love your brother. I don't care about his money. He could be dirt-poor and I would still love him."

"Uh-huh, I've heard that shit before."

"You should be happy for him," Bree said.

"Go 'head, marry him. Once you see what a limp-dick, wet noodle he is, my door is always open. I'll have you speaking in tongues when I'm done," I said, tracing my finger along her cleavage.

"Get off me," Bree protested, slapping my hand away.

"What's going on in here?" Kashawn asked. He entered his old bedroom.

"Hey, baby," Bree said, kissing her pussy-whipped husband-to-be. "I was just admiring your old room."

"Yeah, I like to come in here sometimes when I come over." Kashawn cut a look at me that could have slit my throat if it were a razor.

"Look, this is so cute." Bree picked up one of the *Star Wars* Ewok figures from the dresser.

"Baby, be careful with that," Kashawn said, gently taking the plastic toy out of her hand.

Once a nerd, always a damn nerd, I thought.

"D, Ma needs your help with something in the kitchen."

"I'll leave you two alone then. Just make sure you lock the door this time, bro. You don't want Ma to catch you jacking off in here like she did that time."

"Man, shut up, damn. Go see what Mama wants."

I gave Bree one last look-over with these baby-browns, knowing I would have a piece of her sooner or later just as soon as she got tired of playing doting housewife. Patience was mine and, before long, I knew Bree would be, too.

10

KASHAWN

"Bree!" I hollered, slamming the door behind me hard enough it damn near shook the house to its core. Blood had soaked through the bandana I had wrapped around my hand. "Bree, where are you, woman?" There were two glasses of Vodka sitting on the coffee table. I picked both up and finished them off.

I stumbled upstairs, drunk off my ass. "Bree, do you hear me calling you?" When I got upstairs, she was in bed with her back turned to me. I walked over to her side of the bed. "Baby, you awake?"

She was faking, but I knew just the thing to wake her up. I stood over her and started to undo the buckle of my belt. I thought she would open her eyes once she heard the clang of metal, but, no, she still wanted to pull this pretending-to-be-asleep shit.

"Why did you leave the party? Ma was asking about you. We cut the cake and everything." I unbuttoned the clasp of my jeans, unzipped them, and gently eased my dick out of my underwear. "No answer, huh?"

I started to wave my dick in her face. I grazed her plump lips with the tip of my dick head. Bree eased her eyes open, shocked to the sight of my dick in front of her.

"How about a birthday blow job," I said, laughing.

She slid away in disgust like I was dangling a pair of my dirty drawers in her face.

"You're drunk," she said.

"No shit. How did you guess? Come on. How about that blow job? I still have thirty-two minutes left before my birthday is officially over."

"Get that thing out of my face. What the hell is wrong with you tonight?"

"I'm adopted," I told her as I struggled to keep my balance.

"Adopted? Baby, what are you talking about? What happened to your hand?"

"I just found out that the man I thought was my father, really wasn't, that's all." I stumbled into the bathroom where I fell into the bathtub, taking the shower curtain with me.

Bree stood in the entrance of the bathroom, wearing a white negligée. I swear she looked like an angel as the thick flaxen weave framed her face. Damn, my baby looked good.

"Who told you this, your mama?"

"No, my fucking loser of a brother, but Mama confirmed it."

"Not even a day, and already he's starting shit. Here, let me look at your hand."

I felt Bree unfurl the bandana from around my hand.

"It doesn't seem to be that bad. Just some cuts, that's all. What did you do to yourself, baby?"

"Fuck Deanthony."

"What did you all fight about?"

"I was trying to talk to him, find out where the hell he's been the last three years without so much as a damn phone call."

"Do you really think that was a good time to bring it up?" Bree asked as she nursed the cuts on my hand with a washcloth.

"So you're taking my brother's side now?"

"Kashawn, I'm not taking anyone's side. I'm just saying that I don't think you all should have been fighting at your mama's house like that, and, secondly, it's your birthday."

"I feel like my whole life is a lie."

"Does it really matter? Edrick still loved you like you were his own son." Bree retrieved a bottle of rubbing alcohol out of the medicine cabinet.

"It matters to me. I'm a doctor. I thought I was a Parker, but I really don't know who I am."

"Where was your mom during all of this?"

"Being consoled by Deanthony. She didn't say anything, just stood there like the liar she is and cried."

"Be still. I'm going to pour a little alcohol on this."

The sting was immediate. "Ah, fuck!" I hollered.

Bree coated the cuts with some Neosporin before she wrapped my hand in a long strip of white gauze. "What did you hit anyway?"

"That big oak tree in the corner of Ma's backyard."

"Jesus, Kashawn, you could have broken your hand."

"I was trying to use it to break Deanthony's face."

"So did he say that he was here to stay?"

"I don't know and, right now, I really don't give a fuck. He's not my problem."

"Well, in the future, you might want to not be punching trees."

"I feel like I don't belong anywhere."

"Stop it." Bree began massaging my chest. "You belong to me. Now get ready for bed." Bree pulled off my boots and set them neatly in a corner of the bathroom. "Here, lean on me." We made our way to the bed where she pulled the thick, rose-printed comforter over me. "Do you believe what your uncle told you?"

"Uncle Ray-Ray has never lied to me. It took Deanthony coming home to get the truth. I mean, why? Why did Mama keep this a secret from me for so many years?"

"What are you going to do?"

"I really don't know at this point. I don't want to think about it."

"Maybe you need something to take your mind off of all that."
I felt Bree's hand on my dick. "It's time for me to give you your
birthday present."

Bree slid her fingers under the straps of her negligée, causing
the blush-pink silk to slide from her apple butter-brown breasts.
"Let's see if I can get your mind off the craziness of what happened
today."

Our lips came together in ravenous kisses. Bree's skin was as
soft as Georgia cotton. Her breasts were like pillows against my
chest. My dick rose into a hard salute from its limp position when
the lips of her pussy grazed against the head of my dick. She reached
behind, taking me gently into her palm, and guided me inside her.
My wife felt slick-wet, warm. I held onto her hips as she rode me
like a stallion. Damn, the sounds that were coming out of her as
her pussy hugged my ten inches.

"Feels…so good," she moaned.

I switched our positions: Bree's body under me, my dick stretching
her walls. Fuck yeah. Bree roped her legs behind the back of my
thighs as I plunged my dick in. Sweet, juicy pussy. Bree clawed at
my back like the wild minx she was. I threw this dick up in *Tangela*
hard. No. Fuck, I meant Bree. Why was I thinking about Tangela?
Suddenly, I couldn't stop thinking of her and that night in the
living room, her sin-red lips around my dick, deep-throating. I shut
my eyes as Bree fucked me, yet Tangela's face crept in. I prayed I
wouldn't call her name out while I was fucking Bree. The thoughts
wouldn't stop, but kept coming, running through my dirty mind.
The taste of her pussy, my fingers easing in and out of her.

"Baby, you okay?" Bree asked.

"What?"

"It just feels like you're not with me right now."

"I'm right where I want to be, baby. With you."

The visions of Tangela weren't going to stop, dancing around in my head like dirty sugar plums. I thought if I quickened my thrusts, if I fucked my wife hard enough, then maybe the thoughts of my eating out Tangela would dissipate, but with every hard thrust, the vision of Tangela looking up at me with my dick in her mouth strengthened. It was like there wasn't anything I could do. I was doing well so far in keeping the name of my wife's best friend out of my mouth. I felt myself nearing climax, so I pumped harder, faster inside her. I exploded within minutes. We came together in kisses, skin touching sweat-soaked skin.

"I'm going to take a shower. You can join me if you want," I said.

I had plenty of questions that were in need of answers and I was damn sure going to get them.

11

TANGELA

When I pulled in front of Mama Liz's house, Deanthony's black Avalanche truck was parked behind her ugly, silver PT Cruiser. I mean, damn, I don't know anybody black who drives a PT Cruiser. I parked in front of the house so I wouldn't block anyone in. Judging from the black-and-white tag that was pinned at the rear of the truck, it was a rental. The aroma of ham hocks filled the summer air as I walked toward the front door. I could hear Judge Judy running her mouth from the flat-screen, fifty-inch LG TV that Kashawn bought her last year for Mother's Day. The TV was so loud, I wouldn't have been surprised that the whole neighborhood could hear it. Mama Liz came to the screen door, smiling.

"Tangela, hey, baby. Kashawn and Bree aren't here."

"Oh, I know. I'm actually here to talk to Deanthony about something."

"Deanthony!" Mama Liz hollered.

"Huh?"

"Get up, boy, you have a visitor."

"Who is it?"

"Why don't you get your butt out of the bed and find out."

Mama Liz cut me a smile like she was some sweet old woman, but everyone in the neighborhood knew she could get real ghetto if she wanted to be.

"How's your mama doing, baby?"

Was she serious? We both knew that she didn't give two shits about my mama.

"She's doing all right. She's coming home from the hospital on Thursday actually."

"I've been intending to go see her, but I got sidetracked with Kashawn and Deanthony's party."

Intending to isn't doing, I thought.

"Yes ma'am, I understand."

"Lord, what's taking that boy so long? Deanthony!"

He slowly crept around the corner, scratching his head like he had gone through hell and back. His low-budget ass was dressed to the nines in a white tank top, black, baggy basketball shorts, white socks, and black slippers, looking ghetto but far the fuck from looking fabulous. He squinted his eyes from the bursts of bright light of the afternoon.

"Is breakfast ready?" he asked, looking slightly disoriented.

"Boy, it's one o'clock in the day. I called you half a dozen times to come down for breakfast, but you didn't come, so me and your uncle went on and ate. I have some cornflakes in there you can eat."

I grinned when Mama Liz said that.

"I'm not your housekeeper and this ain't no bed and breakfast."

"Okay, Ma, dang," Deanthony said, acting like Mama Liz was like a gnat buzzing around his ear. He deserved the scolding he got after that shit he'd pulled with Bree.

"Don't okay me. I better not go back there and find that room in a mess, either."

Deanthony rubbed sleep out of his eyes as he stepped out onto the porch. "What up, shorty?"

"Let's go out here to my car and talk." When we got out to my ride, I lit into Deanthony's black ass. "D, what the fuck was that shit you pulled on Saturday?"

"Fuck are you talking about?"

"Don't play dumb. Calling Bree, telling her that the reason you came back was for her."

"I had to make it look good. I am an actor after all."

"Should I be concerned?"

"About what?"

"I don't want you fucking this up. You need to stick with the plan. I didn't work this hard so you could throw a monkey wrench into this shit."

"That *you* worked for? You need me more than I need you right now. I was making big things happen in L.A."

"You mean selling your dick in West Hollywood for money? Those kind of *big things?*"

"Bitch, keep your voice down, damn."

"'Cause of that dumb-ass stunt you pulled on Saturday, Bree might tell Kashawn about your little crank phone call. Even worse, she might come clean about everything."

"She's not going to say shit."

"Oh, so just because you fucked her, you know what she will and won't do?"

"You know what? You need to watch your tone with me, Tangela."

"Oh, really? Well, why you don't tell it to somebody who gives a fuck. Deanthony, I'm telling you, if you mess this up, I will make sure Mama Liz, Kashawn, and Bree see the *big* things you've *really* been doing."

Before I could utter another syllable, Deanthony grabbed me by the throat.

"If I what, huh? If I what? I don't know who you think you fucking with, girl, but I'm not the nigga to cross. Who the fuck are you, anyway, just some crazy psycho bitch pining after my brother who doesn't want her."

I struggled to snatch his hand away from my throat, but Deanthony was too strong. It was official. This fool had lost his mind, if he ever had one to begin with. "Get your fucking hands off me." I could barely push the words up from my throat due to the tight hold from Deanthony's kung-fu grip.

"Not until you and I come to an understanding that I'm nobody's whipping boy I'm not some dog that you can kick around when he doesn't do what you tell it."

I felt inside my purse for something I could use against Deanthony. I yanked out my fingernail file and stabbed him in the arm with the only weapon I had against this gorilla of a man.

"Damn, bitch, are you crazy?"

He turned me loose. It took everything in me to keep from cutting Deanthony. A man puts his hands on me, I instantly see red. But Mama Liz had her eyes glued to us the whole time and I wasn't trying to catch a murder case over Deanthony's ashy-ass.

"You're glad I didn't plunge this in your throat. Don't you ever put your grimy hands on me again, or someone's going to the morgue."

"I'm fucking bleeding," Deanthony said.

"Shut the fuck up; it's just a flesh wound. You'll live."

Mama Liz stepped onto the porch. "D, what's going on out here?"

I eased my nail file back into my purse. "Nothing, Ma, we're just talking."

"Well, I heard you yelling out here. Are you all right?"

Fucking mama's boy.

"Go on back in the house, Ma. I'm fine. Tangela and I are just talking." Deanthony dabbed at the cut on his arm with the tail end of his tank top.

Mama Liz did what Deanthony told her, holding her eyes on me. If looks could kill, she would have slit a bitch's throat.

"I don't know who you think you're messing with. Maybe you

got me confused with some low-budget chicken head, but you got the wrong bitch today. I didn't drive all the way over here on this ghetto-ass side of town to kick up shit with you. I'm trying to make sure we both get what we want. I get your brother and you get to ride off back to La La Land with Bree."

"What the fuck makes you think I need you for that? I've stolen a long line of honeys from under Kashawn's nose."

"But Bree isn't just any bitch. This is the woman you're in love with."

Deanthony laughed like he was crazy.

"What's so damn funny?"

"You trying to sell me on Bree like she's a damn frozen cup. Again, baby girl, I don't need you to tell me how I feel."

"Just remember our plan and don't fuck this up for us."

"Where's the tape?"

"Do you think I would tell you, just like that?"

"I could just beat it out of you."

"And you'll never get the original."

Deanthony looked at me, knowing I had him by the balls.

"Mama Liz's doctor told her to take it easy after that mild heart attack she had last summer. I know. I was there when he told her, Kashawn, and Bree about the fragility of her health. It would just break her heart if she found out that her baby was a high-class escort. You know how Mama Liz feels about people like you."

"You a low-level cunt bitch, Tangela."

"Sticks and stones, baby boy. Just stick with the plan and I'll give you all the copies and Mama Liz never needs to know about your *sexual curricular* activities."

"And how the fuck do I know that you don't have copies?"

"You're just going to have to trust this low-level cunt bitch."

Deanthony gawked at me like he was trying to stare a hole through me. He knew I had his ass between a rock and a hard place with both my hands wrapped firmly around his balls. "So you going to tell me what's up or do I have to stand here looking at your fat-ass face all day?"

"You're going to get Bree to go to dinner with you."

"You saw the look on her face at the party when I walked in. She can't stand the sight of me."

"That was just her being a drama queen as usual. Like I told you before you came back to Tallahassee, she still has feelings for you."

"How can you be so sure?"

"I'm only her best friend. She tells me everything."

"Like what?"

"Things aren't going so well between her and Kashawn. Bree says he's been stressed out at work. Look, you can't mention this to Bree, but…"

"What? Spit it out."

"She tells me that Kashawn's been coming home drunk at crazy hours of the night."

"Kashawn doesn't drink that much."

"How do you know? You've been M.I.A. for three years. You have no idea how bad it's gotten. She told me about his temper, too, which obviously is a trait you both possess." My little white lie I was feeding this fool was quickly going from snowball to runaway boulder.

"I don't hit women, just skank, manipulative bitches like the one standing in front of me." He added, "Does he hit her?"

"She has come to me with bruises on her face."

"I'm going to kill him."

Deanthony's simple ass had taken the bait. Damn, I'm good.

"I advised Bree to leave him, to urge him to get some help, but you know how stubborn she can be. She claims that Kashawn doesn't have a problem. She says that if she loves him hard enough, he'll stop. I'm scared something bad is going to happen if they don't get help."

Deanthony was leaning against my Cadillac Escalade with his arms and feet crossed. "Everything was all good at the party."

"That was all a put-on."

I stood there, feeding him one lie after the next about Bree and Kashawn. I deserved an Academy Award for my performance. I could tell how heated Deanthony was getting. Now I wasn't the only one he wanted to kill.

"I mean, no disrespect to your brother, but—"

"Fuck 'Shawn!"

I paused for a moment to let him stew under the white-hot fire of my lies.

"What's the plan?"

"Kashawn doesn't know it yet, but he's going to cheat on Bree."

"How do you figure that?"

"Her name's Katiesha. She owes me a favor. This bitch can get anyone into bed and she's got mad deep-throat skills."

"I know her. Real low class. She's got a place over on Pepper Drive. I hear she charges something like a grand an hour."

I pulled out a fat ball of cash. "I got it covered. Trust."

"So that's why you want me to take Bree to dinner, so you can get Katiesha in their crib."

"You're not as dumb as you look."

"And how do you expect Bree to come out with me?"

"Damn, Deanthony, if I have to think of everything, what the fuck do I need you for? Sweet-talk her, tell her you're sorry for pulling that high school, crank-call bullshit you did, and that you want to make it up to her. Hell, take her out for doughnuts or something, just make sure you get her out of the house. You can be real convincing when you want to be, something people don't know about you." Flattery doesn't just get you everywhere, but it gets weak-minded men like Deanthony exactly where you want them.

"So you ain't trippin' about this Katiesha chick fucking Kashawn?"

"It's a small price to pay considering when this shit is all over, I will have your brother. I'm going to need you two to stay away from the house for a couple of hours. I'll text you when it's cool for you to bring her back."

"You ain't gonna do nothin' crazy to hurt Kashawn, right?"

"Like I said, I'm just out here to make sure we both get what we want. After we lay the groundwork tonight in splitting Bree and your brother up, everything will be butter. After tonight, she's not going to want to be in the same damn ZIP code as Kashawn."

"You just make sure this shit doesn't get away from you."

"Quitcha bitchin'. I told you I have everything under control. "

"I'll go by the house today and see what's up with Bree," Deanthony said.

"I'm supposed to be meeting up with Katiesha tonight with the money to discuss the details."

"Let me know if she's down or not."

"Oh, she'll be down once I stick this wad of money in her face."

If Deanthony knew what was good for him, he'd stick to the plan. If he fucked me over on this, I was going to flour and deep-fry his ass, Tangela-style.

12

TANGELA

I hated to do this to Bree. Well, almost. She was out of town in Atlantic City with one of her hoochie stripper friends the night Kashawn and I hooked up. You would think the bitch would get a better class of friends once she married into money and didn't have to shake her ass in the faces of old white dudes for chump change. She and Kashawn had gotten into one of their knockout drag-outs about who knew what. Bree had the nerve to ask me to take care of Kashawn while she went off to gamble away his money he worked so hard for. She was making the shit way too easy.

"I know you're busy with your photo shoots and all that for the magazine, but if you could just roll through every now and again, see how he's doing."

Of course, I wasn't about to pass up the opportunity to bend Kashawn's ear about his doting wife. The night before Bree was to return from Atlantic City, I went by the house to check on Kashawn, but not before I freshened up a little, put on one of my favorite outfits that would accentuate my titties and other...*assets*. I took one look at myself in my vanity and knew for damn sure that if he resisted this, he was out of his mind. When I arrived at their house in Ox Bottom Manor, I felt him give me the look-over, ripping my clothes off with those pretty brown eyes. Married or not, he was a man who knew a fine-ass bitch when one was standing on his doorstep.

I pampered Kashawn all that weekend: keeping the house clean that I should have been sharing with him instead of Bree, cooking, as well as washing and ironing his clothes. Hell, I even ironed the man's socks and drawers. I made sure he didn't want for nothing. We spent the weekend finding out new things about one another, like him being a die-hard fan of Allison Hobbs' novels. I still hadn't gotten my copy of *Big Juicy Lips* back yet, but I didn't sweat the shit, considering I'd read the book fifty-eleven times. I noticed the book sticking out of Bree's pocketbook a week ago when we lunched at Bella Bella. That night, Kashawn and I stuffed ourselves to the gills from the lasagna I had prepared for dinner.

"Damn, ma, I didn't know you could throw down in the kitchen like that," he said as we made our way to the living room with two glasses of red wine. We settled on the white leather sofa I helped Bree pick out at Aaron's Furniture.

"Oh, I'm full of surprises," I said with a sinister tone.

"Bree doesn't even cook like that."

"I didn't think she cooked at all."

"She does all right. She's gotten better since we got married."

"Yeah, I saw all the cookbooks in the kitchen drawer." We both grinned at Bree's sorry-ass attempts at being *Top Chef.*

"You can't blame her for trying."

"Back when Bree and I were roomies, that girl could barely boil rice without burning it to a crisp, kept the apartment smoked up. So much so I had to disconnect the fire alarm."

I loved when Kashawn laughed. He had the prettiest white teeth.

"That would explain the burnt smell I would get a whiff of whenever I walked into the apartment."

He looked and smelled so good. I wanted to lick the skin off his body. Simple fact is that Bree didn't deserve a man who treated her like a queen, who worshipped the ground her man-stealing ass walked on.

"You want a little more wine?" Kashawn asked.

"Just a little."

He poured more in both of our glasses. "You know, I owe you an apology."

"For what?" I asked.

"That night at Club Rehab. I was about to walk over and talk to you that night."

"So why didn't you, silly?"

"I honestly don't know. Would you believe that I was shy?"

"You? Noooo," I teased.

"I've never had much luck with women. Even though Deanthony and I look alike, he was more of the chick magnet. Y'all like that bad boy image. If girls were into me, it was either so they could get closer to my brother, or they would pay me to do their home-work."

"Well, if it's any consolation, I think you're hotter than Deanthony. Looks and a big dick can only get you so far. Look at you. You're a surgeon at one of the best hospitals in the country, you have a gorgeous home, and a great wife. You have a shitload more going for you than your brother."

"You think I'm hot, huh?" Kashawn asked, taking a sip of wine.

"Oh, smoking hot. Have-the-whole-crib-burning-down hot."

Kashawn and I chuckled.

"I always thought you were pissed about what went down at Rehab that night."

"That was a long time ago, Kashawn. I'm not the kind of woman who holds grudges."

"I guess Bree told you that we've been having problems?"

"Yeah, but show me a marriage that doesn't have its troubles."

"Seems like all we do is fight."

"I know Bree can be a bit rough around the edges sometimes."

Kashawn turned to me and asked, "How so?"

"I mean, coming from the lifestyle of stripping, she's not used to being so... domesticated."

"I don't see our marriage as that at all."

"Oh, of course not. It's just that maybe she's grown a little weary of cooking and cleaning, which would explain her trip to Atlantic City. It's never enough for her sometimes, nothing is. She can have a ravenous appetite in trying to get what she wants, you feel me?"

"I guess so, yes."

I watched as the seed of disillusionment set into Kashawn's mind.

"So how come you're still walking around here single?"

"I guess I haven't found the right man yet." I couldn't have smeared the bullshit on any thicker.

"I do regret not walking over to you in the club that night. Maybe things would have been a lot different."

Kashawn's face was only inches away from mine.

"You can't help who you fall in love with," I said.

Kashawn moved in closer. I was about to get a kiss from the man of my wet dreams. Back when he used to spend the night with Bree, I used to masturbate under the covers, hearing them fuck behind the tissue paper-thin walls that separated us, wishing that it was me he was deep-dicking. Kashawn's lips felt like warm butter against my own. He slipped me some tongue, but I didn't object. I grazed his crotch to feel a bulge that tented his jeans. My heart was beating like an African drum in my chest with the disbelief that this shit was going down.

Kashawn fought to undo the pea-sized buttons that ran down my blouse. He got tired and tore open my top, causing buttons to pop loose, bouncing on the plate glass of the coffee table Bree had imported from Anthropologie in New York. He flicked at my chocolate chip nipples with the point of his tongue before he sucked them hard past his lips and white teeth into his mouth. He made my sex-charged body quiver, easing a hand up along the inside of my left thigh until he reached my spot. Kashawn teased the lips of my pussy with his digits before he entered me. I wrapped my legs around him like a vise as he sucked each of my breasts, as he fingered my sugar.

Payback's a bitch and her name is Tangela Charlise Meeks, I thought as Bree pranced into my head.

Kashawn went for my panties, peeling them off my plump thighs, down to my gold stiletto, platform fuck-me pumps. The Victoria's Secret drawers snagged onto one of the ten-inch heels. This shit was on and popping. My tight black skirt was hiked above my booty. I was half-ass naked with a soaking wet pussy that was down for whatever Kashawn had in mind. He wasted no time moving down south. Fuck yeah. I thought I was going to nut as soon as I felt the tip of his tongue hit my spot. This brother started doing things with his tongue I didn't know were humanly possible.

"Fuck me," I pleaded. "I want to feel that dick inside me."

Kashawn ignored me and kept eating me out. I basked in the idea of Bree coming home and smelling my pussy on her man's dick, a bitch marking her territory, so to speak. I wanted him to fuck a hole through me that night, but with the serious pussy-eating skills Kashawn was throwing down, I didn't give a damn either way.

Damn, boy, you better get this tongue insured. Full coverage for eating pussy. That night, I had never came so hard in my life.

"Shit, girl, you're a skirter?"

"I am now."

Kashawn rose up from between my thighs, his face wet with my juices. I wasn't content until I got his dick wet. I don't play that one-sided reciprocation shit. I'm a lady who's about pleasing her man. I unzipped Kashawn's jeans as he undid the clasp.

I hooked my sin-red nails behind the elastic ring of his tight-whites and edged them down until Kashawn's thick piece popped free. The veins that ran along his dark-chocolate shaft were like thunderbolts. The fat dick head resembled a chocolate heart if admired from a certain angle. Kashawn looked to be about ten inches, maybe eleven. I wasted no time throwing my lips to his appendage that hung between his muscled thighs. I held the base of his dick between my index and fuck-you finger. My red-hot nail polish juxtaposed with pitch-black crotch hair.

"Suck that dick."

Nothing gets me more horned up than when a man talks dirty to me. I sucked the head of Kashawn's dick as if there was a sweet center I was trying to get to. I eased my lips like a dick-ring around his shit until his pubes tickled my nose.

"Deep-throat me." I took him until his heart-shaped dick head kissed the back of my throat. "Yeah, like that. That feels good."

If Kashawn's dick was this tasty, I could have only imagined how he felt balls-deep in my pussy. I looked up at him as I worked his dick with fire-engine-red lips. I sucked until I felt him tense in my mouth. Within seconds, torrents of cum filled me. I throated his juice like the all-day dick sucker I was. I swigged a little wine to wash Kashawn down.

"Fuck, I needed that," he said, out of breath.

I knew then that sucking dick was a duty Ms. Wifey was not living up to. It goes to show that you don't always have to be a fly on the wall to know what's going on in people's lives. Kashawn and I spent the rest of the night talking as if he was never face-down between my legs.

13

DEANTHONY

should have choked the hell out of her. How in the hell did she know about the shit I did in L.A.? I'm going to get that tape if I have to beat it out of her. I'll go with Tangela on this plan for now until I get what I want, but then after that, all bets are off.

When I walked back in the house, the screen door slamming behind me, Mama Liz was hot on my heels.

"What the hell did she want?" She followed me down the hall that led to my bedroom.

"She just wanted to ask me for a favor, Ma, that's all." I shut the door behind her, in Mama Liz's face. I was pissed and in no mood for her insistent nagging and complaining.

"You need to stay away from that woman. Tangela is nothing but trouble, just like her mama."

I pulled open one of the drawers of the bathroom counter and took out a Band-Aid. I tore off the paper, peeled off the plastic tabs from the adhesive, and stuck the bandage over the damaged area where Tangela had stuck me.

"I'm going to cut that blackmailing bitch off at the knees when I get Bree and the tape." I scrolled through my cell phone until I got to Bree's number.

"Hello?" Bree answered.

"Hey, it's me, Deanthony."

"Why the hell are you calling me? Kashawn is in the kitchen."

"Hold on, Bree, don't hang up. I called because I wanted to apologize for what I said to you on the phone the other day."

"You freaked me out with that shit."

"And that wasn't my intention. Why don't you let me make it up to you?"

"It's fine. Apology accepted."

"Let me take you out for a drink."

"I can't. You know that."

"Bree, it's drinks, just two friends hanging out, strictly platonic."

Silence breached our words.

"Hello?"

"I'm here."

"So how about it? Drinks at the Mockingbird?"

"One drink," Bree said.

"How does seven o' clock sound?"

"Whatever," Bree said coldly, "I need to talk to you about something anyway."

"About what? What's going on?"

"I can't talk about it over the phone, but we'll talk tonight." Bree hung up the phone before I could say anything.

I called Tangela to let her know what was up. "It's a go. We're meeting up for drinks tonight at The Mockingbird at seven."

"Good boy," Tangela said in an annoying patronizing tone. "I told you that you could do anything you put that dirty mind of yours to."

"What are you about to do now?"

"Call her to find out if Kashawn's going to be home so I can put Plan B into action."

"You need to tell me what the hell you're planning so we can be on the same page."

"I don't have to do shit but stay black and pretty, motherfucker.

You just do what I tell you, and Bree could be back in those big, brawny arms of yours faster than you can say cuddle slut. Now let me remind you that if you fuck this up for me, I'll make sure that Bree and Kashawn get a copy of the tape."

"You know what, bitch, there isn't going to be too many more of your empty threats."

Tangela laughed. "Just don't forget what I have on you."

"Fuck you!"

Tangela chuckled. "I'll be in touch."

14

TANGELA

I sat at a table in the middle of the club, sipping a dirty martini as I watched this stripper who looked like her ass was a hundred years old with droopy titties, chittlin' thighs, and crow's feet. I kept thinking, *where in the hell did they get grandma?* This bitch was so old, she probably knew Fredrick Douglass back in the day. I laughed my pretty girl ass off as the stuffed shirts in the place hissed and booed, begging the old bitch to actually put her clothes back on instead of taking off another stitch. I took cute sips of my dirty martini as I waited for them to bring on the next dancer. After about twenty agonizing minutes of watching this hag prance up and down the stage, it was finally over. Good-damn-thing, too, 'cause another second of that, I was going to jab my eyes out.

"Give it up for Ursula Starr!" the DJ announced.

None of these sleazy brothers clapped, and they hissed and booed even louder. This Ursula chick pathetically reached down to scrape the few singles that were thrown to her off the black stage. "Fuck every last one of y'all!" she yelled.

I laughed, thinking, *that's some sad-ass shit right there.*

The DJ, some wigger with corn rolls, stood in front of a turntable mixing one rap song after the next. When he put on Trina's "Red Bottoms," I wanted to get up out of my seat and shake my ass to that jam.

"That's my bitch right there," I said to myself.

"All right, niggas, loosen your ties, get outcha seats, and grab your dicks, 'cause let me introduce you to Tallahassee's baddest bitch in the 8-5-0, Katiesha!"

It was her, the chick I had waited for, the bitch who hated Bree about as much as I did. Katiesha slinked out on stage, wearing a leopard-print two-piece, a blond wig that draped down her back, and black, red-bottom platforms. She had a pretty caramel complexion with round, brown titties and a thick booty. Now, I'm not saying that I'm gay or nothing, but if I was, I would probably holler, no lie.

So that's the infamous Katiesha?

The bitch had given Bree shit for years. Katiesha was who I was looking for, who would be instrumental in the next phase of my plan to break up Bree and Kashawn. The suits were making it rain with dollar bills as she wrapped herself seductively around the steel pole, grinding her pussy against it like it was a dick. She had these fools eating out of her hands, and would soon leave them with empty wallets and brick-hard dicks. I pulled a C-note out of my cleavage, walked slowly past these sex-thirsty men to the stage, and handed the money to Katiesha. All the eyes in the club were on me. These mutts were cheering like a bunch of pussy-hungry frat boys, like they wanted me to join Katiesha up on stage. Dirty fucks. When it comes to pussy, men will do anything, including sit and roll over. The way Katiesha made her ass jiggle and clap on stage, she had them drooling all over themselves.

I couldn't keep my eyes off her, the way she swung herself around the pole like some kind of exotic boa constrictor. She even had a bitch like me captivated by her talent. After her performance, she came out in the lounge area of the club, dressed in a red robe with lace trim on the sleeves and at the hem. The suits pulled at her like she was some famous porn star, all of them aching for a minute of her time, but she kept her light-brown eyes zeroed in on me, knowing, as well as I, that those fools were trifling and low-pro.

"How you doing tonight?" she asked.

"Sitting here, enjoying my drink and the sexy entertainment. I gotta tell you, ma, you were doing your thing up on the stage."

"Thank you. Did you enjoy yourself?"

"Hell yeah. I love how you have these fools puffing and panting on you."

"So what brings you out tonight?"

"I'm just out, seeing what kind of trouble I can get into."

"I feel you," Katiesha said. "So, um…you want to go in back for a lap dance?"

"Lead the way, baby girl."

Katiesha took me by the hand, leading me toward a back room at the rear of the club. The room was dimly lit with a red and black color scheme. The floor was blacker than the devil's asshole, and the walls and plush booth seats were as red as sin. Katiesha picked a private corner of the room where she sat me down.

"I just want to let you know before we get started that it's two-hundred bucks an hour."

"Not a problem," I told her.

I was willing to pay whatever it took to get Katiesha on my team, to do what I needed her to do. I plucked two hundred-dollar bills out of my silver clutch and handed them to her. She stuffed them seductively down into the leopard-print bra part of her bikini. I started to ask her where she purchased it from, but decided against it. Katiesha worked herself between my thighs, grinding her booty in my lap. If I had a dick, I would have been bone-hard that night.

"What do you think I could get for a thousand?"

Katiesha gyrated around slowly with a seductive expression on her face. "Pretty much anything you want, baby." She gleamed. "What do you have in mind?"

"How about just talking?"

"Talk? Talk about what?"

"A mutual friend of ours."

"I don't have any friends."

"This bitch you would know. Bree Parker."

As soon as I mentioned Bree's name, Katiesha gawked at me like it was a mortal sin to say Bree's name in her presence. "Who the fuck are you?" She spoke with venom in her voice.

"Someone who wants to see Bree get exactly what she deserves."

Katiesha kept on dancing. "It's been a hot minute since I last heard that name. You still haven't told me who you are and what you want."

"I have a proposition for you."

"Is this some kind of joke? Did that bitch send you here to punk me?"

"Bree didn't send me. I'm an old roommate of hers. We lived together back when she was stripping here at the club."

"Okay, and?"

"She always talked about how she couldn't stand you."

"Well, the feeling was mutual. How is that stank pussy bitch anyway?"

"We can't talk here. Meet me in the parking lot after your shift is over, and I'll fill you in on everything. I drive a black Mustang. It's parked in the back of the parking lot." I handed Katiesha a fifty-dollar bill to let her know that I wasn't fucking around. "And there's plenty more where that came from if you're interested." I walked out of the back room, leaving Katiesha with her curiosity piqued.

It felt good to breathe in some fresh air, to get away from the stench of period pussy and cigarettes. I waited almost two hours for Katiesha before she made her way out of the club, but I would have waited all night if it meant I would get what I came for. She was dressed from tip to tail in a black jacket, a black corset, and a black mini that was so short, you could see her fallopian tubes. She had on these eight-inch thigh-highs that I would have killed for. Black wavy weave came down over her shoulders.

Ho couture, I thought. I unlocked the passenger-side door for Katiesha to get in.

"Damn, these boots are killin' me," she said as she slid into the passenger seat.

"You know what they say: beauty is pain."

"Shit. You ain't never lied."

"You hungry? There's a Whataburger a block up the street. They have the best double cheeseburgers you ever want to sink your teeth into."

Katiesha was skin and bones, like she hadn't eaten a month from Sunday. "You ain't weird or anything, are you? I'm not into that kinky shit."

"I'm not weird, kinky, or crazy. I just want to do some business with you, that's all. Lady to lady."

"I guess I can use a little something to eat, but can you stop me off to Walgreens to get some cigarettes?"

I started my car. "Whatever you need, ma."

15

BREE

"Baby, who was that?" Kashawn asked as he took me from behind, kissing along the nape of my neck.

"Um…it was Tangela. She asked if I wanted to have a girl's night out tonight. I told her I would call her back and let her know for sure." I felt terrible lying to Kashawn. I'd told so many lies to cover the truth, I had lost count. "I wouldn't object to spending a quiet Saturday night with my man."

"Baby, I have so much work to catch up on here. You should go. It's better than sitting around the house."

"Well, you want me to bring you some dinner home?"

"I'll probably order takeout. It's likely I will be burning the midnight oil tonight with all of these patient files."

"So have you thought about this stuff with your biological father?"

"It's all I've thought about. I need to work right now to take my mind off things."

"You know I'm here for you, no matter what you decide," I said as I seductively roped my arms around Kashawn's torso.

"And I could use that support system right now." Kashawn and I came together in a long kiss.

"Are you sure you want to stay cooped up in your study all night?" I asked, caressing the bulge in his pants I was responsible for causing.

"If I don't try to get some work done tonight, it will only pile up on me."

I licked and kissed Kashawn's top lip. "How about I pile up on you instead?"

When I started for his zipper, he eased away. "Let's do this when I get from under all this paperwork, baby."

"Are you sure you don't want a little taste before you head off to the office?"

"Hell no, I'm not sure," he laughed, "but if I don't leave, I'm going to end up throwing you over this desk and fucking you gorilla style."

"Where's the bad in that?"

"Damn, girl," he said, looking back at me as he reached for the doorknob.

"Your loss." I ran my index finger across my cleavage, something that would give Kashawn the initiative to do what he had to do, so he could fuck me stupid later.

16

TANGELA

For someone who was skin and bones, Katiesha had the appetite of a moose. She ordered just about everything off the menu. Two double cheeseburgers, two large orders of fries, a large root beer, and two pineapple pies. The fast-food greasy spoon was packed with college kid drunks from the bar across the street. I picked a booth seat in a corner where Katiesha and I could run our mouths. The smell of hot grease bit my senses. Katiesha not only finished off what she ordered, but ate half of what I had on my tray. It was like she was a bottomless pit the way she scarfed down burgers and fries. Damn, to be that skinny and not gain an ounce should be a damn crime.

"So what that ho up to these days?" Katiesha asked, stuffing fries into her mouth. "Didn't she get married to some hot-shot doctor?"

"Yeah, Dr. Kashawn Parker," I said.

"I saw a picture of them in the paper. I wasn't feeling that ugly-ass wedding dress she wore. Who is she fooling, wearing white like she's some virgin princess? Bougie bitch. Bree always did think she was better than everybody."

I swirled my straw around in my sweet tea. "More than ever now that she got a ring on it," I added.

"Hell, that doesn't mean nothing. She stoops over and shits like the rest of us."

I don't know what I was sickened by the most: Katiesha's greasy fingers from the hamburgers, or her talking with her mouth full. Who taught this bitch proper table manners, Slimer from *Ghostbusters?* I've seen babies with better manners.

"So what's up? You mentioned something about a business proposition."

"So you know Bree's husband?"

"Who hasn't? I can't stand that bitch, but, damn, she's got good taste in men. The girls at the club steady be talking about how fine he is. Bree better not slip 'cause a bitch might push up on it."

The thought of Katiesha doing anything to my Kashawn almost made me throw up in my mouth, but I had to keep my composure to get this shit done. "And how much would it take for you to *push* up on that?"

"Whatchu mean?" Katiesha dipped two fries into a container of spicy ketchup.

"What would you say if I told you I would pay you five grand to fuck Bree's man?"

"I would say stop pulling my dick."

"Oh, I'm dead serious."

Katiesha started laughing. She took a napkin, realizing its use, and wiped her mouth. Hell, for a minute there, I thought I would have to get this girl a bib.

"Let's go outside. I need a cigarette," she said.

We walked outside where we leaned against my Mustang. Katiesha rested the cigarette between her lips, took out a green lighter, and lit the end until it burned orange-red. Smoke spirited from the cave of her nose, the crease of her lips.

"When are you talking about doing this?"

"Kashawn should be home now."

"Hold up. I know you ain't talking about doing this shit tonight."

"Tonight is the only time it can be done. I might not have another opportunity like this."

"So what's in this shit for you?"

I wasn't about to tell home girl my business. "That's not important."

"You trying to break their marriage up?"

"Question is will you do it?"

"That's it, isn't it? You wet for Bree's man."

I ignored Katiesha, growing more and more annoyed with her trying to get all up in my business. "It has to be done tonight and we need to move fast."

"Well, I've never been one to turn down good money, but make it ten G's and you got a deal."

"Damn, ten grand?"

"Cash motherfucking money."

I didn't want to give into her demands. "Okay, I will give you five now and another five when the job is done."

Katiesha took a drag from her cigarette as she considered my plan. I knew good and well it was an offer she wasn't going to refuse. "That's what's up. Let's do this."

"And this has to be kept between you and me. If I find out that you told anyone, the deal is off, no money."

"I gotchu. I'm down for whatever."

I knew I couldn't trust Katiesha's ass as far as I could throw her. The girl was a stripper after all, which is why I was going to see this through. I already had Deanthony fucking my shit up, and I wasn't about to have her throw a kink into my game.

"I need to clean up first, wash my pussy."

"What?"

"My vagina. You want me to have a clean vagina, don't you?"

"Do what you gotta do."

As Katiesha went to the bathroom to *freshen up*, I couldn't help but think what the hell I was getting myself into with this chick. I called Bree to see what was up. Deanthony should have done his part by now.

17

BREE

Fuck is Deanthony's problem, calling me here? I need to have my damn head examined for agreeing to have drinks with him. As I cleared off the kitchen table, my iPhone rang. I studied the tiny flat-screen. It was Tangela.

"Girl, I'm so glad you called."

"Hey, you all right? You sound upset."

"I just got off the phone with Deanthony."

"He called again? What does he want this time?" Tangela asked.

"He wants to have a drink tonight, make up for calling me and scaring the hell out of me the other day."

"What did you tell him?"

"I told him I would meet up for *one* drink, but I'm thinking about calling him back and cancelling."

"I don't see anything wrong with talking to Deanthony. It's not like you can move to another country."

"I have a bone to pick with him anyway. Kashawn came home last night, drunk and pissed off."

"Why? What happened?"

"Something about Edrick not being their real daddy."

"Damn, that's fucked up. Do they know of the whereabouts of their real daddy?"

"No, and it's been bothering Kashawn ever since he found out. He hasn't slept much and he's spending a lot of time at the hospital and drowning himself in work to take his mind off things."

"So where is he, at the hospital?"

"He's in his study catching up on some work."

I slipped on a simple white tank top and some jeans, nothing special, to meet with Deanthony. My hands were already starting to sweat at the thought of meeting up with D, but I knew Tangela was right. There was no running away from the man, no matter how much I wanted to avoid him. I grabbed my keys to the Mustang and hauled ass out the door.

"So what is Kashawn going to do?" Tangela asked.

"If I know him, he's going to track his real daddy down."

"That's good, though, right?"

"Yes, but I don't want him to set himself up for disappointment."

"If he does, then you will be there to pick up the pieces," Tangela said.

"Tange, I wish you were going with me."

"You want me to meet you at The Mockingbird, lie back in case he tries something sneaky?"

"I would love that, but I want to find out why he came back here."

I remembered the Marlboros I had stashed under the driver's side seat. I struggled to quit for Kashawn, who hated that I smoked. I reached under and pulled the pack from under the seat. As soon as I hit a stoplight, I fished a cancer stick out of the pack and rested it between my lips. With a cheap lighter I'd purchased from CVS, I lit the end and took a drag.

"Well, let me go so I can get this over with."

"Call me after. Let me know how everything goes," Tangela said.

"You know I will."

I pressed the red END CALL button on my cell and dropped it in my black leather clutch. The cigarette was what I needed to calm my ass down. I hadn't set eyes on Deanthony since the birthday party at Mama Liz's. I took a drag off my cigarette and then exhaled, blowing a body of smoke out into the warm spring air.

I was nervous as hell when I pulled into the lot of The Mockingbird. My heart was beating crazy. When I walked in, he was sitting at the bar, nursing on a Bud.

"All right, girl, let's do this," I said to myself. I went over and tagged Deanthony on the shoulder. "Hey."

"Hey, what's up, you made it."

"Sorry I'm late. I know you said seven o'clock."

"It's all good. I just got here anyway."

A cute, brown-skinned bartender walked over to where we were sitting.

"You want something to drink?" Deanthony asked. "Vodka Cranberry, right?"

"You remembered."

"I never forgot."

"A Vodka Cranberry for her and let me get another beer," Deanthony told the young bartender. "So how you been?"

"Honestly. Not that good." The bartender returned with my drink. I swirled the straw around in it. "Kashawn told me what happened at Mama Liz's that night of y'all's birthday party."

"It was in the heat of the moment. He kept riding my ass about why I left Tallahassee and why I came back."

"So why did you?"

"I think you know the answer to that, Bree," Deanthony said. "Everybody seems to care more about why I left than why I came back, like it matters." A look of annoyance ran across Deanthony's mug.

"So when did Mama Liz tell y'all you were adopted?"

"We were about eight at the time. Ma sat me down after dinner one night and told me that Edrick wasn't our real pops, and that he loved us like we were his own. Our dad died in a car accident when

we were real young. She made me swear to never tell Kashawn."
Deanthony took a sip from his drink.

"You should have said something years ago if you knew that
Mama Liz had no intention of telling him. How could you hold
on to a secret like that for this long?"

"I figured he would have found out somehow by now, or Ma
would have told him."

"You're his brother, for Christ's sake, adopted or not." I was so
pissed. I felt a headache coming on.

"I guess she didn't want to face the possibility of losing me and
Kashawn if she told when we were adults."

"He's been walking around here for thirty years, carrying the
last name of a man who isn't his father."

"Ma said that the guy was some crackhead."

I looked at Deanthony like he'd just said the dumbest thing anyone could say. "D, we're going to get married. If his identity is a
lie, so is mine because I've taken Kashawn's last name. And what
if we decide to have children? He's got the name *Parker* on his
birth certificate, on his driver's license, social security card, everything, and you're going to sit here and fix your lips to say that it
don't matter? It should matter to you because it affects you as much
as it affects him. Kashawn hasn't been right since you told him."

"Why, what's up?"

"He came home drunk and pissed off, going on about the fight
y'all had, saying that he wasn't who he thought he was. 'My whole
life is a lie,' he kept yelling."

"He didn't do anything to you, did he?" Deanthony asked.

"Of course not. Kashawn isn't like that. I was able to calm him
down, but I can tell that it's bothering him."

Cubes of ice kissed Deanthony's lips as he took another drink.
The bartender noticed that my glass was empty and asked if I
wanted another Vodka Cranberry.

"No, I need to go. Kashawn is home waiting. He thinks I'm out with Tangela."

Deanthony kept glancing at his watch. "Come on, stay. Have another drink. I will talk to my brother and straighten everything out."

"You are the last thing he needs right now."

"Bree, look, we're brothers and brothers fight. Kashawn'll be all right."

"You don't get it, do you?" I asked, raising my voice. "This shit wasn't like some fight on the playground where he got sand kicked in his face. He found out that the man he admired and respected isn't his biological father, but that he's the son of a man he's never seen or met, a man who probably doesn't even know that you all exist because you and Mama Liz kept him in the dark all these years."

"Look, I admit that Kashawn never should have found out like that, and you know that I never meant to hurt him, to have him find out the way he did."

"If I know Kashawn, he's got a lot of questions about who his real father is, and I don't want him to get hurt if he decides to go looking for answers."

"I don't think that it will come to that."

"Deanthony, you know once he sinks his teeth into something, it's hard to pull him loose. I just don't want him to set himself up for devastation, whatever he finds."

"I'll talk to him. Everything will be fine," Deanthony said.

"Whatever he decides, I'm going to stick by him."

Deanthony's phone rang. He answered the call. Suddenly, a stoic expression came over his face. "What? Who is this?" He directed his attention to me. "What about my brother?"

"What's going on? Did something happen to Kashawn?"

"We need to go. Something's going on back at your house."

"What is it? What happened?"

Deanthony hauled ass out of the bar, frantic.

18

TANGELA

We pulled a couple of blocks away from Kashawn and Bree's crib, somewhere we couldn't be seen. Ten minutes later, Kashawn pulled into the driveway.

"Damn, he just as fine in person," Katiesha said.

"Focus, girl, focus," I told her. "Now run our plan by me one more time. What did we discuss?"

"Tangela, I'm not fucking stupid. I know what to do."

"I know, but I just want to make sure we're on the same page, that's all."

Katiesha sighed as if I had been prepping her for some kind of national spelling bee. "I go to the house, ring the doorbell, tell Kashawn that my car broke down, and ask if I could use his phone to call a tow truck."

"Yes, good. And once you're in, the rest is up to you."

"Don't trip. No man can resist these bountiful titties of mine." Katiesha adjusted her breasts in the black genuine leather corset.

"And more importantly, make sure that Bree sees you."

"Oh, trust, I will give that bitch a show she will never forget."

"If shit pops off, get out of there."

"I'm not worried about nothin' poppin' off. That bitch can't beat this ass."

Katiesha got out of the car and started toward Kashawn and Bree's, one of the biggest houses on the block. I would have given anything to be a fly on the wall when Bree walked in to find Kashawn and her worst enemy in bed, fucking. I grinned, knowing that it was a given that Katiesha was going to get that ass whipped by Bree. Hell, I was counting on it.

19

KATIESHA

A in't this a bitch! I never thought that I would run into someone who hated Bree's ass as much as me. It goes to show that
there is all kinds of cray-cray out here, some real straitjacket
kinda bitches. My little low-income, one-bedroom crib didn't have
shit on Kashawn and Bree's mansion. That bitch had done well for
herself. I could have married into money. This white sugar daddy
that had a sweet tooth for young chocolate would always come
into Risqué, slapping down major cake just to see me dance. The
geezer was like ninety-somethin' years old. He had a nurse who
would wheel him into the club. She would sit there and pretend
to read a magazine while he waved one hundred-dollar bills in my
face. He told me that if I married him, I wouldn't want for anything. I was going to take him up on it until the man up and died
on a bitch, so there went my meal ticket.

I felt like I stuck out like a sore thumb in the well-to-do neighborhood, like all eyes were on me. I walked up to the big, wide, white
door and pressed the doorbell. I could hear the echo of the ring
inside the house. I tugged my skirt down, checked my titties as I
waited for Kashawn to answer. I was nervous as hell. I looked back
at Tangela sitting in her ride, looking. I heard footsteps coming
closer toward the door.

"All right, 'Tiesha, put your game face on, mama."

When that big door flew open, this six-foot-four mocha Chocolatte brother with deep brown eyes and juicy-ass lips stood in front of me. I had no idea how gorgeous Kashawn was. The newspapers didn't do his fine ass justice. All I could do was stare.

"Can I help you?"

"Huh? What? Oh, my bad. Sorry to bother you, but my car broke down a few blocks down the street and I was wondering if I could use your phone to call my friend to come get me?"

"Yeah, come on in." Damn, his voice alone was enough to make my pussy tickle.

I stepped over the threshold, entering Kashawn's palace. With brandy in one hand, he searched his pockets with the other for his phone. "Here we go," he said, swiping it from a small table behind one of the pretty white leather sofas.

I dialed a fake number, held it up to my ear, and faked a conversation with someone made up. I had to pull a name quick out of my ass. Kashawn had his TV on, tuned to CNN. "Anderson, this is Katiesha. My car broke down again. Can you come get me? I'm over here on... What's the address here?"

"1413 Thornburg Court."

"1413 Thornburg Court. Yeah, Anderson, way out here. "I'll be outside waitin'." I handed the phone back to Kashawn. "Thank you."

"You're welcome. What's going on with your car?"

"It won't start. I don't know what's wrong with it this time. That damn car is always breakin' down."

"You want me to go take a look at it? You said it's down the street, right?"

"No, it's cool. You don't need to do that."

"Are you sure? It's no problem. I own an auto parts store, so I know my way around cars. It would save your friend from having to drive all the way out here."

"No, it's all good. He said he's out here in the area anyway."

"You sure?"

I gave Kashawn a flirtatious smile. "Yeah, he's on his way."

"Well, it's pretty dark out there. You can wait around here for him if you want."

"I don't want to put you out."

"It's not a problem. Just hang tight until he shows up."

"Thank you. Anderson takes his time getting anywhere, so it might be a while."

"You want something to drink while you wait?"

"I'll have a beer if it's not any trouble."

"No trouble. I'll be right back," Kashawn said. He set his glass on the coffee table and hauled off to the kitchen. As he rummaged around for a can opener, I reached inside my purse to pull out a tiny plastic bag of GHB. "So what kind of car do you drive?"

"It's a 2001 Oldsmobile Bravado. I just got it, actually," I lied.

"What lot did you buy it off of if you don't mind my asking?"

I slipped a tiny white pill in his drink and swiveled it around in the glass of liquor and ice. "Kareem's Auto on Apalachee Street."

"I know them. Be careful with those guys. I know a guy who used to fix cars for them who told me that a lot of the cars they have suffered water damage from Hurricane Katrina."

"That would explain why I've been having so many problems with it."

Kashawn unscrewed the top off a bottle of beer and walked out of the kitchen, back to where I was standing. "People I've talked to who have bought cars from them come to the store to buy new parts for parts that have rusted out from all the water damage." Kashawn handed me the cold beer. "Here you go."

"That's what's up then. I'm getting rid of it. That SUV ain't been givin' me nothin' but trouble since I got the thing." It's a wonder my nose wasn't growing with all the lies I was telling. I watched

Kashawn take a swig from his beer. It wouldn't be long before the drug took hold. "This is a nice house you have here."

"It oughta be. It cost me enough."

"You know what? I thought you looked familiar. I saw you and your wife in the paper. What's your name?"

"Kashawn Parker, and, yes, that was us." He smiled like he took pride in knowing I noticed him.

"And Bree Parker is your wife. Y'all make a beautiful couple."

He took a sip from his spiked drink. "Thank you. I was a ball of nerves that day."

"I bet your wife was climbing the walls."

"She claims…that, um…that she was all right once she saw me standing at the end of the altar."

I could tell that the drug was starting to take effect, judging from the way Kashawn was losing his ability to stand. "I've always dreamt of gettin' married, but I guess it was never in the cards."

"The right guy is out there for you. He just hasn't found you yet." Kashawn looked as if he was about to lose his balance.

"You all right?" I asked, knowing good and damn well he was anything but.

"Yeah, just a little dizzy."

"You should lie down."

"I think you're right."

Kashawn couldn't keep his balance and was about to take a nosedive into the coffee table until I wedged myself under his right arm to keep him from falling.

"Let me help you upstairs."

Kashawn was listless, dragging his feet across the white marble floor. It took some *She-Hulk* kind of strength to get his ass upstairs.

I laid him gently on the king-sized bed like he was fragile, fine china. I sat on the bed next to him, admiring his boyish good looks.

I caressed his chiseled jaw, ran my fingers over his full lips that I reached over and kissed. His chest was warm to the touch as I slipped my fingers between the open grooves of his lavender dress shirt. I looked around the bedroom that was bigger than my bathroom and living room combined. There was a huge vanity strewn with earrings, necklaces, and diamond rings.

Here Bree was, living high off the hog, while I scraped for every nickel and dime I made. It wasn't right that she should get the fine hubby, the big crib in the well-to-do part of town with all the white folks and their ripe green yards where shit was pretty and worry-free. I took a tour of the bedroom. The white and peach bathroom was the size of my garage. Bree had the walk-in closet that I had only dreamt of having. There were columns of shoes that went to the ceiling while Prada, Chanel and Louis Vuitton lined the perimeter of the closet. Bree's white mink was the first thing that caught my eye.

"I bet this shit here cost more than my mortgage."

I got undressed and tried on the fur. It felt like it was made for me, the way it hugged my naked body. I tried on Bree's rings, sliding a different piece of bling on each finger. "Yeah, a bitch could get used to this right here. The glamorous life."

An unconscious Kashawn reflected back at me in the vanity mirror. I turned to him. "All right, time is money. Let's get this shit started."

I walked over, undid the clasp of Kashawn's peanut butter-tan slacks, unzipped them, and slowly reached under the waistband of his drawers. His dick felt fat and limp to the touch. Kashawn didn't budge.

"Hope I didn't give him too much of that shit." I held my index finger under his nose. "Yeah, still breathing."

When I tugged his dick out, I was dumbfounded by the size. It had to be eleven inches, easy. Dick so thick, I almost couldn't get my fingers around the shaft. I kept an eye on him as I started to tease his dick with the tip of my tongue. It started to bone up. Kashawn was out cold, but his dick was wide awake. I took the thick head into my mouth, hugging the plump, tasty tip before I began throating his appendage until the thing was hard enough for my pussy. I eased on top of him. As I straddled him, his meat baton kissed the lips of my pussy. I reached back and aimed his engorged thickness in.

"Oh shit," I said, letting loose a sigh of ecstasy as I used him to enter me. I rode him like he was one of those mechanical bulls at AJ's Bar where I like to go to on ladies night. "Damn, this dick is good."

I clawed at his chest as I rode Kashawn, my pussy hugging all eleven chocolate inches. I smiled as I watched his dick piston-pump my pussy. Had I had a cam, I would have recorded the shit, being the kinky bitch I am. Put a deep-dicking like the one I was getting on YouTube. To have Bree walk in on me putting this gushy down on her high-class doctor husband would have to do. As I was working Kashawn, he started to come to.

"Bree?" he whispered.

"Hey, baby," I said, caressing his face. "Relax. Let me get this nut out of you."

Just as I was working him over, his dick slamming into my sweet spot, I heard a car door slam. "Right on time, wifey." I began to moan loudly on purpose so Bree could hear me fucking her man. I could hear her coming, each stair creaking to her weight.

20

BREE

I jumped out of Deanthony's SUV and ran inside, hollering for Kashawn. I froze at the foot of the stairs when I heard salacious moans reverberating from upstairs. My concern for Kashawn started to fade when anger crept in. As I eased up the carpeted steps to our bedroom, I grew more pissed. The bedroom door was cracked open slightly. *His ass doesn't even have sense enough to lock the fuckin' door.* Shock ran through my whole body when I saw this petite, bony, butt-naked bitch on top of Kashawn.

"Damn, you got some good dick," the woman said.

"What the fuck!"

This bitch turned her head to look at me. "Bree, this is your man? Girl, he knows how to break a bitch off."

"Katiesha?"

It was this skanky bitch I knew from when I worked at Risqué. I could see nothing but red, like all sense of reason and rationality had left my body when I saw that skank on top of my husband. Instead of Kashawn getting up, he just lay there like he was in some kind of unconscious haze, like he didn't know where the fuck he was, but that was all right, because I would soon slap him out of it as soon as I put an ass-whippin' on this bitch. I lunged for Katiesha, grabbing her by her nasty-ass weave. I flung her off Kashawn and onto the floor.

"Bitch, get the fuck off me," she protested.

I started punching her in the face with a closed fist, beating the shit out of her. Katiesha pushed me off, but I slapped her down.

"Help!" she started yelling. "This bitch is crazy."

"Skank-ass ho!" I yelled as I punched and slapped her. I was wailing on her ass good until I felt arms wrap around my mid-region, pulling me off Katiesha.

"Bree, stop, damn, you're going to kill her."

"That's the idea," I said as I struggled to free myself from Deanthony's hold on me. "Put me down. I'ma kill this bitch!"

Katiesha slid off in the corner of the room like the snake she was. She held her hands up to her face, blood staining her busted lip. "Bitch, you always been crazy."

The cops had arrived out of nowhere. This big-ass white man, who was the size of a refrigerator, stood in the bedroom door. He noticed Katiesha crying, frightened and bleeding in the corner. Fuckin' bitch! The linebacker of a cop rushed to her aid. I turned to Kashawn, more than ready to wail on his black ass for messing around on me with this hood rat.

"Nigga, wake your ass up!" I yelled. I slapped him across his face until Deanthony stopped me.

"That bitch is crazy, arrest her," Katiesha yelled.

I was trying to hear nothing coming out of her ho-ass mouth. Good thing for her po-po came, 'cause I would have stomped her ass into next week. "Of all the bitches to cheat on me with, you fuck this bitch, and in our house, Kashawn, in our fuckin' bed?" He acted like he couldn't hear me. "Wake your ass up!" I knew he was faking.

"Ma'am, what happened here?" this cop asked me.

"What the fuck does it look like?" Katiesha hollered. "She just came charging her ass in here and started hitting me. Bitch, I'm going to sue your crazy ass."

I slapped Kashawn again across his face. "Wake the fuck up."

"Bree, stop," Deanthony said, pulling me away.

"Why isn't he waking up?"

Deanthony quickly rushed to Kashawn's side where he attempted to shake him into consciousness. "'Shawn, wake up, bro. 'Shawn!"

"Sir, you need to stand back," the cop warned.

I felt Kashawn's forehead. "He's hot. Come on, man, stop playing."

I noticed his eyes roll back into his head. "Bitch, what did you do to him?"

Another cop entered the room. This one was thin, tall, and bald-headed. He looked Cuban. He wrestled Deanthony to the ground like D killed somebody. I shook Kashawn as hard as I could, but he wouldn't wake up.

"Somebody help me!"

Deanthony yelled and cussed at the Cuban-looking cop as the man pinned him down, clicking cuffs around his wrists.

"Officer, let him go, he's my brother-in-law."

"I don't care who he is. When a police officer tells you to stop, you stop."

This was some fucked-up shit. "Y'all help my husband, damn."

Cuban Cop finally called it in after he had Deanthony cuffed. Kashawn looked at me, moving his lips like he was trying to say something. I pressed my ear to his mouth, yet nothing but jumbled nonsense was coming out.

"What about me? I'm bleeding over here," Skank Ho' said.

"You slipped him some of that nasty shit you on, didn't you? What the fuck did you give my husband?" I charged at her, ready to put another beat down on Skank Ho's ass until Refrigerator Cop pulled me back and slapped handcuffs on me. "Kashawn, it's going to be okay, baby. The ambulance is coming." I pulled against the cuffs. "Fuck you arresting me for? I found this ho on my property, in my house, in my bed, fucking my man, and y'all are putting cuffs on me?"

"Ma'am, please, you need to calm down," Refrigerator Cop warned.

"Kashawn, I love you. I love you, baby."

21

DEANTHONY

ree and I waited with bated breath in the lobby of the hospital for news on whether Kashawn was going to pull through. I called Ma and told her that something happened to Kashawn and that we were at Tallahassee Memorial Hospital. She started screaming on the phone. I told her that Kashawn was fine, that she needed to get to the hospital as quickly as she could. I left out details about him being drugged until she arrived. They held Katiesha at the police station for questioning, but the Cuban-looking cop who cuffed me told me that the bitch refused to talk. Bree hadn't been able to stop crying sense the paramedics brought Kashawn in.

"How did this happen?" Bree asked.

I thought of Tangela, how her stink was all over this. I was kicking myself in the ass for going along with her plan, trusting that it would work. Now my brother was in the damn emergency room, fighting for his life. And, of course, that bitch was nowhere to be found. Bree and I jumped up when we saw Jayson Wilkinson, a friend of Kashawn's since their days in medical school, enter the lobby. He was a year older than Kashawn with short brown hair and blue eyes.

"Jayson, how is he?" Bree asked.

"We took some blood and found high doses of gamma hydroxy-butyrate in his system."

"What is that?"

"The street term for it is GHB."

"Oh, my God," Bree said.

"Jay, is he going to get through this or what?" I asked.

"It was touch and go at first, but he's going to be fine. He just needs bed rest."

"When can he go home?" Bree asked.

"We will monitor him overnight, but he should be able to go home tomorrow."

"Thank God," Bree said, pressing her hand to her chest in relief. "Thank you, Jayson. Thank you so much," she said as she hugged him."

Moments after getting the good news that Kashawn was going to make it, Ma and Uncle Ray-Ray arrived with nosey-behind Yvonne tagging along. They came in frantic, searching my face for an explanation.

"What happened? Where's Kashawn?"

"Hello, Mrs. Parker," Jayson said, greeting Mama Liz.

"Jayson, how are you? How's my boy?"

"As I was telling your son and daughter-in-law, we found a potentially lethal dose of GHB in his system, but he should be fine."

"GH what?" Mama asked.

"It's a lethal narcotic. I'm assuming that the drug was slipped in his food or drink somehow."

Ma looked as if she couldn't quite wrap her head around what was being explained to her.

"But the good news is that he's going to be okay."

"Thank the Lord."

"Well, if you all don't have any more questions, I have some patients I need to check on."

"Thank you again, Jayson," Bree said.

"Who would do this? Who would want to harm my boy?" Ma turned her attention toward Bree, giving her a devilish look that if it could kill, would have cut Bree in half. "You did this, didn't you? You tried to kill my boy."

"What?"

"Ma, don't."

"I warned Kashawn about you. I told him that nothing good is going to come out of being married to a girl like you. Bitches like you ain't nothin' but trouble, comin' from that kind of lifestyle."

"Ma, stop. Bree didn't have anything to do with what happened to Kashawn."

"And for your information, I came home and found him in bed with someone else. So before you go blaming me, why don't you go and ask him what he was doing in our bed with another woman."

"He wouldn't stray if you would sit yourself down somewhere and be the wife you're supposed to be."

I wished I could say that I was surprised what came out of Ma's mouth, but I wasn't. I mean, shit, she had said worse than that. Bree was already pissed from the mess she found Kashawn in, and for Ma to get up in her face and blame her for Kashawn nearly over-dosing on GHB, was the epitome of fucked up. I looked at Bree and could tell that she was two seconds from wrapping her hands around Ma's throat.

"Lord, give me strength," Ma hollered.

As I consoled her, Cuban Cop appeared.

"Mrs. Parker, I was wondering if I could ask you a few questions." He plucked a small pad with a black cover from his left breast pocket.

"What is it this time?" Bree said, crossing her arms in front of her chest.

"It's about what happened at your home this evening."

"I already told y'all what happened. I came home and found my husband in bed with that waste of skin. What more do you need to know?"

"Who is she talkin' about, Deanthony?" Ma asked.

"Bree, come on," I said.

"I got a call, well, Deanthony got a call, telling me that I should get home because something was wrong with Kashawn."

"Sir, do you know who it was that called you?"

Bree and Ma looked at me, searching my face for an answer to Cuban Cop's question. I thought of Tangela and the video she had of me, but then I thought of Kashawn and how he almost died because of her fucked-up plan that had gone astray.

"The call came from Tangela."

"Tangela?" Bree said.

"She was the one who called and told me that something was wrong with Kashawn."

"What's her last name?" the cop asked.

"Meeks. Tangela Meeks," Bree said, "but she didn't have anything to do with this. She was just giving me the heads-up. Katiesha is who you need to be talking to. What did that hood rat tell y'all anyway?"

A nurse walked past, urging Bree to keep her voice down.

"Ms. Brooks isn't talking. She's asked to see her lawyer."

"Why am I not surprised?"

"So how do you know Ms. Brooks?"

"We worked together at Risqué."

"The club over off Highway 20," the cop said.

"That's the one."

Ma rested her head in her hand, embarrassed.

"So what happens now?" Bree asked.

"Nothing."

"What, you're kidding, right?"

"There's nothing to hold her on. We don't have any evidence proving that she drugged Dr. Parker. She's not talking and, luckily for you, she's not going to file assault charges. We don't have a choice but to release her."

"She almost killed my husband and y'all are lettin' that bitch go?"

"I'm sorry."

"I don't believe this. Y'all know Katiesha did this. You need to put that low-budget hood rat under the jail. Throw the book at her. I wish *I* had a book to throw at her. A big-ass dictionary, a case of encyclopedias."

"Next time, Mrs. Parker, if you want to blow off some steam, try martial art classes. It works wonders, trust me."

Bree looked at Cuban Cop with disbelief as he walked off. "I bet had my husband been white, that crazy bitch would have been tried and given life without parole."

"Bree, we need to talk," I said.

"About what?"

"Let's talk in private."

"What the hell is going on?" Ma asked.

"Y'all go see how Kashawn is doing. I need to talk to Bree about some things."

"Where are you going?"

Bree and I made our way to one of the patios outside of the hospital. My heart was beating crazy in my chest, knowing that I was about to come clean about everything. Bree tucked her hair behind her ears, anticipating what I had to say, but just when I was about to tell her what was up, I noticed Tangela making her way toward us. It was like her ass appeared out of nowhere. She looked at me with a sinister smile across her mug. It took everything in me to keep from lunging at her, but I kept my cool around Bree.

"Bree, hey, Mama Liz just told me what happened." Tangela and Bree came together in a hug.

"Hey, girl, I'm glad you came."

She was wearing a black blouse, a leopard-print skirt, and black platform shoes. Thick braids draped over her back. Funny how she showed up in the nick of time. "I got a call from Mama Liz telling me that Kashawn was in the hospital. I rushed right over when I heard."

Tangela pretended to play the compassionate best friend trying to come off like she gave a fuck. I wanted to throw up.

"Is he all right?"

"He was drugged," I said.

"What?"

"I came home and found him in bed with this bitch I used to work at Risqué with," Bree said. "She drugged Kashawn. The doctor said they found GHB in his system."

"Oh, my God!"

Fake-ass bitch.

"Did this girl say anything to the cops?" Tangela asked, glancing at me with a nasty glare.

"The cops said she refused to say anything. I tried to kill her ass when I saw her in bed with my man. Can you believe they let that bitch go? They said they didn't have anything to hold her on."

"Damn, that's fucked up."

I was getting sick to my stomach, watching Tangela play the sensitive best friend. I needed to get out of there. Tangela's presence had released a stink in the air.

"Deanthony, how are you holding up?" Tangela asked. This bitch had balls.

Well, being that that bitch you sent almost killed my brother, all I want to do is stomp you into the ground. "I'm good now that I know that my brother is going to be okay."

"Jayson said he can go home tomorrow."

"Thank God."

"I'm going to go see how Mama's doing," I said.

"Deanthony, if you need anything, don't hesitate to call me. Baby girl, you know that goes double for you. We got to keep it together for Kashawn. He's going to need the support of his family and friends to get him through this."

I walked off, knowing that if I stuck around, them pigs would be pulling me off Tangela. "I will see you upstairs, Bree."

"Deanthony, hold up." Bree turned and walked toward me and threw her arms around my neck. "What did you want to tell me?"

"You're family, B. That's what families do," I said, glancing over her shoulder at Tangela.

Tangela stood there with her arms crossed, baring her scarlet-red fingernails like she wanted to bury them in my back much like she had done to Bree. "It can wait."

"Are you sure?"

"Yeah. We'll talk later."

My brother ending up in the hospital was not a part of the plan. I loved Bree, but this shit went too far. Tape or no tape, my brother's life wasn't worth Tangela's bullshit.

22

KATIESHA

When those pigs released me and gave me back my purse, I made damn sure there wasn't a penny missing. Cops around here could be some dirty bastards. Protect and serve, my ass. I'd called Tangela six times and the only thing I done got was her voicemail. I knew that bitch was going to pull that shit, but she's tangling with the wrong bitch. I didn't play that. She's as dumb as her ass looks if she thought she was going to cut loose without paying me the money she owed. I had done my part, now she had better live up to her end.

All my life motherfuckers had been trying to get over on me. Sweet-talk a bitch until they get what they want, but when I called in a favor, I couldn't find their sorry asses. Got enough of that shit in Ohio, which is why I moved to Florida. Between my mama and the shit storm my cousin, Brittnee, threw me up in, I had to bounce.

"Don't think you're going to sit your fat ass in my house and not work," was the last thing I remember my mama saying to me. "If you don't wanna go to school, then you're going to work. I didn't raise no lazy-ass child. You're going to learn that it ain't easy out here without an education. Welcome to the real world, girl." She went on and on and never asked me why I dropped out of that hell hole to start with.

I didn't tell nobody. Who would believe that the school slut got raped by the political science teacher? That's what Mr. Rick said when I threatened to go to po-po and tell 'em what he did to me.

In his class, in an after-school tutoring session, he started messing with me, feeling up my leg, touching my booty and shit. When I tried to get up to leave, he pinned me on his desk, held my arms down, ripped off my panties, took his dick out, and fucked me.

I wanted to tell Mama what was going on, but like everybody else, I knew she wouldn't believe me. Not somebody who thinks that all I do is lie all the time. Had I told anybody at school, that shit would have spread like a grease fire. Everybody would have known by lunch, probably every high school in the county. I was a good student before Mr. Rick did what he did. I made As and Bs, and the honor roll a couple times. I thought about going to fashion school in New York. I used to make my own stuff and everybody at school would ask me where I got my clothes. They didn't believe me when I told them I made most of my stuff. I always have my nose in a magazine. I live for *Vogue* and *Cosmo*. Every month, I go to Target and buy the new issues to check out that season's collections by some of my favorite fashion designers like Donna Karan and Karl Lagerfeld.

I sat in the dressing room at Risqué sometimes and stared at the gowns for hours until it was time for me to go on stage. I loved reading about famous fashion designers traveling to places like New York, Paris, and Milan for fashion shows.

"That's going to be me someday," I used to tell Mama.

She would sit there and take a drag off of one of her cancer sticks, and moan, "Uh-huh."

"I am. Watch and see."

I didn't give a damn what she thought. I was hell-bent on making sure that I didn't end up like her: living in the projects—on welfare. Unlike her, I had plans that didn't include sitting around next to the mailbox, waiting for a damn welfare check every month. I swore that I would never end up like her.

I was so messed up over what Mr. Rick did to me, by the time I was a junior in high school, I went from As and Bs to Ds. Plus, I got real depressed, having to see Mr. Rick at school every day and knowing what he did to me, knowing he would do it to some other girl if he wasn't already. I would sit and wonder how many girls he had raped before me. I knew for damn sure that I wasn't the only one. I couldn't take going to school and have him stare at me in the halls. It was like that bastard was raping me all over again. I would imagine him in the teacher's lounge, laughing, telling all my favorite teachers what a slut I was, telling them one lie after the next.

I was about to head to my next class when I bumped into him in the hallway, and all that bastard said was, "remember what we talked about. Not a word."

I was done after that. I left school and never went back. Ma's clueless ass never would have found out about my not going to school if they hadn't called her and told her that I hadn't been in three weeks. She tried to get me to go back, but I told her that if she made me, I would run off and she would never see me again. Ma gave in and told me that if I was so headstrong about being an uneducated dumb-ass for the rest of my life, I might as well get out and work, so I got a job cleaning up nights at Kent State. I caught on quick and got pretty good at it. After only six weeks, I got a raise. I use to flip through *Vogue* magazine on my lunch break.

I got up one morning and spent half of it in the bathroom throwing up. I knew I was pregnant. I knew it was that bastard's baby, because despite what people at school thought about me, I wasn't a slut. Letting Carlton Lewis feel my titties behind the baseball bleachers a few times didn't make me a slut. That same week I was throwing up, I went to Walgreens and bought a pregnancy test. I didn't even wait until I got home to take it. I did it right there in the bathroom. It was only a few minutes before I found out what I already knew. I was pregnant. I went to the clinic and saw this light-skinned nurse who drew blood and told me how far along I was.

"You're two weeks' pregnant."

It was like I didn't even hear the word *pregnant*, but two weeks, and my stomach felt like it had caved in. I had a feeling, but hearing it from a nurse made that shit written in stone. The fucked-up thing was when I told Ma, she sat there on the sofa, fingering collard greens off of one of her cheap Family Dollar plates like telling her I was pregnant wasn't a big deal.

"I'm not surprised," she said. "I knew it was only going to be a matter of time before you got your load, spreading your legs for all those nasty boys to run up between."

That day, I was officially done with her telling me what a ho I was and that I would never amount to nothing. So I hauled ass to my room, grabbed my suitcase, and packed up everything I bought with my own money. Ma stood there in the door of my room with her hands hooked at her hips, watching me pack.

"Where the hell do you think you goin'?"

I didn't say anything as I stuffed as much as I could in my white-and-black bangle-print suitcase and started for the door. Ma pushed me back in the room when I tried to leave.

"I asked you a question, girl."

I gave her a look that would kill, letting her know that I wasn't playing with her. "All you ever do is call me a ho and walk around the house looking at me like you wish you had never had me."

"Watch your mouth," Ma said, willing her index finger at me like it was a sword.

"I'm not staying in this house another second with your crazy ass. From here on out, I'm not taking any shit from you or nobody else."

"You walk around here like you better than everybody else with your magazines and shit. How you gon' be a famous fashion designer now with a bun in your damn oven?"

"Here's what, Twanette..." I called her by her name because as far as I was concerned, I didn't have a mama anymore. "You don't have to worry another day about what I'm doing. You stay on your side of Ohio, and I will stay on mine."

I bolted past her with my suitcase and walked out the door. No matter what I did, I was always going to be a disappointment to her. I didn't know where I was going, but was happy that I finally found the nerve to push myself from under Twanette's thumb. Brittnee was the only one I could think to call. We were more like sisters than cousins. We'd always been thick like that. When I told her about the fight I'd had with Ma, she told me that I could stay with her as long as I wanted. She was the only family I knew and had. My daddy was living somewhere in Phoenix, but I never knew the man. I told Britt about the pregnancy. I knew she wouldn't say anything. Britt had always been real good about keeping secrets. She's three years older than me. My birthday is in May and hers in March.

I was sitting at the kitchen table, spreading mayonnaise on four slices of bread while Britt cooked up some homemade hamburgers, when I told her about Mr. Rick raping me.

"Did you go to the cops?"

"For what? You know how pigs are. They don't give a damn about you if you ain't white and rich."

"Yeah, but, damn, Katiesha, you can't let that rapist fuck get away with what he did."

It was like every time I heard the word *rape*, it felt like a hot fork down my back.

"I don't want nobody to know my business," I said.

Britt looked at me like I didn't have any sense. "So you're just going to let his ass get away with what he did to you? If it was me, I would go to him, tell him that I'm carrying his baby, and that if he didn't want anyone to find out, he would have to pay some serious cake." Britt placed a plate of cooked hamburger patties in the middle of the table. "Hold up. Are you even going to have this kid?"

"I don't know. I'm only seventeen. What the hell am I going to do with a baby?"

"Well, that's up to you. Whatever you decide to do, I'm here for you." Britt set a plate of seasoned curly fries next to the burgers and sat down. She took a drag from her cig before she stubbed it out in an ashtray that was sitting next to a set of salt and pepper shakers.

"What would you do?" I asked.

"Me? I couldn't take care of no kid. I'm too damn selfish. I like other people's kids, yeah, but…uh-uh, I'm not mama material," Britt said, blowing smoke into the air.

With lettuce, tomatoes and condiments splayed out on the table, we started making our hamburgers. My stomach was growling at how good they smelled. Britt had a full-time job working as a production assistant for WTZL. The money was nothing to write home about, but you let Britt tell it, and you would think she was working for Tyler Perry or somebody. Britt was the most headstrong person I knew, couldn't tell her nothin'. Like me, she was about doing shit her damn self ever since her mama kicked her out the house when Britt told her she was gay. You would think she was a dude if her titties weren't so big. She might not have been a man, but I'd seen her fuck dudes up like one. She had this huge collection of *Jet* magazine beauties in this shoe box she kept. She knew that I was cool with gay people. I always said, love who the fuck you want.

I loaded my burger up with the works: lettuce, tomatoes, ketchup, mustard, and pickles. My first bite was a big one. "Mmm…damn, this is good."

"Good, ain't they?" Britt asked. "I like to cook the onions right in the meat. That's my secret."

I had so much on my hamburger, mustard and ketchup squished out onto my fingers. I took a napkin and wiped them clean. "Girl, I'm pissed that he did that shit to me. It's like…if you can't even trust teachers, who the fuck do you trust, you feel me? Parents kick us out, and you ain't got nobody."

"You trust yourself. 'Cause at the end of the day, yourself is all you got."

"You ain't never lied."

I took another bite of the good-ass burgers Britt had made. "So have you talked to your mama?"

"I've called, but she don't answer. I've gone to the house, but she don't come to the door. I see her peeking out of the living room window, so I know she's home."

"Damn, that's fucked up."

"It is what it is. I'm done. This is the one life I get, and I'm living it. Plain and simple. If she wants to talk to me, then she knows where I'm at."

I was the first family member Britt came out to before she told her mom. She cried when I told her I knew, and that I was cool. But it was hard for her mama to deal, so she told Britt to make a choice: Jesus, or her being gay, that if she chose her sexuality, she had turned her back on Jesus, and turning her back on Jesus, meant she turned her back on her family. I hated when people hid behind the Bible to justify their own ignorance. Britt packed up her stuff that night and left.

I wanted her to stay with me, but Ma said, "I don't want no dyke staying up in my house. I don't give a damn if she is family."

Britt stayed at the YMCA for a few weeks until she was able to get a job and an apartment. She was this close to being homeless. It went to show if you don't have family, you got nobody.

23

KATIESHA

A few weeks had passed. I had come to two decisions: to keep my baby, and to confront Mr. Rick that his raping ass was going to be a daddy. I picked up some more shifts at the college cleaning up, which put me at almost thirty hours. All the bills were split in half, including the groceries. Brittnee and I were doing real good. We would stay up for hours, watching movies, shooting the shit about how we used to be when we were kids. I officially dropped out of Shawnee High School and enrolled at Sharon Lynn's School for Girls on the east side of town. It was way cooler than that shit stain that I hated going to day after day. All the kids were down, and I liked starting over without the rep of being known as a slut. None of them knew who I was. I might as well have been from Russia or someplace, which was more than cool with me.

Britt and I found out where Mr. Rick lived through his last name. It was real easy to find somebody these days. Britt insisted on going with me to make sure that he didn't try nothin'. We took the J train to Milford Avenue where he lived. Britt fished a piece of paper out of her jacket pocket where she had written down Mr. Rick's address.

"2414 Milford Avenue. This is it."

We could hear him hollering at a game from inside his house, which was one of those low-income, one-bedroom setups. Fuckin' loser. Britt rang the doorbell.

"Who the fuck is that?" he yelled from inside the house.

Neither one of us said anything. We heard him inside stomping toward the door to answer. Britt's hand was stuffed down in one of her jacket pockets. I could make out something shiny and black between her fingers, but before I could say anything, a gust of wind slapped me in the face when Rick answered.

"What the hell do—" Before he could spit another word, Britt stuck the barrel of a semiautomatic in Rick's stomach, forcing him back into the house. "What the hell?"

"Shut the fuck up," Britt yelled. She gripped the gun tightly in her hand, her finger pressed behind the trigger.

"Britt, what the fuck, girl?" I asked. "Where did you get a gun at?"

"My fuckin' fairy godmother." Britt waved the gun at Mr. Rick. "Sit yo' ass down."

"If you all want money, I got some stashed. I can get it."

"Shut up."

I could tell from the expression on Britt's face that she was dead serious. "What are you doing?" I asked.

"I'm gon' make this bastard confess what he did."

"Bitch, put that burner away," I said.

"Not until he confesses what he did to you, to both of us."

"What are you talking about?"

Britt shot a razor-sharp glance at Mr. Rick, who was by now starting to sweat, realizing that Britt wasn't playing. "He knows what I'm talkin' about. Tell her what you did." Britt pressed the nose of the gun against the right cheek of Rick's face. "Tell her what you did to me, rapist."

"Katiesha, I don't know what all this is about," Mr. Rick said.

"We were downstairs in the field house, under the gym. It was after softball practice. He asked me to help him put away some equipment. He was a coach, so I didn't think nothin' of it. Everything was good until he grabbed my ass. When I knocked the shit out of him, that only made him madder. He pulled at my shirt. I tried to fight him off me, but the more I struggled, the crazier he got. I tried to get away, but he ran after me. He pulled me into one of the storage rooms, pushed me to the floor, and forced himself on me. I scratched and pushed, but he just kept on. That's how he got the scar on the side of his face."

"That's bullshit. Katiesha," Mr. Rick said. "She's crazy. Don't believe her."

Britt kept the gun pointed at Mr. Rick's face. "After, he told me the same thing he told you, that if I ever I told, he would kill my brother and moms, so I didn't say nothin'…until now. Now I got your ass exactly where I want you."

"You ladies need to think about what you're doing," Mr. Rick warned. "Don't throw your life away over this craziness."

"Oh, now you want to play mentor now, huh?" Britt said. "'Cause of what you did, my head is all fucked up. I still be havin' nightmares about that day." With the gun aimed, Britt took something out of the inside pocket of her jacket.

"What is that?" I asked.

"A tape recorder."

"Britt, this ain't the way to do this shit."

"Listen to your cousin," Mr. Rick said.

"Shut the fuck up."

Britt looked at me like I had committed a mortal sin. "Tiesha, I thought you would be with me on this. This bitch needs to confess."

"Yeah, but, Britt, this isn't the—"

Suddenly, Mr. Rick rose up and grabbed the barrel of the gun. He and Britt struggled. My heart felt like it was pounding in my stomach. She fought like she wasn't about to give up the gun. They knocked over lamps and vases in the struggle. I jumped on Rick's back, digging my nails into his face, scratching at his flesh like a wild animal. The three of us fought until I heard a loud bang that had my ears ringing. Still holding onto Mr. Rick, I collapsed with him onto the floor, landing on my stomach. As I slid from under him, he was still alive, holding his hands at his gut where blood started to stain his white tank top. Rick was going on like he was struggling for breath. The blood kept coming, growing into a bigger and bigger blob like some kind of plague spreading.

"We need to do somethin'," I said.

Britt stood there frozen, with a crazy look in her eyes, holding the smoking gun down to her side.

"Britt, did you hear what I said? We need to call nine-one-one. He's dyin'!"

Britt didn't say nothin'. After a few minutes, Mr. Rick had stopped struggling for breath. He had gone still and quiet. He was dead.

"We need to clean up."

I turned to her in a state of panic. "What?"

Britt started rummaging through Rick's pockets.

"What the fuck are you doing? We need to bolt."

"We need to make this shit look like somebody robbed him." She grabbed his brown leather wallet, took out one hundred dollars in twenties, and handed me the money.

"I don't want that shit. That's a dead man's money."

Britt stuffed the cash in one of the front pockets of her baggy jeans. "You still superstitious like that." She took the gun and shoved it back into one of her jacket pockets. Britt went to the kitchen and grabbed a wet dishcloth out of the sink and started wiping down the door.

"What are you doin' that for?"

"Damn, girl, don't you ever watch those detective shows? The killer always wipes off everything he's touched so he won't leave any prints for the cops. Did you touch anything other than the door?"

"We need to get the hell outta here. Somebody probably heard the gun go off."

"Did you touch anything else?"

"No, I don't think so, no."

Britt started feeling around on her jacket and jeans.

"What are you doing?"

"We need to make sure a button or whatever didn't come off in the struggle. I've watched enough *CSI* episodes to know that's how they get you."

I checked myself to make sure nothing came off of me when I fell. I kept looking at Rick lying there dead, blood staining the beige living room carpet.

"Forget him," Britt said. "Ain't nobody gon' miss that pervert. Who knows how many girls he's raped? Hundreds, fuckin' thousands probably. The way I see it, we did all them, and all the girls he hadn't messed with yet, a favor by sending that demon straight to hell."

"Come on, girl, hurry up."

Britt carefully started turning over tables and chairs to make it look like it was a break-in.

"That's enough. Come on, let's go." I hauled ass toward the door when Britt stopped me.

"Hold up."

"What?"

Britt eased the door open, peeked her head out to make sure everything was cool. "Okay, come on."

On the way home, Britt threw the gun in a ditch. I kept thinking about Mr. Rick and all the blood. Dead was the last time I saw him.

When we got back home, Britt was cool as a cucumber. She took a cig from her pack of 305s, and lit the end of it, taking a couple of long drags. I, on the other hand, was climbing the walls.

"Britt, are you serious right now?"

"What?" She pushed smoke from one side of her mouth.

"Fuck do you mean, 'what'? You just shot that man."

"You were there, Katiesha. You saw the gun go off. That shit was an accident. And what the hell is up with you anyway? I thought you would be glad his ass is dead."

"What if the cops come sniffin' around, askin' questions?"

Britt took another drag from her cig. "Just say we don't know nothin'. Cops come around here. They know they ain't gon' get shit."

"What if someone saw us?"

"Nobody did. We were careful."

I felt like I was going to throw up. I knew then that if I didn't put some distance between myself and Britt, I would end my ass up in one place: prison. "I need to get the fuck outta here."

"Where you goin'?"

"Fuck if I know as long as it's away from here."

"You mean you need to—"

I looked at Britt to hear what she had to say. "What?" I looked to see that I was bleeding. "Oh, my God." I ran to the bathroom and pulled my jeans down. My panties were soaked with blood. I knew enough to know what was up.

The next thing I knew, I was in bed. Britt and some old lady were hovered over me. I jerked up.

"Lay down, cuz. You need to rest."

This lady, who I had never laid eyes on in my life, was tall and thin with a short, salt-and-pepper Afro and wire-frame glasses on her face. "Make sure she takes these. Two every eight hours for the pain." The woman packed up whatever she had used to butcher me. "You're going to be okay. Just make sure you get plenty of bed rest."

It felt like my insides had been ripped out and stuffed back in again. The lady took her bag and walked out of my room. I watched Britt give the lady some money and send her on her way.

"What the hell did that bitch do to me? What happened?"

"You, um…"

"What? Brittnee, tell me," I said, grabbing at her arm.

"I'm sorry, cuz. You had a miscarriage. You lost the baby."

I touched my stomach and broke down crying knowing I had lost my baby. Britt tried to calm me down, but I snatched away from her. "Bitch, this is your fault."

"My fault? I didn't do nothin'."

"All this shit with you killin' Mr. Rick. Why did you go over there with a fuckin' gun? All I wanted to do was talk to him. I didn't say shit about a gun." With tears streaming down my face, choking me, I got up out of bed.

"Katiesha, what are you doin'? You heard that doctor. You need to rest."

"Fuck you. Who was that, some kind of back-alley psycho bitch? How could you let her anywhere near me?"

"You had passed out. There was blood all over the bathroom floor. I had to call somebody. You would have died, girl."

I plucked my suitcase out of the closet and threw it on the bed. I tossed all my clothes into it. It felt like my insides were going to bust open, but I kept packing.

"Where the hell are you goin'?"

"I'm going to see if Marquise will let me stay with her until I decide what to do."

"Katiesha, don't be stupid. You can't go nowhere in your condition." Britt pulled at me to keep me from leaving, a scene that was all too familiar.

"I don't want to be anywhere near you when the cops come around, and they will, trust and believe."

Britt's look turned cold. "Fuck you tryin' to say, Katiesha? You gon' snitch?"

"I don't need to run and tell nothin'. You'll fuck up again. You're sick, Brittnee."

"I don't believe this. I put a roof over your damn head and food in your mouth, and you turn on me? You take a nigga, who raped you and got you knocked up, over me and you say I'm sick? Bitch, please. I tell you this, though, if I find out you went to the cops, I'm gonna forget you family."

I couldn't believe she was threatening me. My own cousin.

"It's like I say: trust nobody but yourself. It ain't your enemies you need to watch your ass with. It's your own flesh and blood plunging a knife in your back," Britt said.

I kept packing, wanting nothing but to get out of there, away from Britt.

"Fine. Take your ass on then. All you do is eat me out of house and home anyway. Let's see how long you last in these streets without me watching your back."

I cut past Britt toward the door.

Two weeks later, I got word that the cops were looking for me and Britt. I figured they must have found something or someone said they saw us leaving his crib. Britt was blowing up my phone every two minutes. I didn't want to talk to her, so I cut off my phone. When I turned it back on, there were seventeen messages on my cell, all of them from Britt's crazy ass.

"What the hell did you tell the cops, bitch? We need to be on the same page, 'cuz."

I stopped listening by the time I got to the eleventh message where she talked about me being nothing but a liability and being a loose end. Britt had lost what was left of her mind. She was full on cray-cray. I found out that Britt had gotten pinched by the cops for some shooting that happened over on Collinwood Boulevard. I knew it was only a matter of time before po-po came looking for me, so I quit my job and bought a bus ticket to Florida. There was nothing but a black cloud over my head in Ohio anyway. I needed a fresh start.

I used the money I had saved to put a deposit on an apartment. With the money I had spent to get to Tallahassee and buying food, I was blowing through my savings fast. I needed a job and quick. I was busting the pavement, putting in applications when I saw a flyer that was advertising for topless dancers at Risqué. I had the body and a decent set of titties, so I figured why not? I had never stripped before, but thought how hard can it be? I went to the club that same day. It was as sleazy as I thought and smelled like stale cigarettes. I walked in with this black dress on, the neckline cut low, showing just enough goodies. I had these fools drooling from their mouths and probably dicks, not even ten minutes after walking in.

I sauntered up to the bar and asked this girl where I could find a dude that went by the name Blue-Black. She pointed me in the direction of this dark-skinned man who was sitting in the corner of the club. He was as black as pitch, sucking on a cigar, blowing a fat body of white smoke into the dimly lit club as he watched some chick shake her big ass on stage. Blue couldn't take his eyes off my tits, but I didn't care. I was used to my twins being stared at as if they were sweet snow cones.

"You ever danced before?"

"No, but lookin' at white girl up there, I know I'm a hell of a lot better than her."

Blue chuckled. "What's your name, Lil' mama?"

"Katiesha."

"All right, Kat. Kitty-Kat. Let's see what you got. Snowflake, get off the stage!"

"You want me to dance *now?*"

"Hell yeah, now. I'm not gonna give you the job without seein' how you shake your ass first."

Any other time, I would have told someone like Queasy to kiss my ass, but since I was new in Tally and needed a job, I sucked it up. White Girl mean-mugged me as I stepped on stage. I looked over at the DJ, who started to play "Red Bottoms" by Trina. I started dancing all sexy, like I was making love to Blue.

"Take your dress off," he yelled from the back of the club.

I was hesitant at first, but said fuck it and unzipped out of the little black number until all that was showing were my bra and panties. After twenty minutes of dancing like a slut, Blue yelled at me.

"All right, Kat, you got the job. Can you start tonight?"

"Yeah, that's cool."

"Welcome to Club Risqué, New Booty."

It wasn't that good of a new beginning, but it was *my* new beginning.

24

TANGELA

I wish Ma could see me now. I have my own home, I work at the most high-end salon in Tallahassee, and, to top it all off, I'm head over heels in love with a wonderful man. I'm also smart enough to know that it won't make a damn bit of difference to Mama. I can hear her now:

"The house looks smaller than the pictures you showed me."

"There's a salon in Fort Lauderdale that's nicer than this one."

If it's there to be ridiculed, Mama's going to be the one to blow my house down. Ever since I was a little girl, she has always had something to say about anything and everything I've done or attempted to do. When I wanted to try out for cheerleading, she told me I was too fat. If I wanted to run for student body president, she would say I wasn't smart enough. When I told her that I wanted to be a Girl Scout, she told me that she had never seen a black Girl Scout before. What mother says that kind of shit to their daughter? Only thing that woman would give me props for was doing hair. "If you're lucky, you *might* make someone a half-decent wife," she said to me once.

One thing for sure was that I was good at doing hair. Pretty much taught myself how to braid by watching my big sister, Taniesha, do her friend's hair. They used to come to the house, wanting their nappy-ass heads braided or permed for dates and proms. Taniesha would charge them twenty dollars a head when she first started, but when word got around that she was the go-to girl, Taniesha went up to forty dollars. She would get so busy, she would have to set girls up for appointments.

Mama didn't have a problem with it as long as Taniesha didn't let it interfere with her college education. I would clean up all the hair and made sure all of Taniesha's hair curlers, scissors, and hot combs were clean. She would give Mama half. Even though Mama never lifted a single lazy-ass finger to help Taniesha, she still wanted a cut.

"As long as you're using my house to do hair in, you gotta pay up. You oughta be glad I'm letting you stay here rent free."

Mama is the meanest woman I know. I guess you could say I inherited that mean streak from her.

I would sit for hours and watch Taniesha do hair. She did braids, twists, perms, blow-outs, everything. Taniesha was eighteen and I was two years younger. Whenever she got busy, she would have me answer the phone and make appointments. I loved helping out my big sister. When I wasn't busy, I would practice doing hair on old dolls I outgrew. It wasn't long before I got just as good as Taniesha. People started asking me to hook them up with new dos if Taniesha got too backed up or was at school. Everything was cool until she got caught up in Eldridge Harris' shit. He was Taniesha's boyfriend at the time. Could tell that he was nothing but trouble. He was tall and boney with skinny legs and was blacker than roofing tar.

I remember he was blind in his left eye. The eyeball was white and nasty. Shit always creeped me out. Taniesha said he lost it as a child when he was running through the woods by his house one day and caught a twig in the eye. Nasty eyeball of his made him look mean. Eldridge would always come over with these flowers that looked as if he had yanked them out of someone's yard. The dirt and roots were still attached. Mama treated him like he was some kind of Boy Scout when he was a snake in sheep's clothing. I saw clean through Eldridge while he had Mama and Taniesha eating out of the palm of his drug-pushing hand.

Wasn't long before Taniesha took a turn for the fucked up when she started staying out all times of the day and night. Started looking like skin and bones, like she hadn't eaten in days. Taniesha went from having pretty, cocoa bean-brown skin, long pretty hair, and a body to die for, to looking a haggard, cracked-out mess. Eldridge had turned my sister into a damn junkie. Taniesha had stopped doing hair, so I took the reins. Mama was working double shifts as a waitress at Huddle House, so she was never around to see how fucked up things had gotten. I think she knew exactly what was up, but didn't want to face the fact that Taniesha was on junk.

Her friends, Akeila and Milan, were always asking me about her. I would cover for her by telling them that Taniesha was out of town, visiting my cousin in Buffalo. Milan and Akeila would give each other that look like they knew I was lying. Fort Lauderdale is small, so I knew it wouldn't be long before Taniesha was spotted on the streets somewhere, if she hadn't been already. When I was able to nail Mama down long enough to tell her what was up, she would only turn the conversation around on me.

"You've always been jealous of your sister."

"Are you serious? What exactly am I supposed to be jealous of?"

"She's smarter, prettier, and thin. Taniesha can't help that she got her looks from my gene pool and you got yours from your no-account damn daddy."

I couldn't say I was surprised by the venomous words that were coming out of her sewer of a mouth. It was, by far, one of the shittiest things she had ever said to me. Course, she was drunk off her ass, but I've always thought that people use booze as an excuse to do and say dumb shit, and then want to come off the next day like they don't remember what they said or did. That was one thing I *was* smart enough to understand.

"Leave your sister alone. She's tired from school to be bothered by her bratty, meddling little sister."

Oh, she's tired all right.

I was officially done with trying to convince Mama that Taniesha, her *perfect* and pretty daughter, had a problem with drugs. But, then again, she had her own Christmas list of issues. Liquor being one of them. Mama spent many a night under a bottle and would often come home drunk as a damn skunk. If I was going to help my sister, I was on my own. Taniesha was too sick and messed up to get help herself. I was only sixteen and had no idea where to start.

When Taniesha did manage to find her way home, she was so drunk and cracked out, she spent most of the day in her room with the door shut. My sister had lost so much weight. She would get herself together about as much as a crackhead could, and then was off with Eldridge again. I wouldn't see her weeks at a time, not knowing if she were alive or dead in a ditch somewhere. Mama also managed to pull her ass together long enough to get to work, only to come home reeking of gin. I couldn't help them both, so I chose Taniesha over Mama. The night of my plan, I waited until Mama left for work. She was covering a shift for one of the waitresses, so she had to pull a double at Huddle House. She didn't mess with me about getting a job since I took up much of the slack doing hair.

Mama had to be to work by six and left around a quarter 'til. As soon as I saw her get into the truck driven by her flavor-of-the-month boyfriend, I put my plan into action. Taniesha had been in her room all day, sleeping off her high. I cracked the door to find her sprawled across her bed with her dress hiked above her butt.

She was hovered over a pool of vomit that had the entire room reeking with the worst kind of funk. It was my first time seeing Taniesha like that, and it wasn't hard to see how far she had fallen.

I took one of her arms and threw it over my shoulder and lifted her out of the bed. Got to the point where she weighed less than me so she wasn't heavy. I literally dragged her to the bathroom as she went in and out of consciousness. Taniesha smelled like she had not bathed in days, probably longer than that. I managed to peel off this black pencil dress she was wearing that she had gotten from Top Fashions, a store that's a stripper's and hooker's dream. I knew that Taniesha wouldn't be caught dead in a dress like that and figured that bastard, Eldridge, made her wear that slutty ensemble. I gently eased her into the tub. I thought of Eldridge and how strung out he had her.

"I don't even want to know what he's got you doing."

I was shocked to find track marks down both of her arms. It was worse than I thought. I turned on the shower and let the cold water run on her street-battered body, which was enough to shake Taniesha out of her drug-induced slumber. She screamed so loud, I thought she would send the whole neighborhood shuddering. You would think Taniesha was being burned with lye, the way she was hollering. I doubted she even knew where she was. She screamed so much, I had to slap her to calm her down.

"Taniesha, it's me," I yelled. But she kept screaming like her skin was on fire, so I slapped her again. "Girl, shut the hell up."

She finally stopped. I took some soap and washed her. Lather ran down her arms, over fresh track marks that looked like she had been picking at her flesh with an Exacto knife. I took a mirror from one of the drawers of the vanity and held it up to her muscle-wasted face.

"Look. Look at yourself. Girl, you sick. You need some help."

Taniesha pushed my arm away, knocking the mirror out of my hand, causing it to shatter on the bathroom floor. "Get the fuck off me. What are you, a dyke or somethin'? Get the hell outta my room." Taniesha attempted to lift herself out of the tub, but was too weak. "Get out. I don't need your damn help."

"I'm not going anywhere."

"Eldridge got you strung out on that shit, didn't he?"

"You don't know shit, Tangela. Eldridge treats me good. He loves me. He buys me whatever I want, takes me out to eat. He does more for me than you and Mama ever did."

"Bitch, don't even try it. You know I've had your back since the third grade when you stole ten dollars out of Mrs. Bullock's purse. Do you know how many times I have covered for you, have lied for you every time Milan and Akeila ask where you at? I'm the one who has taken up the slack when you're too fucked up on shit to do hair. I've done nothin' but look out for you."

"Well, ain't nobody ask you to do shit for me. Fuck do you want, a medal? This is my life." Taniesha was slung over the rim of the bathtub like the drugged-out, trifling mess she was. "I don't need you. I can take care of my—" More throw-up obstructed Taniesha from finishing her sentence.

"Yeah, I see how well you takin' care of yourself. Sit down in the tub."

"Fuck you, Tangela." She swiped the back of her hand across her mouth. I took a towel from the rack between the sink and the tub, and started to clean up the funky-smelling vomit that felt warm and slimy as I wiped it up with one of my Mama's good towels before I took it and pushed it deep down in the hamper. When I tried to finish washing Taniesha, she said, "Get off me. Bitch, I ain't a damn bull-dagger."

I didn't take what she was saying to heart, knowing it was the junk talking. "Fine. You clean enough anyway." I turned the shower off. The more I thought of Eldridge, the more pissed I became.

Love, my ass. If that's love, you can have that shit.

I grabbed one of Mama's robes and handed it to Taniesha. When she managed to find the strength to lift herself out of the tub enough to put on the robe, I couldn't believe how much weight she had lost, how she had wasted down to nothing. My eyes began to fill up with tears.

"I don't care what you say. I'm your sister. I'm going to look out for you no matter what."

Taniesha caressed my face and then slapped me hard across it, sending stings of pain to course through. "Mama always said you was a weak bitch."

Whoever said words will never hurt was full of shit. They hurt. They cut, rip, and tear.

For a good, solid week, Taniesha was clean and back to her old self, eating well and doing a few heads. Everyone was glad to see that she was doing hair again. I was just glad to see my sister healthy. Taniesha was gaining some weight, looking real good. She was even talking about going to beauty school with me to take a few classes, maybe get our license. It wasn't long before Eldridge started snooping his ass back up around the house, sweet-talking Taniesha, saying he missed her and wanted her to come back. It wasn't long before she started to sink back into her old ways. Eldridge had a hold on Taniesha that wasn't so easily broken. I told Mama what was going on, but she was so deep in denial and wrapped up in her own addiction with booze, she didn't give two shits about her two daughters being in peril.

I went out one night to search for Taniesha after not seeing her after two weeks. It was killing me, wondering if she was alive or dead. I figured she was laying up with that bastard, Eldridge, somewhere much like Mama, who on her days off, was drunk under her latest conquest, some greasy white man of a trucker she met at work, no doubt. The night I went looking for Taniesha to bring her home, I sneaked into Mama's bedroom where she and the trucker were in bed sleep, butt-naked and drunk. The room reeked of sex, sweat, and vodka. I thought I was going to throw up, but I managed to keep it together long enough to grab the car keys out of Mama's purse. Taniesha and I were pros at sneaking out of the house whenever we wanted to go to the movies or a house party someone was throwing in the neighborhood.

On my way out, I stepped on a plate of chicken bones that was sitting at the foot of the bed, but it wasn't loud enough to wake either of them up. Luckily, Mama can sleep through a five-level hurricane. The trucker was snoring loud enough to wake the dead. *Calling the hogs* is what Mama calls it. If Taniesha was with Eldridge, I knew I couldn't wander onto the streets without protection. Mama kept a gun under her sweaters in a chest. I eased it open and found not only a .38 semiautomatic, but a half-bottle of gin that was hidden away like a bad secret she wanted to keep covered. I had never shot a gun, but knew I would learn quickly if I had to put a bullet in someone's ass if somebody came between me and my sister.

I didn't yet have my license, only my permit. The most Mama would let me drive would be down to the corner Family Dollar and back. I swore I would take the money I was making from doing hair, save it up, and get me a car. I was too old and too damn cute to be riding the cheese mobile. I hated how she would let Taniesha get away with murder, while whatever I tried to do to please her, to make her proud of me, was never enough. But look who's bailing who out...again? Look who's left behind to clean up their damn messes? Mama had always played pick and choose over me and

Taniesha, all because I was some one-night-stand mistake, while Taniesha's daddy was supposed to be the love of her life. If he loved you so, why did he run off with another woman, leaving you to raise a child by yourself? I might not have been grown, but I was grown enough to know that shit ain't love. Whoever my daddy was, I got my strength from him. I love Mama, but she's weak. She went on and on about Taniesha. Pretty this and smart that, but why weren't you helping me to get her away from that pimp, Eldridge? No, you were too busy lying under some loser to give a damn. You know what, fuck that. I didn't have time for this. I had a sister to save.

I searched every corner store, park, playground, from Rawson Street to Whitlock Avenue, looking for Taniesha. Nothing. "Hold up. Sicklen Street. She might be there."

Word was that Eldridge had a place on Sicklen where he stayed when he was under fire by the po-po. I had heard that Eldridge was wanted in the connection of about five murders across town. I wasn't sure how true it all was, but there's usually a little truth to everything. Once I got to Sicklen, I suddenly had one of my bad feelings. I kept calling Taniesha on her phone, but it would go straight to voicemail.

"What's up? You know who you've reached and you know what to do. Peace."

"Taniesha, hey, this is your little sis leaving you another message. Girl, where are you? Mama's worried sick," I lied. "Please call me when you get this message. I love you."

There was a thug on each corner, slinging dope, and girls wearing next to nothing trying to pick up tricks. I had Mama's gun in the passenger seat, covered over with magazines. I drove until I reached Eldridge's crib that was in this ratchet neighborhood. His black Cadillac Escalade high on .26s was parked in front of his crib.

The rap music was so loud that I thought it was going to shake the ground open, causing the rundown, abandoned crack houses to be swallowed whole by some unforeseen force. This side of town looked like the land time forgot.

I took Mama's gun and tucked it in the waistband of my jeans under my shirt. I could hear a commotion of curse words from behind the door before I even walked up to knock. I wasn't planning on bodying nobody, but scare these bastards, if anything, to get me and Taniesha out of there. At first, I knocked gently on the door, knowing these fuckers wouldn't hear my faint, non-threatening knock. I tried to be all hard, but I was scared shitless. I knocked again, harder this time, but nobody came to the door. In that neighborhood, I was getting nervous. I knew if a girl like me went missing, no one would give a damn. This time, instead of knocking, I banged on that bitch with the side of my fist.

"Who the fuck is that?" I heard someone ask. It sounded like Eldridge's voice.

I rested my hand on the butt of the gun, ready for whatever. As soon as the door flew open, I aimed the semiautomatic in the face of this meaty-ass, dark-skinned, African bastard, wearing a white tank top, black baggy shorts, and white socks with black Nike flip-flops. A gold grill capped his teeth. His cigarette dropped from his lips when he found himself staring down the barrel of my gun.

"What the fuck?" Eldridge mouthed.

I couldn't hear what he was saying through the loud music. The front room reeked of dank. There was a bucket of chicken, forties, and money on the table. I loved N.W.A., but that shit was getting on my nerves, so I shot at the large sound system that was sitting in one of the corners of the room.

"Whoa, whoa, damn, girl, you crazy?" Eldridge asked, shielding his face with his hand.

"Where Taniesha at?"

"How the fuck should I know. I haven't seen that bitch in days."

"Stop lying. I know she's here."

"You need to turn around and walk yo' ass back out that door before I forget you're Taniesha lil' sister."

"I'm not doin' shit until I walk out of here with Taniesha."

"Bitch, he told you—" Before Tank Top could finish his sentence, I shot him in his right foot. "AAAGGGHHH!" He fell to the floor, holding his foot. Eldridge gave me this sinister look, knowing that I wasn't fucking around. "Bitch fuckin' shot me! Man, shutcho ass up!"

I held the gun directly at Eldridge's face, itching to pop the next bullet between his bloodshot eyes. "Where the fuck is my sister?"

"She's in the room in the back," Tank Top yelled.

"Man, shut up, damn."

"Walk," I told Eldridge.

"Bitch, walk where?"

"To the room. If you did something to Taniesha, there won't be a hole deep enough to throw your ass in. Now move."

Eldridge led the way down the hall to the bedroom. Taniesha was lying unconscious on the bed, naked.

"Taniesha, it's me Tangela." When I tried to wake her up, she moaned in protest. I was happy to see that she was alive. Barely, but alive. "What the hell did you do to her?"

"Nothin' she wasn't begging me for."

"Why won't she open her eyes?"

"She's high, that's all. You got what you came for, now why don't you and your ho-ass sister get the fuck out of my crib."

As I struggled to get Taniesha dressed, I noticed a needle and a small bag of heroin on the bedside table. "You the one who got her hooked on this nasty shit."

"I didn't do nothing to her she didn't want to happen."

"Fuck that. If she hadn't have met you, none of this would be happening to her." I walked up to Eldridge and held the barrel of the gun directly in the center of his forehead.

"Girl, you need to donate your brain to science, 'cause you obviously ain't using it."

"Fuck you."

"You think you the only female that has pointed a burner at me?"

"I should do everyone a favor and splatter your head all over these fuckin' walls."

"You better, 'cause I'm comin' for you if you don't. You, Taniesha, and your damn mama, bitch."

"Tangela, what the fuck are you doing here?" Taniesha asked.

"Girl. I'm here to take you home."

"This is home."

"This place ain't your home. This bastard don't care about you. He just wants to keep you messed up on junk and then turn you out on the street when he's done with you."

"That ain't true. Eldridge loves me."

"That's right. I love you, baby. You my girl."

"Shut up! Don'tchu talk to her."

"You heard her. She *is* home. So why don't you get out of here and maybe I'll forget this shit happened."

"I'm not leaving here without her."

Taniesha barely had her clothes on, but she was decent enough to go out in public. With the gun aimed at Eldridge, I lifted Taniesha up off the bed and dragged her out of the room, down the hall, past Tank Top, who was unconscious, his foot a bleeding mess.

"If I see your head peek out of this door, I will shoot it off."

I eased Taniesha into the passenger's side before I rushed around to the driver's side. When Eldridge peeked his head out, I let off a shot.

"Bitch, this ain't over."

I ignored his empty threats and hauled ass out of there.

On the way home, Taniesha was hunched over, holding her stomach. I thought she was going to throw up, so I rolled the window down. "Tangela, I'm sick."

"Don't worry, sis. You'll feel a lot better when I get you back to the house. You need some food in you, that's all."

I drove home as fast as Mama's PT Cruiser would take us, flying past stop signs and red lights, and surprisingly not getting stopped once by the cops.

"Okay, Taniesha, we're home." She wasn't saying anything. I shook her to try to get her to wake up, but she wouldn't. "Taniesha, stop playin', wake up." I couldn't tell if she was breathing, so I felt for a pulse. There wasn't one. "Taniesha, wake up! Please, sis, wake up!" I got out of the car and rushed to her side and pulled open the door. I shook her repeatedly, but she wouldn't open her eyes. "Taniesha, please wake up, Please!" I took my sister into my arms, dragging her out of the car. I screamed, begging her to open her eyes. She felt cold. There was no life in her once pretty face. My big sister was dead.

Taniesha was buried on Saturday, March 12, 2011, at Southwood Cemetery. The day of the funeral, I could barely hold it together. The church was so full, there weren't enough seats for everyone. Family and close friends, including Akeila and Milan, were at the funeral. People spoke so well of my big sis, about how nice and generous she was to everyone she met. Before we'd even arrived at the church, I could smell gin on Mama's breath. I couldn't stomach to look at her because I blamed her partly for what had happened to Taniesha. Had she not been so fucking selfish and in denial about what was up, Tanieshaa might have been alive today.

After her death, Mama's drinking spiraled out of control to where I couldn't take it anymore. I had already lost one person I loved to addiction and couldn't bear to see Mama go down that same road of self-destruction. I left Fort Lauderdale. I left her a note explaining that I wasn't going to stick around and watch her destroy herself. I moved to Tallahassee where I later enrolled in some beauty and cosmetology classes at Lively Technical Institute. After six months, I got my license to do hair. I wasn't just doing it for myself, but for my beautiful big sister, who taught me everything I knew.

25

BREE

I had been counting down to the second of Kashawn's home-coming. Jayson had given him a clean bill of health and I was happy knowing that I wouldn't have to spend another night in the house alone, to roll over to find Kashawn's side of the bed empty and cold to the touch. I got the idea to throw him a home-coming party, inviting all his close friends, along with Tyrique, Lathan, and Maleek. I could have done without Mama Liz, though. She thought I didn't notice her cutting me these nasty looks every time I so much as breathed in her direction. At that point, I was damned if I did and damned if I didn't. Once she got something in her head, it was hard to convince the old bitch otherwise. But whatever. I was married to Kashawn, not her. Ever since the night Kashawn was brought in, she'd been up under him like some damn lioness fighting to protect her cub from danger. I guessed that danger being me. I was done with her. Maybe Kashawn could get through her plate of armor.

Deanthony had really been there for me since that whole fucked-up night. He had spent the last few weeks even getting the house clean and ready for Kashawn's homecoming. I didn't know what I would do if it wasn't for him. The day of the party when Kashawn was supposed to come home, Mama Liz volunteered to go pick him up from the hospital. Uncle Ray-Ray was out on the deck, manning the grill, cooking up a mess of barbecue ribs, chicken, hot dogs, and sausages for the guests. That man had the whole neighborhood smelling good. Guests kept bugging him about wanting to get his secret barbecue sauce recipe, but he stayed tight-lipped about it.

"I'm taking it to my grave," he said. He don't know 'til this day that Kashawn let me in on the secret ingredient that had everyone's mouths watering and stomachs growling for his famous barbecue. Uncle Ray-Ray had told me something about brown sugar and lemon juice. Uncle Ray-Ray would cut Kashawn a new asshole if he knew he told me of the secret ingredient.

I was anxious to see my husband, to feel him in my arms again, but Mama Liz insisted on going to pick him up. I didn't push it and let her do her thing. She probably thought I was going to drive Kashawn off a damn cliff or something. I held back and entertained our family and friends. I made sure that everything was perfect. I was his wife and it was about damn time I acted like it. I made sure there was plenty of booze and beer, especially Heineken, Kashawn's favorite. I remembered he told me once that, if he had a choice out of blood or beer running through his veins, he would choose beer, and it would be Heineken. Every crack and crevice of the house was stuffed to the ceiling with people. Hell, you would have thought it was Kashawn's wake. The hors d'oeuvres I had prepared flew off the tray before I could even set them down on the table.

"So what time are they supposed to be releasing Kashawn?" Ebonya asked, sucking Corona from the bottle through a straw.

"His doctor told me around two-ish. Mama Liz went to go get him."

"Girl, what did you do, invite the whole neighborhood?"

"Child, I know, right? Half of these people I don't even know."

"That's what I was telling Tyrique."

"Some of these people are from the neighborhood, and I only invited a few. Girl, I can't stand party crashers."

"That only goes to show that Uncle Ray-Ray's barbecue has a way of bringing black folks together," Ebonya said. Tyrique walked over and joined in the conversation.

"Ty, do you know who all of these people are?" I asked.

"Some of them I recognize, yeah. Most of them are from the hospital, I think. I guess they heard about 'Shawn being in the hospital and wanted to show their respects."

"I guess it doesn't matter. We got plenty of food. It isn't like I can tell all these people to leave," I said, sipping beer from a red Dixie cup. I should have gone with Mama Liz's idea to have a simple intimate dinner with family and close friends instead of stuffing the house with a bunch of people.

"So how are you holding up?" Deanthony startled me, standing over my shoulder.

"I'm anxious as hell. I should have gone myself to go pick him up. I hope he won't be mad that I didn't go with your mama to get him. I love your mama, but you know that I can't be in a confined space with that woman for too long."

Deanthony chuckled, knowing exactly what I was talking about. "You had to keep shit running around here. I know 'Shawn, and I think he'll understand."

"Mama Liz is back," Jayson announced.

I checked my hair and makeup in one of the hallway mirrors. I looked sickening in my red Michael Kors pencil dress newly purchased from Macy's that I struggled to stuff my booty and hips into. Lathan, Maleek, and Jayson had been checking me out all day. I even caught Tyrique stealing a few glances when he thought Ebonya wasn't watching him like a hawk. I was serving it, giving red carpet realness. I got Kashawn's dick brick when I wore tight clothes.

"Come on here, girl, they're on their way," Ebonya said.

"Do I have any lipstick on my teeth?" I turned to her and asked.

"No, you good."

"Okay," I said, rubbing my palms together. "Damn, I feel like a mail-order bride meeting her husband for the first time."

"You so silly, girl, come on."

The nine-inch fuchsia pumps I had on were killing me, but, damn it, beauty is pain. Everyone was standing around, sipping from the containers of their chosen drinks, waiting anxiously for Kashawn to walk through the door.

"Hush, y'all quiet down," I said. My heart was pounding like a percussion drum that sank at the floor of my stomach when Mama Liz walked in without Kashawn in tow. "Mama Liz, where's Kashawn?"

"When I got there, they told me at the nurse's station that some-one picked him up already."

"Who?"

"A nurse said it was some woman."

Damn, lady, you never ask the important questions.

"What woman?"

"They didn't tell me. They just said that she said he was a friend of the family."

They didn't tell you? You didn't bother to ask?

"Let me call his cell, see what's going on."

Just as I was dialing Kashawn's number, Tangela and Kashawn walked in.

"Surprise!" everyone yelled.

Kashawn beamed, smiling from ear to ear, as family, friends, and party-crashing neighbors clapped to his arrival. "What's all this?" he asked.

I breathed a sigh of relief. "Welcome home, baby," I said, roping my arms around his neck in one of the biggest hugs I had ever given him. I knew something was up when he gave a kind of half-embrace instead of the big grizzly-bear hugs I had gotten used to. "How you feelin'?"

"Good. I'm just glad to finally be up out of that death house," he announced.

A synchronization of laughter filled the living room.

"Welcome home, bro."

When Deanthony embraced Kashawn, he acted like Deanthony had cooties or something. Doubt Deanthony even noticed how shady Kashawn was being. When Uncle Ray-Ray walked in from the deck, Kashawn broke past the both of us to greet him.

"Hey, boy, I'm glad you're home." Uncle Ray-Ray wore a big, white apron that was soiled with barbecue sauce like he had been slaving over the grill all day. "You hungry?"

"Starving. I smelled your barbecue down the street."

"That's the idea," Uncle Ray-Ray said, laughing.

Kashawn barely looked at me, and he didn't utter a word about the dress I wore exclusively for him. There was no way I was going to walk around, looking this good for him to ignore a bitch.

"All right, y'all, the meat is done. Come and get it," Uncle Ray-Ray announced. Everyone cheered, ready to quench their appetites with barbecue ribs, chicken and hot dogs.

Tangela crept up behind me, wearing a tight white dress with the usual plunging neckline that exposed her larger-than-life breasts. "Hey, girl, my bad if I worried everybody. I thought it would be a nice surprise to bring him home. Sorry I didn't call to let you know what was up."

"Girl, it's all good. I mean, look at Mama Liz. We're just glad to have him home."

"How are you doin'?"

"Other than the fact that Kashawn looks at me like I'm the Anti-Christ, and Mama Liz has been a tick on my ass about everything under God's blue sky, I'm holding it down."

"She still giving you shit?"

"She hasn't said anything to me directly, but I know she still blames me for what happened to Kashawn."

"You got to do what I do. Kick dirt over that bullshit and move on."

"Did you see how Kashawn treated me when he walked up in here? And he's been throwing shade at Deanthony, too. I know Deanthony noticed it. Did he say anything to you in the car?"

"Nothing out of the ordinary. He seemed like he was okay. Honestly, he was quiet the whole way here."

"Well, what's up with this cold shoulder stuff? Look at me. I'm giving Kashawn video vixen glamour, and he's acting like that?"

"Bree, he just got out of the hospital. He's tired, that's all."

I let loose a sigh. "True. Listen to me overreacting."

"There will be plenty of time to talk to Kashawn. Then when you done talking, throw some sexual healing down on his ass. He'll pep right up."

"True that." I laughed. "Let me go see how he's doing."

As I walked out toward the deck, I was headed off by Mama Liz. "Listen, this is Kashawn's homecoming. I don't want you and Deanthony starting nothing."

"No disrespect, Mama Liz, but Kashawn is my husband. I know what's best for him."

"Maybe so, but he was my son before he *ever* became your husband. We'll see how long *that* lasts when he comes to his senses and divorces you."

Oh, my God. This woman was seriously about to make me lose my shit. And up in my own home, at that. Who in the hell did she think she was talking to? What I did know was that she was over-due for an old-fashioned cursing out, but out of respect for my home, Kashawn, and my guests, I held my tongue, something I wasn't accustomed to doing. I had plenty of beef with Mama Liz, and not the slabs that Uncle Ray-Ray was slathering with barbecue sauce, either. I kindly pushed this overprotective woman out of my way.

"Excuse me. I'm going to go see how *my* man is doing."

I needed to get away from Mama Liz as far as I could before I forgot she was my mother-in-law. People lined up at one of the tables that were set up with heaps of meat and bowls of cole slaw and potato salad. They were armed with paper plates, waiting to savor Uncle Ray-Ray's infamous barbecue. Deanthony sat at the patio table, swigging down his fifth beer, gawking at me like I was one of Uncle Ray-Ray's baby back ribs. Kashawn was standing in the backyard, under an oak tree, nursing on a Heineken, talking to Tyrique.

"Hey, baby, can I talk to you for a minute?"

Kashawn gave me a kind of side glance as he took a swig from his beer.

"Let me go before all the barbecue's gone," Tyrique said. "Welcome home, man. Glad you're okay."

They gave each other dap, coming together in a warm hug. "Thanks, T. I appreciate that."

"What's going on with you?" I asked.

"What do you mean?"

"You've been ice-cold to me all afternoon and you've been mean-mugging on Deanthony since you got here."

"Oh, so now all of a sudden, you give a damn about how Dean-thony's feelings?"

"What does that mean?"

Kashawn leaned against the tree, cocking his foot up against its trunk. "Why didn't you come pick me up from the hospital?"

"I wanted to, but your mama insisted on going instead. She said when she got there, a nurse told her that you had already been picked up by Tangela. I was going to call you to see what was going on, and that's when you and Tangela walked in."

"How convenient for you."

The ghetto Bree was about to cut loose. "What is up with this passive-aggressive shit?"

"Mama's been telling me about what's been going on around here with you and Deanthony."

"What? What kind of lies has she been feeding you about me now?" I noticed Mama Liz standing at the foot of the deck steps with her arms folded across her chest, giving us one of her matter-of-fact glances as she watched what was slowly becoming a fight.

"So that girl that poisoned me, you saying you don't know her? Ma told me that y'all used to dance at Risqué together."

"It's true. I've never lied to you about my past, Kashawn. I told the cop that when he questioned me about her, but since we are on the subject of Katiesha, what were you doing in bed with that bitch?"

"I was in the study working when I heard the doorbell. This woman is standing there and said she was having car trouble and asked to use my phone to call someone."

"And then what happened?"

"She used my phone, said someone was coming to pick her up and...that's all I remember. Next thing I know, I'm waking up in the damn hospital."

"Are you serious? Do you really expect me to believe that?"

"It's true, Bree. Why would I lie about something like that?"

"Do you know how you sound right now?"

"I know how it sounds, but I'm telling you that's what happened."

I was pissed to the tenth degree. My head was swimming, not knowing what to believe.

Kashawn pushed himself away from the trunk of the oak tree. "So who is she?"

"It doesn't matter. The cops couldn't charge her with anything."

"Answer my question," he said. "Who is this girl?"

"When I started dancing at Risqué, I came on the heels of Katiesha, who, at the time, was the queen bitch on the scene. She got the nickname Green-Eyed Diva because she was always jealous of every new bitch that Blue hired."

"Who is that?"

"He's the owner of Risqué. Katiesha couldn't stand me from the word *go* when I came up and liked me even less when I started pulling more coins than her. Nakeema and Latrice schooled me on the fact that she was the one getting all the lap dances, but all that changed when Blue hired me. I came to work one day to find my locker broken open with all of my clothes cut up. I asked who did it, and no one said shit, but I knew Katiesha had fucked with my stuff. She and this old-ass bitch Ursula were the only two bitches who didn't like me. From that day on, I kept both eyes open."

"The owner, this Blue person, didn't do anything?"

"Hell no. He didn't give a damn as long as we didn't fuck with his money. Things only got worse as weeks went on. One night when I got off work, I found that my car had been keyed. That night was the final straw. Katiesha was out on stage when I ran out and started beating her ass. Chet, one of the bouncers, rushed in and pulled me off of her. Good thing, too, because I probably would have put that bitch in a coma. That was my last night there. Blue had fired me, but I didn't care because I left her spitting blood and teeth. I got enough money saved up and was done with Risqué.

That's why I went ape-shit when I saw Katiesha in bed with you."

"This is just…"

"Just what, Kashawn?"

"I don't know if I can deal with this kind of behavior. Do you know Jayson told me that I needed to get an STD work-up, that this…Katiesha might have given me something?"

"What!"

"Yeah. On top of all this shit with finding out about my dad, I have to deal with this."

"Kashawn, I'm so sorry."

"I just don't know if I can deal with any more surprises from your past, Bree."

"Do you blame me for what happened?"

"That's not what I'm saying."

"You know, while you were laid up, somebody had to run the house and Deanthony was the only one who stepped up when all your mama did was point fingers and treat me like I was some kind of she-demon. Between her and Yvonne keeping me under a microscope, I'm surprised that I've been able to keep it together."

"Why do you always have to blame my family for everything? Mama hasn't been nothing but supportive. You have to understand that all this is a lot for her to swallow."

I couldn't believe what I was hearing. Kashawn usually had my back when it came down to Mama Liz's criticisms and shady glances. "What the hell has she done to you?"

"Bree, stop. I think we need to take responsibility for our own actions here."

"I don't know what you want me to say. I've tried to be nothing but a good wife to you."

Kashawn looked at me like he was trying to see through my soul. "I need to ask you something and I want you to be honest with me."

"What? Ask it. What?"

"Is anything going on with you and my brother?"

It was the question I hoped he would never ask for fear of having to tell Kashawn the truth. "What are you talking about?"

"I see how you get when Deanthony is in the room, like you can't be still. You only get like that with him. I noticed it at my birthday party. Be honest with me. Is anything going on between the two of you?"

"You know what, fuck you. Here I am, trying to hold our life together, and you want to accuse me of fucking Deanthony. Fuck you!" I yelled, shoving Kashawn in his chest, forcing him to land back on the heel of his right foot. I hauled back and slapped him across his face. When I attempted to hit him again, he grabbed me by my wrist, locking his hand hard around it like an iron brace.

"Did you fuck him?"

I paused, feeling tears come up. "Yes. Yes, I fucked him. Is that what you want to hear? I fucked Deanthony. It didn't mean anything."

"It must have meant something."

All eyes were on us when I came clean about my adulterous confession.

"Mama is right about you. I should have left you at that club where I found you. You're nothing but a damn gold digger."

"You've been waiting to find the bad in me. Any excuse to quit me. Well, congratulations, mama's boy. I guess I'm a gold-digging slut. I'm not the perfect woman you said 'I do' to, and you are not a perfect man. You want me to sit at home and bake cookies and plant tomatoes in the backyard like your meddling mama, but I'm not her, Kashawn. I'm your wife, and if you don't like it, then maybe we should stop being married."

"I have a reputation in this community and I'm not going to

have my wife make a fool out of me. I see how these men look at you, like they want to fuck you, walking around here in those tight clothes like some slut."

I had heard enough and stormed back toward the house.

"It just goes to show that you can take the girl out of the strip club, but you can't take the strip club out of the girl. What the fuck am I doing with you?"

I turned around with rage and tears in my eyes. "I thought it was because you loved me."

Tangela rushed to my defense as I sauntered toward the deck, but I wasn't trying to hear what she or anyone else had to say. Everyone played it off like they weren't witness to our fussing and fighting. Mama Liz looked off like she couldn't stomach me.

"Congratulations, you got your son back." I jumped in my car and hauled ass. The last place I wanted to be was around Kashawn.

26

KASHAWN

My heart raced. My blood surged through my veins like white fire as images of Bree and Deanthony fucking danced in my head, his hands on her breasts, his face planted between her thighs. I thought of how often they were doing this behind my back, fucking in my bed. How could I not see it? I knew something was up when I caught them together in my old room at Mama's the night I brought Bree to meet everyone. I saw how Deanthony was looking at her at the birthday party like she was a slab of fucking beef.

I wanted the earth to open up and swallow them. I couldn't shake the image of her sucking his dick or Deanthony eating her out.

"Kashawn, baby, are you all right?" Ma asked. She tried to ease my hurt.

"Mama, not now."

She couldn't make this go away. Hell no, not this. I broke past her, past a cluster of family, friends, and hospital coworkers. "Where the fuck is he?" I entered the living room. Bree was gone. Good. Fuck her. Ma and Yvonne were right about her. She's a whore.

I fucked Deanthony. I fucked Deanthony. I fucked Deanthony.

Her words were razor-sharp barbs ripping through my mind. I was so stupid. How the fuck could I have been so naïve? I should have left that slut where I found her. I should have married a white woman.

I had Deanthony in my sights. Our eyes met past the house full of people. *Yeah, bitch, your secret is out.*

"You had to do it, didn't you?" I yelled. All eyes were on me. "You just had to fuck her. Is she why you came back? You two thought, what, that you could take up where you left off?"

"Kashawn, let's go outside and talk about this."

"Talk about what, huh? Talk about what, motherfucker?"

I wanted to kill him, rip his fucking head off.

"It just happened, bro. We weren't trying to hurt you."

"You weren't *trying* to hurt me? Were you *trying* not to hurt me when you stuck your dick in my wife?"

Gasps of shock and awe filled the room. "Kashawn, stop that in this house," Ma protested.

"Why don't you tell me... no, tell *all* of us how good my wife is in bed? Her pussy's real good, isn't it?"

"Kashawn, don't do this. Not here," Tangela said, taking me softly by my arm.

I charged past my guests toward Deanthony. I was on his ass like white on rice, slamming his face into the wall. He pulled at me as I punched him continuously in the face with my hand tight at his throat. His lip was split. Blood trickled down his chin.

"'Shawn, stop. That's your brother!"

He deserved the ass-kicking he was getting.

"Fuck him. I don't have a brother!"

He slid to the floor. I kicked him in the stomach and ribs. I punched until I felt arms under me, yanking me off Deanthony's sorry ass.

"Get off me! Get the fuck off me!"

Uncle Ray-Ray pinned my arms behind me. He was bigger than me, strong as an ox.

"Just like old times, right, bro? I can't have shit because of you!

You've always wanted what I had." I spat on Deanthony like he wasn't shit and, as far as I was concerned, he wasn't. "Are you happy now? You ruined my fucking marriage!"

Tyrique and Jayson helped him to his feet.

"Leave him there. Let his ass bleed," Kashawn said.

Jayson gave Deanthony a handkerchief to wipe his lip.

"Get him out of here. We're not brothers. You're dead to me, bitch. Get the fuck out of my house."

27

DEANTHONY

Meet me in the garage. This calls for a celebration, Tangela's text message read.

I made sure that no one saw me as I made my way to the garage where Tangela was waiting, exhaling smoke from a cigarette. The faint fumes of oil and gasoline permeated throughout.

"Bitch, are you crazy, smoking up in here? The whole place could go up."

"Did you see that in there?" Tangela grinned.

"The whole fucking house saw it."

"And we didn't have to lift a finger."

"Did you see Bree's face?"

"Oh, please, she isn't doing nothing but putting on one of her performances so somebody can feel sorry for her, and it looks like it's working on you," Tangela said, taking a drag from her cancer stick.

"This is my fucking family you playin' with." I applied more pressure to my lip to stop the bleeding. A busted lip was what I deserved and a whole lot worse. If I were in Kashawn's shoes, I would have kicked my ass too.

"Fuck this. I'm done."

"You can't throw the towel in now, not when we're this close. Kashawn and Bree are both vulnerable. All we got to do now is seal the deal."

"I need to call her to see if she's okay."

"Hell no, she's not okay. She just confessed to sleeping with you in front of all her family and friends. I wouldn't be surprised if she never showed her face here again. Nobody will say it, but Kashawn looked ridiculous walking around here with someone like Bree on his arm. I mean, damn, we're talking about somebody who used to shake her titties and ass up in men's faces for money."

"Shut your fuckin' mouth."

"Awww, what's the matter? Did I hurt your wittle feelings?"

"You don't give a fuck who you hurt. You don't care who you hurt to get what you want."

"Nigga, whatever. Don't play that holier-than-thou shit with me. You want Bree for yourself and always have. All I'm doing is pushing things along so we'll both get what we want."

"Not like this."

"How else was it going to go down? What, you're just going to walk up to your brother and confess your love for his wife? You thought you were going to walk back into his life after three years and take what's yours without cracking a few heads?"

"I didn't want it to go down like this."

"D, what difference does it make how it went down as long as the end result involves me getting Kashawn, and you and Bree get to ride y'all asses off into the sunset?"

Every word that came out of Tangela's mouth set my blood to boil when she talked about Bree and my brother. I couldn't stand the sight of her. "I could break your damn neck."

"What the fuck is your problem?"

"You're my damn problem. Because of your scheming, my brother could have died."

"I'm assuming you're talking about that shit with Kateisha. I didn't say nothing to that bitch about drugging Kashawn. I told her to get him in bed, that's—"

Before Tangela could say another word, I lunged at her, locking a hand around her throat. "You almost get my brother killed and you have the nerve to show your face here."

"Nigga, get your hands off of me."

"I could snap your neck like a glow stick and no one would miss you."

Tangela reached inside her purse to pull something out, but I grabbed at her arm. It wasn't a fingernail file this time, but a .38.

"What the fuck you think you're going to do with this, huh?" I took the gun and pressed it to Tangela's temple. "Are you fucking mental, bringing a gun to my brother's house?"

"Go ahead, do it. Pull the fucking trigger."

"I oughta put you out of your sad-ass misery."

Tangela pressed her forehead hard against the barrel of the gun. "Do it. Kill me with all these people around. You can't. You know why? Because you don't have the fucking balls."

"Bree has no idea who you are." I took the gun off her head. "Bitch, you ain't worth the bullet."

"That's what I thought. I never should have brought you in on this. I knew your punk ass would crumble like a cookie."

"Everything you touch turns to shit."

"I just thought of something. How about I kill Bree? I'll blast her ass right in her own driveway."

"Don't you touch her."

"Killing you would be too easy. Why waste a bullet on you when I have this?" Tangela took out her phone and showed the video of me fucking a man in a gay porno. "All I have to do is send this nasty shit to Mama Liz. What do you think she would think, seeing you butt-ass naked, giving it to some old white man up the ass?"

"Fuck you."

"Maybe, but knowing where your dick has been, not fucking likely.

Looking at this shit. I'm going to have to go get tested for HIV. Who the hell knows what you gave me."

When we heard a knock on the garage door, I tucked the gun in my jeans, under my shirt, while Tangela hauled her ass out of the side door of the garage.

I walked up the stairs that led back toward the house. Yvonne was sitting at the kitchen table, doing what she does best: eating. Her plate was so full with barbecue chicken, baked beans, and potato salad, it was literally running over.

"Why are you sweating?" she asked.

"Nothing. I saw that we were running out of cups and came out here to get some more."

"Uh-huh," she uttered.

I went over to the sink to wash my hands. She looked funny, sitting there chomping away at chicken like it was the last thing she would ever stuff her fat face with.

"How's the chicken?"

"Unc put his foot in them as always."

"I thought you were on a diet?"

"I start it tomorrow."

"Uh-huh. I've heard that before."

"How's the lip?"

"I think I'll live," I told her, drying my hands with paper towels.

"So, what were you and Tangela talking about? I saw you follow her out there in the garage."

Yvonne's big ass don't miss a beat. "We were just talking."

"About what?"

I started laughing as I dried my hands. "You ask me that like I would actually give you an answer."

"Why is it that everywhere you go, D, you leave behind a trail of shit? No matter what you do, trouble ends up finding you."

"I would ask what your problem is, but I don't want you to think that I actually give a shit."

"Why you can't leave Bree and Kashawn alone?"

"Why don't you get you some business instead of sticking your pig nose in everyone else's?"

"Everything has been fucked up since you came back in town."

"Well, you will be happy to know that I'm not going anywhere, so you, Bree, Kashawn, and everybody else might as well get used to me being around."

"It's obvious you're not over Bree."

"Yvonne, you know what you need? Some dick. Capital D-i-c-k. If you got a little, you would be too busy getting fucked to be in other people's business." I grinned at the sight of Yvonne's mouth stained with grease. "Get yourself an African man. They love big girls."

"Is Tangela your next conquest?" Yvonne ignored my usual digs at her.

"You give me way too much credit, cousin."

"You should leave and take Bree with you. Kashawn can do bad all by himself."

I was about to curse my nosey cousin out when I heard mama screaming. We both ran out on the deck where people were clustered around Uncle Ray-Ray lying on the living room floor. I tore through the crowd like a hurricane through a crop of houses. Kashawn was hovered over him, giving him mouth to mouth and chest compressions. Uncle Ray-Ray's pie-shaped face was flushed and sweaty.

"He's having a heart attack," Tyrique said. Ebonya held herself snug against his chest.

"Somebody call nine-one-one," I yelled. Ma was wailing and screaming, hysterical. "Come on, Unc, stay with me. Why the fuck are y'all just standin' there? Call nine-one-one!"

Tyrique took out his phone and dialed. Uncle Ray-Ray's lips were dry. Beads of sweat peppered his face.

"The ambulance is on the way," Tyrique said.

Tears pooled up in my eyes as I watched Kashawn struggle to breathe life back into the man who was like a father to me.

28

BREE

The day of my wedding my whole breakfast came up. Bacon, boiled egg, grits, English muffin. I was a hot mess of nerves. If it wasn't for Tangela, they would have had to scrape me off the ceiling with a spatula. I had turned into a raging bridezilla, the one thing I said I was never going to turn into. Kashawn went all out to make sure that I would have a wedding that would put Tallahassee on the map. I had never seen so many flowers in my life. Mama Liz and Tangela made sure that everything was perfect, that the wedding went off without a hitch. It didn't hit me until I stepped into my Vera Wang original. I struggled to hold back tears when I looked at myself in the full-length mirror.

Had someone told me that I would be marrying the man of my dreams, I would have said they were crazy. Girls like me don't get married, and girls like me sure as hell don't get married to doctors. If anything, I figured I would meet some loser, get knocked up, only to end up on welfare as a single mother, another statistic. Chicks like me don't fall in love. I thank the Lord every day for Kashawn. Let me stop. I've done enough crying today.

The colors I chose for the wedding were white and lavender. Light lavender dresses for my bridesmaids with a bouquet of white roses and lilacs. Lavender has always been my favorite color, ever since seeing the color scheme of lavender and yellow in one of my aunts' bedrooms. I even thought to dye my wedding dress lavender, but, honey, you don't alter Vera Wang. Nakia, Josette, and even Latrice's big behind looked gorgeous in their Ronald Joyce dresses. The four of us wore white sling backs with matching Victoria Jane pearls. My hair was done up in pretty fishtail braids with lilacs placed perfectly throughout. I let this sister, Ava, do it. She has this shop in Governor Square Mall. Radiance, it's called. I wanted Tangela to hook me up, but she doesn't do wedding hair, so she recommended Ava. I had my reservations about her at first, but Tangela swore by her.

"Girl, if she messes it up, I'm gonna make sure she never twists another braid in this town again. Bree, trust me. I told Ava what you want, and she told me that it's no problem."

After about two hours, home girl had me looking like a queen by the time she was done. She was officially my go-to for any hair catastrophes I had in the future, or just when I wasn't in the mood for one of my do-it-yourself jobs that consisted of twisting my hair up in a ponytail.

I wanted to have the wedding at our house, but Mama Liz insisted we get married at her church. I figured the house was perfect. It was big enough to hold all five hundred guests, and the backyard was damn near the size of a football field.

"Oh, my God, Bree. Girl, you look so beautiful," Josette kept saying.

You would think the way Tangela, Nakia, and Latrice were fussing over me, that they were getting married, but I'm not going to lie, I loved every pampered minute. I looked at myself in the mirror and couldn't believe that I was in a wedding dress, a Vera Wang wedding dress no less. It was a complete and total transformation. There was a knock at the door.

"Latrice, will you see who that is?"

Latrice answered the door to find Uncle Ray-Ray standing there, dressed to the nines in a gray tuxedo with a white shirt, a gray-and-white tie, and sterling silver cufflinks. It was the first time I had ever seen Uncle Ray-Ray look so clean and sharp outside of a T-shirt and jeans, wearing an apron that was always smudged with grease and barbecue sauce.

"Here y'all are. Mama Liz is wondering where the rest of the bridal party is."

Tangela, Latrice, Nakia, and Josette started to scramble.

"Y'all better get down there before she throws a fit."

My three bridesmaids filed out of my bedroom one at a time.

"Girl, you look gorgeous," Nakia said as she kissed me on the cheek.

"Thank you, baby girl."

Uncle Ray-Ray stared at me in the mirror like I was Tallahassee royalty.

"So what do you think?"

"I never had a daughter, but if I did, I would want her to look exactly like you on her wedding day." Uncle Ray-Ray's words nearly brought me to tears.

"You know, ever since the day I joined this family, you have been nothing but sweet to me, while Mama Liz and Yvonne have had nothing but beef with me. I'm still not sure yet if I've convinced them that I'm good for Kashawn."

Uncle Ray-Ray placed his hands softly on my shoulders. "It doesn't matter what they think, or whether or not you're right for my nephew. They're not marrying Kashawn. You are."

"And I've been telling myself that ever since."

"Bree, I know that it hasn't been easy, but you seem to be holding your own with the two of them. Trust me, they are not easy women to get along with."

"You ain't never lied. I can't seem to do anything right by Mama

Liz. Even on my wedding day, I feel like I'm walking on pins, needles, *and* thumbtacks around her. I don't know what else I can do, short of offering her my firstborn."

Uncle Ray-Ray chuckled. "Like I said, they'll come around. It's not like they have a choice. And let's not make this day about them. This is your and Kashawn's wedding. And, girl, his heart is going to melt when he sees how beautiful you are today."

"You think so?"

"No doubt about it. Kashawn is a lucky man."

"All I want to do is make him happy."

"And you will. I know my nephew. That man is head over heels in love with you."

"He better be. He spent enough on this dress," I joked.

Uncle Ray-Ray held out his arm to escort me downstairs. "Well, we better not keep your guests waiting. Let's get this show on the road."

I kept saying in my head that I wouldn't cry as I made my way downstairs. When the organist began to play "Here Comes the Bride," everyone turned in my direction. Within seconds, all eyes were on me and I felt like straight-up queen royalty. When I saw Kashawn waiting for me at the end of the aisle, my nerves had subsided. I knew that everything was going to be okay, that as long as we had each other, we could get through anything.

I was about to order another Vodka Cranberry when my phone rang. It was Ebonya. I answered it. "Hey, girl."

"Bree, where are you?"

"I'm at Mockingbird Bar. Why?"

"You need to come to the hospital. Something's happened."

I instantly felt a panicked feeling wash over me. "What is it? Is it Kashawn?"

"No, it's Uncle Ray-Ray. He's had a heart attack."

"Oh, my God, okay. I'm on my way."

29

BREE

I t was a rainy Saturday afternoon the day of Uncle Ray-Ray's funeral. Kashawn was pretty much in a daze all day, staring at the storm-gray casket as they lowered his uncle into the ground. Kashawn's hand felt cold, like the life had been drained out of him. I would look into his light-brown eyes, only to find him listless, overcome with grief. Mama Liz rocked back and forth in a white fold-out chair, her mouth moving like she was singing to herself. Mount Zion Church was packed to the rim with family, friends, and people from the neighborhood. Even after the ushers brought out chairs for people to sit in, there was still standing room only in the small white church.

I had no idea Uncle Ray-Ray had so many friends. People from south Florida to Alabama came to pay their respects. More than a dozen people got up and spoke about him, sharing funny stories, most of all talking about how he cooked the best barbecue in Tallahassee. Deanthony sat by himself eating, nursing on what I think was his fifth or sixth beer. He looked defeated, like there was no strength left in him. Miss Corrine, a neighbor of Mama Liz's for thirty-four years, fixed Deanthony a plate of fried chicken, black-eyed peas, greens and corn bread. He took it in kindness, but all he did was pick over the food with a plastic fork. Kashawn didn't have an appetite for nothing, either.

There was enough food to feed a Third World country. Platters of both fried and baked chicken, slices of honey ham, a mess of three kinds of greens, corn bread, black-eyed peas, lima beans, roast beef, and an assortment of pies and cakes occupied long fold-out tables. Someone even brought 'coon, something I had no intention of putting my mouth on. I was country, but not *that* country. I remember Uncle Ray-Ray had some barbecue 'coon at the birthday party, but I didn't have the stomach to put my hands on any of it. All I had was a piece of bread pudding Ms. Corrine had made. I badly wanted to go over and see how Deanthony was doing. I was there for Kashawn, but no one seemed to care about Deanthony. These men out here try to be so tough, but death will bring the hardest man to his knees. Ebonya eventually walked over to see about Deanthony.

The plate of food that Mama Liz had made for Kashawn sat idle between his feet.

"Hey, you've barely touched your plate. You need to eat something."

"I'm not hungry."

"You should go see how your mama's doing."

Kashawn glanced over at her, Ms. Corrine cupping Mama Liz's hand in hers. He walked over to his mama and sat on the other side of her, pulling her into him, the two of them rocking simultaneously, back and forth.

"Girl, he won't eat anything," Ebonya said, folding her fingers over Tyrique's white silk handkerchief.

"I'm going to miss Uncle Ray-Ray. He was such a sweet man."

"Girl, I know," Ebonya said. "He would give you the shirt off his back."

"And he never let anyone go hungry. When he lit that grill up, everybody was welcome. Not one soul did he turn away."

"Not a single one. Nobody will ever say that he didn't do anything for anyone. He was like a father to a lot of kids out here when their biologicals didn't give a damn."

"He welcomed me into the family with open arms when Mama Liz had her reservations about me because of my past."

"Bree, has she always had an issue with you?"

"She would smile in my face, yeah, but would talk bad behind my back. Kashawn is always telling me about something she's said about me, but I just keep doing me."

"Girl, that's all you can really do."

"Everyone has a seedy past. No one's perfect."

"Have you and Kashawn talked since the argument at the homecoming party?"

"Things have been so crazy making preparations for the funeral that we really haven't had the opportunity to talk. Honestly, I have no idea where we stand. We said some nasty things to each other."

"Can I ask you something? You can tell me to mind my own business if you don't want to answer."

"Not at all. What's on your mind?"

"Is it true about you and Deanthony?"

"It happened a long time ago, before Deanthony left town. Ebonya, I regret every day that I let that happen. I was in a bad way. Kashawn was always working late nights, I was home alone all the time. I know that's no excuse to cheat on your man, but—"

"Girl, you don't have to explain a thing to me. I know exactly how you feel."

"I haven't gone over to see how he's doing because the last thing Kashawn needs to see is me sitting up around Deanthony after everything that's happened."

I couldn't believe we were talking about this subject at a funeral. Scared that someone was ear-hustling, I turned the subject back to me and my issues with Mama Liz when Tangela walked in wearing a black, tight Chanel dress, black shades, and long, thick weave draped down her back. The coat of scarlet-red nail polish was matched by a pair of scarlet-red heels. Even at the funeral, she had the men's heads turning while their wives were quick to slap their eyes back into their dirty minds as Tangela paid her respects to Kashawn and Mama Liz. Deanthony gawked at her like the devil himself had walked into the room. It was official. Something was up with those two. I had noticed the sly-ass looks they were giving each other at the hospital and again at Kashawn's home-coming party, like they were in some stand-off at high noon.

"Hey, girl, how are you holding up?" Tangela sat next to me, taking my hand into hers.

Ebonya sucked her teeth and said, "Girl, let me know if you need anything." She walked away.

"Thank you, Vita, for sitting with her," Tangela said, butchering Ebonya's name.

"I'm just trying to keep it together for Kashawn."

"How's he doing?"

"He's in mourning. He hasn't said much since the hospital."

"Is there anything I can do?"

"I appreciate that, Tangela, but you're being here is enough," I said, hugging her hand.

"Well, you know I got your back, no matter what."

"I know." I smiled.

"Have things gotten better with y'all since the argument at the welcome-home party?"

"I was just telling Ebonya that Kashawn and I haven't had time to really sit down and talk about things. I didn't feel it was appropriate to talk about anything with the planning of the funeral."

"Of course," Tangela said, "I can understand that."

"I just want us to start over, forget last week ever happened, a clean slate."

"So, he's good after that mess Katiesha pulled?"

I was taken back that Tangela would fix her mouth to even so much as spit that hood rat's name. "Girl, I'm not even trying to waste brain cells thinking about Katiesha right now. Best thing she can do is stay her ass wherever she's at."

"Did Kashawn remember what happened that night?"

"He said Katiesha came to the house to use the phone after her car broke down. Says he doesn't remember much after that."

"Do you believe it?"

"I don't know what to believe, but I'm going to find out what really went down that night."

"What are you talking about doing?"

"I'm going straight to the source. I'm going to talk to Katiesha."

"Do you think that's a good idea? You two are like oil and water."

"Oh, trust, I would rather stick a rusty butter knife in my eye than to see that bitch again, but something hasn't added up since that night. How did she know where I lived and how does she know Kashawn?"

"Bree, don't you think that you have suffered enough? Don't you think it would be better if you moved forward and forget about that ho?"

"I got to do this. I can't get that image of her fucking Kashawn out of my head. Finding out what really happened that night is the only thing that will give me a piece of mind. And, hey, if I end up beating her ass in the process, so be it."

"Bree, don't do something that's going to get you locked up."

"How can I regret getting to the truth?"

"I'm saying be careful. This bitch did key your car. Who's to say that next time, it might be your face?"

"If anything, she will end up being the one getting cut up. Mark my words. Katiesha is going to tell me what happened that night."

"When are you talking about doing this?"

"I'm going to go look for her ass tonight."

"Tonight?"

"I figure she'll be working tonight, or at that shit box of an apartment she stays at over on Pepper Drive."

"Girl, that part of town is dangerous."

"I grew up in a part of town like that, remember?"

"And what if you can't find her?"

"A hood rat like her won't be hard to find."

"Well, there's no need of you going on this suicide mission by yourself. I might as well go with you."

"Hell no. Tangela, I can't ask you to do that."

"There is no way you're going to Risqué by yourself."

"Tangela, this is my business."

"Girl, don't be crazy. I'm going with you and that's final."

I sighed, knowing that once Tangela's mind was made up, there was no changing it. "Okay, fine. We'll go check out Risqué first. She might still work on Sunday nights. Meet me at Risqué around ten."

"Bet," Tangela said.

"I'm going to go see how Kashawn and Mama Liz are doing."

"Okay, I'll be outside having a cigarette if you need me."

"Thanks, girl, again, for coming."

"That's what friends are for."

30

BREE

I t was storming the Sunday night I went looking for Katiesha. Being that I can't stand to drive in the rain, I started not to go out. Kashawn and I were like a wet Band-Aid, barely holding together. I left him in bed, sound asleep. Well, not so sound, considering his snoring was like a table saw going off. I still couldn't believe Uncle Ray-Ray was gone. That man was like a father to me when I didn't know who my real father was. His famous barbecue will not be the only thing I will miss about that big ole chocolate *daddy bear.* That's what I would call him sometimes. Daddy Bear.

I looked at my watch and it was twenty minutes after ten, and Tangela still had not shown up. I called her for the third time, and again her phone went straight to voicemail. "Damn, bitch, where are you?"

Hard to believe that it's been five years since I was last at Risqué. D'Shon, my piece of shit, dope-pushing boyfriend at the time, had kicked me out because I wouldn't push rock for his dusty ass. I had moved down here to Tallahassee by way of D.C. to get away from my control freak of a mama who had a revolving door policy when it came to men, dragging them home as if they were wet alley cats who thought I was the sprinkles on top of whatever Mama was serving. Most of them stuck around long enough to take what they could from her and then they were out the door. They were always coming around trying to get a piece of me, feeling and rubbing on me and shit.

I'll never forget this nigga, Clint, she used to fuck with. He was the one who got Ma hooked on coke. Big, black, and dirty in every sense of the word is the best way to describe him. He was always coming over with gifts, bags and bags of clothes from Macy's. I knew all the stuff was probably shit he stole, but me and Ma didn't care. When I did go to school, I was always in the freshest gear. Clint would buy us stuff; take us out to places like Red Lobster and Olive Garden to eat. He was cool until his ass started getting too comfortable. He kept Ma and tried to get me hooked, but I was too smart for that shit. I saw what crack had done to her and I wasn't about to go down that same fucked-up road.

The night Clint came into my room and raped me, Ma was passed out on the sofa. He was so stank that night like he had his hands up a dog's ass. I remember that it was the smell that woke me up. I felt the weight of him when he sat down on my bed, smelling like a skunk. When he put his hand on my shoulder, I told him to get the fuck out of my room. I have never forgotten what he said to me that night.

"I want to taste you."

I couldn't get away because he was standing his big-belly ass in front of the door. I screamed, but Mama could sleep through anything, even when she wasn't high, which wasn't often. Clint caught me and pushed me down on the bed. I kicked and kicked until he grabbed my legs and yanked me across the bed. He tore off my nightgown and lay on top of me. That bastard was heavy as hell. I tried to push Clint off, but he was built strong. He started kissing me, grabbing at my titties. The tighter I attempted to keep my legs closed from his invasion, the rougher Clint got, forcing them open. His breath smelled like ass and gin. When I screamed as he pulled my panties down, he put his hand that was like the size of a baseball mitt over my mouth and told me that if I screamed again, he would kill me and Mama. He held me down as he forced his dick inside me.

Before Clint, I had never really had sex. There was this boy, Dino, at school who I let feel me up behind the gym bleachers, but that was it. Clint didn't see me reach for the pencil I had sitting on top of my notebook from the math homework I was doing. The end of it was good and sharp. I took it and, as hard as I could, jabbed the pencil in his neck. Yeah, that got his ass off me quick. He hollered, not focusing on the strength he used to hold me down, but the pencil that was sticking out of the side of his neck. Clint made this loud thud when he hit my bedroom floor. I got out of there and ran as fast as I could out of the house. Ma told me that he didn't die. I wanted that raping-ass fuck dead for what he did to me. I knew that if I stayed, things would only get worse. The day I decided to leave, Ma was lying on the sofa, slobbering, with a cigarette clutched between her fingers. I was always telling her to watch her damn cigarettes, that she was going to burn the house down, but she never listened to me. I didn't leave a note or nothing, figuring she wouldn't notice that I had left one anyway.

I stayed with this girl named Keasha, who ran a small junior food store over on Orange Avenue. She would let me sleep in an extra room she had upstairs, and, in return, I would keep the store clean, mop the bathrooms, and run the store while she went to run errands. Keasha was both like the mama and the big sister I always wanted. She pretty much raised me as her own when I told her what Clint had done to me. I didn't think of Ma that much. Out of sight, out of mind as far as I was concerned. Months later, I found out that her apartment caught fire. The news said that she must have been asleep when the place went up. "Goddamn cigarettes." I cried like a baby at the funeral. She wasn't the ideal mother. She'd made some mistakes, but she was the only mother I had.

After the store got broken into and vandalized, Keasha didn't have money for repairs and had to close the store. Things got real bad after that. Keasha started drinking and would come home drunk and take her frustrations out on me. When she tried to beat on me, I knew it was time to move on and leave her with that shit. I wrote her a letter, thanking her for everything. I threw what little I owned in a garbage bag and left. I was fifteen. I stayed at the Y a few nights. It was filled with nasty-ass homeless pervs, so I didn't lay my head there long. I didn't have a dime to my name. I hustled until I was seventeen, sleeping mostly in abandoned apartments. I was always trying to figure out where my next meal of something to eat would come from when I saw this flyer on the abandoned window of Keasha's old store about Blue-Black looking for dancers. I figured I had the ass and the titties, so why not. It was a hell of a lot better than flipping burgers at Mickey D's.

The day I walked into Risqué, dudes looked at me like I was a piece of meat. Blue asked me how old I was. I lied and told him I was nineteen. He laughed like he knew I was lying. My first impression of Blue was that he looked a little like a fat-ass Bernie Mac. He was tall, six-three, six-four maybe, shit-brown eyes with black processed hair combed in waves. He had big everything. Big hands, big arms, big legs, big chest, and a big dick he made all the new girls suck. Blue told me that I would have to suck his dick if I wanted the job, that it was something all the girls did. He talked about me sucking his dick like it was no big deal. I thought about Clint and him raping me four years earlier, but I had to put that shit out of my mind and do the do if I wanted the job. Shit, it wasn't like I didn't know my way around a hard dick by then no way. Out on the streets, that pride shit goes right out the window when you stuck between not eating and sleeping in a warm bed versus the lobby of a bus depot.

The first night I started, I had them thirsty fucks eating out of my hand, making four to five hundred a night and a stack on the weekends. I bought some new gear and got myself one of those nice apartments on the east side of town near Florida State University's football stadium. Even though I was pulling enough cake that I didn't need a roommate, I wasn't used to living by myself, so I put an ad on ApartmentSeekers.com, advertising for a female roomie, someone clean, and not some catty, cutthroat, man-stealing bitch like the girls from the club. Tangela was the first to answer the ad. We had the same taste in movies, clothes, and music. She was my kind of bitch. We have been inseparable ever since.

Tangela knew that I said to meet me at ten o' clock. Fuck it. I don't have time to wait on her. I folded the hood of my black raincoat over my head, stepped out of the car in the heavy downpour, and started toward Risqué. I was a little nervous, but I was more than ready to kick some stripper ass if need be that night. If I had to go upside Katiesha's head in order to get the answers that I came for, then I was down. The plan was to go in and not pop off.

Wishful fucking thinking, I thought.

In Risqué, there was no telling what could get started. Chet, one of the bouncers out of ten I remember Blue having on staff, was standing outside under a red tarp. He was dressed from tip to tail in black. A black windbreaker, black jeans, and black Timbs. Chet used to be a linebacker for the Tampa Bay Buccaneers until he blew out his knee playing against the Chicago Browns back in the day. Supposedly, he and Blue have been boys since they were in diapers. Chet was the size of a Hummer. He looked at me inquisitively as I neared him.

"Chet, what's up?"

"Bree, is that you?"

"Who the hell you think it is?"

Chet pulled me into arms that were the size of tree trunks, giving me one of his big grizzly hugs. It reminded me of the hugs Uncle Ray-Ray used to give. "How you doin', ma? Where you been at, shorty?" This fool didn't know his own strength, squeezing me like I was a turnip he was trying to get juice out of. He finally turned me loose without cracking a bitch's rib.

"Enjoying married life," I told him, showing him the rock on my finger.

"Oh, yeah, yeah, yeah, I heard you got hitched. A doctor, right?"

"Kashawn Parker, yes."

"Ain't he that dude that's in the corny car commercials on TV?" I looked at Chet and sucked my teeth.

"I laugh my ass off every time that commercial about acid reflux comes on," Chet said, grinning through the set of gold-capped teeth in his mouth.

"Laugh if you want to, but he's going all the way to the bank with the cake he makes doing those commercials." I loved singing Kashawn's praises, letting these simple-ass niggas know that I had come up, especially the naysayers who didn't think a bitch like me would amount to shit.

"No disrespect. I bought a Cadillac off one of his dad's lots. They hooked a brother up. See it out there parked in the back of the lot?"

I looked past the pouring rain at the cranberry-red whip that sat idle from the school of other cars. "Nice," I said.

"That's my baby right there, my pride and my joy."

"Well, you look good, Chet. I see you haven't missed a meal," I teased, patting his belly like he was a big ole Saint Bernard.

"I'm trying to lay off the salt and sugar, but, damn, girl, married life looks good on you," Chet said, checking me out from head to toe. "I bet you don't miss this place."

"Baby boy, not even a little bit. I came by to say hey to some of the girls. Is Blue working tonight?"

"You know how he do, in the office counting money."

"Figures. Can I go in? I'll try to avoid him."

"Yeah, girl, go on in."

"Thank you, baby," I said, giving him a kiss on the cheek. That would be enough to keep his dick brick for the rest of the week. He held the red pleather-covered doors open as I walked in.

The smell of beer and cigarettes filled my senses. It felt surreal, like I was walking in for the first time. Ursula, Katiesha's running buddy, was working it to some Rick Ross. She was butt-naked, but I would have paid the scallywag to put her clothes back on with titties that sagged to her knobby knees. Her cottage cheese ass was nothing nice in the neon-green G-string. From her dried-up chocolate weave to her Payless Shoes heels, Ursula looked a hot ghetto mess. It hurt my eyes to be witness to those droopy boobs. I was a bit more surprised that she was still shaking her low-budget ass in this cesspool at her age. A stripper has a five-year shelf life. After that, it's time to get off the pole. None of the suits were paying any attention to her. It wasn't that busy. Most of the losers were saddled up to the bar, nursing on watered-down drinks and overpriced beer.

Hell no, I didn't miss this shit hole. All eyes were on me as I sauntered across the club to the bar tended by this chick dressed in jeans and a black leather bra that barely held her breasts in. Her arms were huge. She looked like one of those weightlifting chicks. Montez, this law school bookworm, used to sling drinks back during my booty-shaking days. Nothing had changed much.

"Hey, is, um, Katiesha on tonight?" This muscle-bound bitch wasn't paying me any attention, so I walked around in front of the bar and sandwiched myself between these two suits who were checking out my booty. "Hey, do you know a dancer here by the name of Katiesha?"

"I'm not sure. I just started my shift thirty minutes ago," she yelled through the thump of the club speakers. "If she is, she's probably in back."

"Cool. Appreciate it." I leaned back from the bar, out of the sight of the drunken suits that should have been home with their wives instead of drooling like sloppy hogs over stripper pussy.

"Can I buy you a drink, baby?" she asked.

"Vodka Cranberry."

"You got it."

I was flattered that she was flirting with me. It'd been a long time since a lady has done that. I took a seat in the corner of the bar as I watched her make my drink. She had pitch-black hair that was pulled back slick and tight in a pony. Her lips were as red as cherry tomatoes. If I had a dick, it would be brick-hard for girl right now. She looked Latina, maybe a little chocolate mixed in. I would probably holla if I weren't married, if I swam in the *lady* pond. She didn't have an ounce of fat on her. Definitely the type Blue would hire.

"There you go. Best Vodka Cranberry you will ever drink."

I took a sip and she was right.

"How is it?"

"You ain't lyin'. That's good."

"Bet your ass it is, girl. I'm Marisol," she said, holding out her hand for a shake.

"Bree."

"So what do you want with Katiesha?"

I had to think of something quick to say. "She's my cousin. I just got into town and she told me to meet her here."

"Damn, is everyone in her family as fine as you?" Marisol asked, caressing my hand.

"Yeah, girl, we're all amazons. Listen, baby, I would love to sit here and kick it with you, but I gotta find my cousin."

"C'mon, what's the rush?"

"I drove all the way from Virginia. I'm tired, you feel me?"

"All right, well, if you need anything, just whistle. Marisol will take care of you."

I finished my drink and made my way backstage to the dressing rooms. I was lucky that Queasy still didn't have security worth a damn. I sneaked in back, ear-hustling on what these bitches were talking about. Nakia's mouth was the loudest over everyone else's.

"Y'all hush that fuss in here. Time is money, bitches."

A simultaneous roar of surprise echoed through the dressing room. Nakia, who wasn't wearing nothing but a silver G-string, wrapped her arms around me, her bare breasts pressing up against mine. Latrice, Nakia, and Josette all gathered around me like I was a celebrity. Grandma Ursula continued caking makeup on her alligator face. All the girls smothered me with hugs and kisses. Other than Ursula, I had made them all bridesmaids at my wedding. I thought Mama Liz and Melinda were going to have a coronary when I included them in the festivities. These four women were like sisters to me. They had taught me everything.

"Girl, what have you been up to?" Latrice asked.

"Where did you go on your honeymoon?" Nakia asked.

"Do you live in a big house?" Josette asked.

"Girl, I can't complain."

"The wedding was so beautiful," Josette, the hopeless romantic baby of the group, said. She had come on a week after I'd left.

"Girl, it was. You looked so good in your wedding dress," Nakia said. "Like a fairy princess."

"Trust. It's not all roses and champagne. We fuss and fight just like everyone else, y'all."

"Well, honey, you better keep him happy 'cause there's always another bitch waiting in the wings." Ursula walked over, tearing through the girls like she was head bitch in the bunch.

"What the hell do you mean by that, Ursula?"

Ursula stood her stride with her arms folded in front of her floppy titties. "I'm just saying. What you won't do, another bitch will."

I came this close to splitting that ratchet bitch's jaw in half. "Trust and believe, I got my man on lock with this pussy. And all y'all up in here know that I will get a ho together if I so much as see her bat an eyelash at Kashawn."

I looked dead at Ursula as I made my point. She was always saying shit out of the side of her neck. Much like Katiesha, she was not above trying to move in on somebody's man. Not even ten minutes had passed and I was already heated over that fucked-up shit Ursula had thrown my way.

"Down, girl," Nakia said, wedging herself between me and Ursula. "Ursula, go back to your cage. You're on again in ten minutes."

Not that anybody wanted to look at her wrinkled, fat ass jiggling in their faces. Ursula huffed like she wanted to pop off. This bitch just didn't know. It wouldn't be no skin off my titties to fuck her all the way up. I quickly remembered why I had come. Forget this idle chatter bullshit.

"Nakia, can I talk to you privately in the hall for a minute?" I didn't want to say anything in front of Ursula, knowing she would tip Katiesha's ass off.

"Yeah, girl, what's up?"

"Nakia, hurry up," Latrice said, "You know how Blue get if we don't come out on queue."

"Girl, keep your tampon on. I won't be long."

Nakia and I stepped into the hall that was lit with this ugly, orange-red lighting that made you feel like you were standing under a heat lamp.

"Ursula is still a bitch, I see. I came this close to pimp-slapping that moose."

Nakia burst out laughing. "Girl, you so crazy. I didn't want y'all fightin' up in there, breakin' shit. So what's up?"

"Have you seen Katiesha?"

"She's off tonight. Ursula took her shift. Why, what's up?"

I was kind of hesitant to tell Nakia about what had happened, but I knew she could keep her mouth shut when need be.

"I got a bone to pick with that bitch, namely hers."

"What her ass did now?"

"I caught that skank fucking my man, that's all."

"Girl, what, seriously?"

"And she damn-near killed him with some shit she had slipped him. Turns out Kashawn is allergic to some component in whatever she poured in his drink. Girl, when I came home and saw her, I saw fuckin' red. I tried to beat the black off that ho until the cops showed up."

"Damn, somebody called po-po?"

"I guess it was one of the neighbors."

"Did they arrest you?"

"Other than treat *me* like I was the damn criminal, hell no. They just asked Katiesha some questions about what happened when she almost killed my husband. They gon' tell me that they didn't have shit to hold her on because she refused to talk, but she's going to talk to me. I *will* find out what went down at my crib. That's why I'm trying to find her."

"Girl, she's hardly ever here, and when she is here, she's fucked up on somethin'. Queasy says he's gon' fire her ass the next time he sees her. She comes in looking tore up, track marks bigger than dinner plates down both her arms. Javion is the one who got her turned on to heroin."

I almost felt sorry for Katiesha. Almost. Everybody got it bad. Don't give her the right to fuck somebody else's man.

"So what are you goin' to do when you find her?"

"As much as I want to finish fucking her up, I just want to talk to her. That's it."

"Have you gone by her crib?"

"That's my next stop."

"You want me to go with you? Pepper Drive is nothin' nice this time of night, girl."

"No, I got this."

"You sure? I can get Josette to cover for me."

"I'm sure. I grew up in a neighborhood like that. I'll be fine."

"Well, okay, but here, let me get your number before you go."

I dug in my purse for a pen and something to write on. "Here, give me your hand." I jotted my cell number down in Nakia's palm. "Call me, girl. We'll go do lunch at The Silver Slipper or something."

"I heard about that place. I hear they got good food."

"It is. The escargot will make you want to slap your mama."

"Escargot?"

"Yeah, snails."

"Uh-uh, you can have that. I'll get me some spaghetti and meatballs or something, girl. I can't mess with nothin' like that."

"You so silly. All right," I said, giving Nakia a hug. "And that about Katiesha is between me and you, cool?"

"B, come on, you know you can trust me."

"Thank you, baby."

"Be careful. Let me know what happens and don't be a stranger."

"I promise."

I went back to the dressing room and said bye to the girls. "All right, y'all, I'm out. I gave Nakia my number, so maybe all of us could hang out." Everybody except for Miss Saggy Titties hugged me bye.

"Bye, Wifey," Latrice said.

"Don't shake it too hard, bitches."

I got out of there before I started crying and made my way at breakneck speed toward the exit before Blue saw me. I was almost home free until I felt someone pull at my arm.

"Where you rushin' off to, Hot Pink?" Blue asked. I hadn't been called that in five years. "You here to beg for your job back?"

"Nigga, you wish," I said, snatching my arm out of his kung fu grip. Blue had let himself go. A beer belly had taken the place of his washboard stomach. His arms were now fat and flabby and, judging from the crow's feet around his eyes, the years had not been kind to him. Blue smelled sickly-sweet of cheap K-mart cologne. I figured Marisol must have tipped him off. "I just came by to say hey to the girls, Blue."

"Heard you got hitched. How come I didn't get an invitation?"

"I don't know," I said, giving him a fake, inquisitive look. "It must have gotten lost in the mail."

Blue grinned. "You still got that mouth on you, Hot-Pink."

"Don't call me that."

"Remember how you got that name?"

"I've chosen to forget a lot when it comes down to you and this shit hole."

"Ouch. That hurts my feelings, Hot-Pink."

"Shit. You gotta have a heart to have feelings."

"You sure you don't want to come back?" Blue asked, scanning my body from my head to my French pedicure. "You made me a shit-load of money, girl."

I slapped his hand away when he grabbed my ass. "Fuck off of me."

"Damn, still got that juicy booty, too." Blue leaned into my left ear and whispered, "Why don'tchu come in back, give me one of them primo blow jobs for old time's sake?"

I pushed him back against a table, sending a half-glass of beer crashing to the floor. He gave a sinister laugh that sounded like it had come up from the recesses of his beer gut, past his raspy throat. The two packs of 305s a day had caught up with his Jabba the Hut-ass. I darted out of there like I was on fire.

"Take it easy, Bree," Blue said.

I ignored him as I hot-footed it out into the rainstorm and back to my SUV. I wanted to go home and scrub my skin raw after coming up out of Risqué. I hauled ass, hoping that I would never have to step a toenail in that open sore again.

31

TANGELA

"Katiesha, you need to get out of here. Take the money, leave town, and go wherever you want. Atlanta, New York, L.A., hell, Hawaii if you want to."

Katiesha took another long drag from the crack pipe, letting the smoke fill her lungs. "You ain't *telling* me to do nothing, number one, and, number two, I don't have to do a damn thing but stay black and be drop-dead fucking gorgeous."

Was this bitch serious? Katiesha pushed a body of the toxic smoke into the already pungent living room that looked as if Hurricane Katrina's cousin had blown through this bitch.

"What you need to do is pay me what you owe me and get the hell out my house."

"I told you when we made the deal that I didn't want no drugs involved. And what do you do, shoot him up with that shit you put up your arms."

"How was I going to put a big nigga like him down without using a lil' some-some? You told me to go over to B's crib and get him into bed, so that's what the fuck I did. I did the job you hired me to do, shit." Katiesha's eyes were sleepy-looking. Her words came out jagged and slurred. "When you told me it was Bree's man, I was all about it. Bitch was always walking around with her nose in the air. Think because she married, she better than a bitch. She stoops over and boo-boos like the rest of us."

"You won't get any argument from me, but you need to lie low for a while until I can get Bree off your scent."

"Fuck her. I'm not scared of that bitch. Let her come for me. I got something for her."

Katiesha could barely stand, talking about what she was ready for, looking a straight-up crack ho mess. Judging from her dirty muscle T-shirt and the dirty, denim cut-offs she sported, she was in no shape to go another toe to toe with Bree. Her apartment was a pigsty and she literally smelled like a used tampon. I held the back of my hand up to my nose as I dry-heaved.

"You don't give a fuck about me. You're just here to make sure I don't say nothin' to that snooty bitch. I don't give a shit about her or your fat ass. Maybe I'll tell Bree anyway. I wonder what she would do if she found out her *BFF* tried to break her and her man up."

The more Katiesha ran her mouth, the angrier I got. I was sick of her, and had put up with more than enough of her mess. "You really think she would believe you? You're nothing but a fucking crack whore. Your credibility is shit."

She gripped the glass crack pipe like it was the key to the city. "Maybe so. Maybe not."

I fished a thick white envelope stuffed with five thousand dollars out of one of the pockets of my trench coat and handed it to Katiesha. "Here, bitch, take the money before I change my mind."

Wobbling on those sore-riddled po-go sticks she called legs, Katiesha snatched the envelope out of my hand, sending it crashing to the coffee table of dirty plates and Absolut liquor bottles. "Fuck that. You want me to keep my mouth shut about what you did to Bree? You want me to hit the bricks? Well, it's gonna cost you."

"It's five stacks in that envelope. You better take it."

"I want another ten grand."

"What?"

"Bitch, did I stutter? You heard me. You can't wipe their ass with five G's these days. Ten thousand, or I tell that bitch everything."

"Where the hell am I going to get that kind of money?"

"That's not my problem. That's my price if you want me to keep these lips on lock."

This dizzy bitch had balls to blackmail me for more cake. All she was going to do was put it in her bony-ass arms anyway.

"Fuck you. I'm not giving your ass another dime."

"You sure you wanna do that?" she asked before she lit the end of the pipe and took another hit.

"I'm done putting up with you. I've given you money; I've even taken your ass to the dope man to buy crack. I'm not giving you another cent."

"That's your choice, baby girl." Katiesha grabbed her cell off a dirty pie plate and started to dial.

"Who are you calling?"

"I looked Bree up, got her digits right here in my phone."

"Put the phone down, bitch."

"It's ringing."

"Hang the fucking phone up."

Katiesha smiled, exposing teeth that were as yellow as corn-bread mix. I scavenged my purse for my gun, realizing that I had left it in the glove box in my car. So I picked up one of the vodka bottles by the neck.

"Ho, I'm not going to tell you again."

"Fuck you."

Without a care in the world, I lifted the heavy bottle up and cracked Katiesha over the head with the blunt end. I thought it would break like they do in the movies, but no. Katiesha dropped the phone and held her right hand up against the right corner of her head. Blood poured from the gaping wound, down her face, dripping from her chin, staining her cutoffs.

"Bitch, you done lost your—"

I hit her again before she could say another word. This time it was across her face. I heard her jaw break. Katiesha spurted blood from her mouth.

"Why the fuck couldn't you just take the money?"

I stood over her and kept hitting until her head was a mash of blood, bone, and flesh. Katiesha wasn't moving. She was dead. The vodka bottle made a thud when I dropped it to the floor. There was blood all over the sofa, floor, and coffee table, as well as on me. Her phone was covered in blood at the foot of the sofa.

"Fuck! Fuck!" I shouted as I smashed her phone under my platform heel. "You should have taken the fucking money!"

I looked in the large mirror that hung on the wall behind Katiesha. Blood spattered my face and hair. I rushed to the bathroom and wiped my face with a towel that hung from a towel rack next to the sink. I stared at myself in the mirror in a daze of shock and disbelief. I frantically started to clean the sink and floor with the towel. I took my trench coat and the blood-stained towel, and stuffed them in the small trash can next to the toilet. I took the bag and dropped the vodka bottle in with my coat and the towel. I wiped whatever I had touched, which wasn't much in that filthy place, and hauled my ass out of there.

32

BREE

Katiesha's maroon Cutlass was sitting in the driveway when I pulled up alongside the curb in front of her crib. I noticed the light in the living room was on, so I knew her ass was home. The rain kept stopping and starting up again, going from a drizzle to a downpour. Why I wore platform heels in this nasty weather, I will never know. With all this rain and water, it was a wonder I hadn't fallen and busted my ass yet. I grabbed my purse and walked up to the door. I rang the doorbell, but she didn't answer. I rang it again and still nothing, so I knocked a couple of times. I tried to see in through the big front window, but I couldn't see shit 'cause of the ugly, booger-green curtains she had over the window. I thought about leaving. It was late and I was dog-tired, not to mention my feet were killing me from my red suede pumps that were officially ruined from all the rain and mud. I was about to leave until I saw a trail of something rolling from under the slit of the door.

"What the hell is this?" I stooped down and ran two fingers over the liquid. "Shit."

When I turned the doorknob and pushed the door open, a body was lying slumped on the sofa. The trail of blood was coming from the rug that was soaked with it. I rushed to Katiesha to see if she was still alive. I could barely recognize her. Her face and head looked like it had been bashed in.

"Freeze!" I heard a voice holler.

I turned around to face the cop that was standing in front of me with his burner aimed.

"Put your hands up!"

It was the baldheaded Cuban cop that had cuffed Deanthony that night at my house. Lewis, I think his name was. I learned early in life that if cops told you to freeze, you froze. I knew too many dumb brothers who tried to stand the cops down, only to end up being toe-tagged.

"Get down on your knees and cross your legs."

"I didn't do this!" Fear rushed over my face; tears started to wail up in my eyes. Lewis stood behind me and cuffed my hands behind my back. The steel felt cold around my wrists.

"This is Officer Lewis. We have what looks like a 187 at 1312 Pepper Drive. Suspect is in custody."

"Listen to me. I came in and found her like that."

"Ma'am, you have the right to remain silent. Anything you say can and will be used against you in a court of law. You have the right to an attorney. If you cannot afford an attorney, one will be appointed for you. Do you understand these rights I have just read to you?"

"I didn't do it. I didn't kill her."

Lewis walked me outside to his patrol car. Red and blue lights lit up the muggy, wet night. A crowd of people was starting to gather. Kids and grown folks alike.

"Call my husband."

"Ma'am, you will get to call someone down at the station," Lewis said as he stuffed me in the backseat of his car.

As people looked through the fingerprint-smudged glass at me like I was a blood-thirsty fugitive that was on the loose, the tears came and kept coming. I couldn't stop them and just let them come.

33

TANGELA

I guess that bitch Katiesha is going to start appearing in my dreams now. She wasn't the first person I ever bodied. That title belongs to Dante Sullivan and he isn't the one to let me live it down the way he fucked with me in my nightmares every night. The dream is always the same. I'm standing in my kitchen on a beautiful Saturday morning, making myself a bagel and a caramel macchiato. I turn around and there he is, Dante, standing there in front of me with these cold, dishwater-white eyes with rotting flesh and blood running out of his mouth. I start to scream, but no sound comes out. Dante was dead, but not really alive. He was like a zombie or some shit, I guess.

Before I could make a move, he plunges a knife into my stomach. I look down, shocked by this knife sticking out of me. Blood starts to stain my powder puff-pink robe as the metallic taste of the crimson-red liquid fills my throat. And all I can do is cough it up as Dante screws the knife in deeper. I wake up in a cold sweat, screaming and disoriented, realizing that I'm safe, if not sound in my bed. I feel my stomach to find that there's no stab wound, no blood stain on my robe.

I scream my head off, but no sound comes out. Sometimes I even think I can smell his cologne in the house. Cool Water, the same fragrance he wore the night I sent his lying-ass to hell for breaking my heart.

The first time I saw Dante was at Grown Folks Night at the Moon. My all-time favorite R&B group, New Edition, was in Tallahassee. Sexy-ass Ralph Tresvant, Ricky Bell, Johnny Gill, Michael Bivins, Ronnie DeVoe, and Bobby Brown, didn't miss a beat, tearing it up from the floor up that night. I didn't give a damn what anyone thought, Ralph Tresvant was the most gorgeous man alive. Ricky Bell was my next fav. I would fuck all five of them, but would marry Ralph. *Mrs. Tangela Tresvant* has a nice ring to it. New Edition sang all their greatest hits: "Candy Girl," "Cool It Now," "Can You Stand the Rain," and my all-time favorite New Edition song *ever*, "Mr. Telephone Man." I'd listened to that whole album about a trillion times. I wanted to marry Ralph Tresvant and have, like, twenty babies with that beautiful man.

Dante looked a little like Ralph, I remember. I was sitting at the end of the bar, nursing on a whiskey sour, when I noticed him staring at me at the end of the bar. He was fine as hell, looking like something out of *GQ* or *Esquire*. I smiled at him, giving him permission to come down and say hello.

"Is this seat taken?" he asked.

Hell no, I thought. "Not at all. I was saving it for you," I said boldly.

Dante had this deep, smoky voice that made my toes curl and pussy quiver. He saddled up next to me, the smell of his cologne infiltrating my senses.

"Hi, I'm Dante."

"Tangela."

He took my hand into his palm and softly shook it.

"I was watching you in front of the stage earlier. You've got some nice moves," Dante said.

"Thank you. I love New Edition. I have all of their albums, including all of their best-of stuff. When I heard on the radio that they were going to be doing a one-night show here in Tallahassee, I bought my ticket the same day."

"Now see, already we have something in common. You're a bigger fan than I am."

"It's always nice to meet a fellow fan. That's that good old school R&B and not that mess they got playing on the radio nowadays."

Dante had chestnut-brown skin, a short, low-cut haircut, and dark chocolate-brown eyes, with a smile to die for, like my future husband Ralph Tresvant

"So, Dante, what do you do?"

"I'm an attorney at Foote, Williams, & Sullivan. I'm the Sullivan in there."

"Oh, hold up. I think I've seen y'all's commercials on TV."

"That's us."

"Wow, you look even better in person. Television doesn't do you justice." When it came down to men, I was always laying the compliments on thick.

"I'm glad someone thinks so. I hate doing those things, but we all agreed that it would be a good idea for drumming up new clients, let people know that we're out there."

"I feel you. Nothing wrong with that."

"So what about you? What do you do?"

"I'm a stylist at Radiance Salon."

"How long have you been a stylist?"

"Let me see, going on about eight years now."

"And you like what you do?"

"I do. It pays the bills and some of the clients can be a pain, but it can be fun, too, like when we have Grandmother Appreciation Day. Women bring in their mothers and grandmothers to get their hair done, and when we get women in from the shelter to get done up for job interviews. I like when we do a lot of work for the homeless shelters and charities, so those are the times when the job is great, when I can give back to the community."

I realized that I was running my mouth, giving too much information to this fine-ass man I had just met all of five minutes ago. "I'm sorry. Am I talking too much?"

"Not at all. I'm fascinated. I think it's great what you're doing. We're trying to do some pro-bono at our firm. There are a lot of people out there who can't afford a lawyer who are in real trouble, so one of the things we want to do is offer up representation for those disenfranchised who can't afford the high cost of an attorney."

"Well, now that I know a lawyer, I know exactly who to call if I ever find myself in a mess. I definitely want you on my side, for sure."

Dante grinned. "Everyone talks about how they hate lawyers. What's that running joke? What do you call a bunch of lawyers at the bottom of the ocean? A good start, but when they get into a bind, who do they call?"

"A lawyer," I said, finishing Dante's sentence.

"Exactly. It's all a joke until someone gets arrested and accused for murder."

"I could not agree more. All of a sudden, an attorney is your best friend when you could be facing life in prison or a needle in your arm."

I realized that the conversation had taken a turn for the morbid and quickly veered into something more lighthearted, like discussing Dante's dick size.

The bartender noticed that my glass was empty and walked over to where we were sitting. "Can I get you another whiskey sour?"

"Yes, please, thank you."

I hoped Dante didn't think I was one of these drunken messes that were stumbling around the club for a man. There is nothing less classy than seeing a sister bent over the shitter, puking her pretty little guts out, only having to be carried over the shoulders of a couple of bouncers, or worse, by some man who had slipped some of that Georgia Homeboy in their drink. That's why I kept my shit classy at all times. You never know when a fine man like Dante is going to come along. Judging from the pecs tight under his shirt, he's no stranger to the gym. Thanks to the way Ralph was gyrating on stage, my pussy was sopping wet and hungry for some sweet dick.

Dante and I talked until they hollered last call.

"I hoped I haven't kept you out too late," he said.

"Not at all. I'm actually off tomorrow, so I don't have anything planned. Would you like to come back to my place for a nightcap?"

A nightcap? Really, Tangela? Who the hell talks like that?

"Sounds good. Lead the way."

Dante followed me back to my house where we continued to get acquainted over glasses of brandy. I was anxious to throw my pussy to Dante's meat.

"How about a tour of the place?"

"Lead the way."

"This is the living room. In there is the kitchen where I throw down."

"You like to cook?"

"Oh, baby, I don't *like* to cook. I love to cook. And up here… is the bedroom."

As Dante followed me upstairs, I could feel his eyes on my ass like hot beams. When we reached my bedroom, we didn't waste any time. I started to undo the buttons on my blouse. Dante took me into his muscled arms, placing one hand lovingly around my waist and the other firmly on my booty before he pressed those juicy, sexy-ass lips of his against mine. He plunged his tongue in as I ran my hand along the bulge that tented his jeans. Dante smeared me onto the bed, his kisses wet and deep. He tugged his jeans down around his bubble-booty. I was surprised to find that

Dante didn't have on a stitch of underwear. Here was this man of sophistication, walking around free-balling.

Y'all freak-nasty asses never cease to amaze me, I thought.

"Wait," I said. I reached into one of the drawers of the bedside table and took out a condom. I wasn't about to catch an STD or a baby. I didn't care how good you looked. I didn't play that shit. "Protection always, boo."

Dante took the rubber and tore open the gold cellophane with his milk-white teeth. Like me, he was good and ready to fuck. Dante unrolled the rubber over the fat crown, down the shaft of his dick. I whimpered when I felt him slide it inside me.

Damn, that feels good.

I wrapped my legs tight around the back of Dante's thighs, kneading his shoulders as he fucked me hard and hot. I held him in my arms as we both came to what could have been labeled as an earth-shattering climax.

Dante began to get dressed, slipping his arms back into the sleeves of his shirt.

"You want to stay the night? I could make us breakfast. I make some mean apple cinnamon pancakes."

His ass was bare to me as he pulled jeans up over his apple butter-brown mounds.

"I wish I could, but I have an early morning meeting. I would like to see you again."

I knelt behind him on my knees on the bed and started to massage Dante's shoulders. "I think that can be arranged."

Dante took out one of his business cards and handed it to me. "Give me a call. We'll have lunch."

"I'm going to hold you to that."

We kissed each other good night. Dante's lips felt like warm marshmallows.

"Are you sure you can't stay?"

"I would love nothing more than to wake up with you next to me, but there are some things I need to take care of before this meeting at the office tomorrow. How about a rain check?"

Dante pulled his car keys out of the front pocket of his jeans and gave me a last kiss good night.

A week had passed and I hadn't heard so much as boo from Dante. I didn't want to think that he had only used me for sex, that I was some notch on his proverbial bedpost. I called the number he gave me, only to be sent to voicemail after three rings. He sounded as sexy on his machine as he did in person. I usually made it a rule to never call a man, but let him call me. I didn't want to give these fools the impression that I was some dick-thirsty bitch. After the fourth call that week, I decided that I wasn't going to bug him.

"If he wants to talk to me, he will call me. Ma Bell runs both ways."

I kept myself occupied with work and doing some things around the house I kept putting off because I was lazy, like organizing the kitchen pantry and color-coordinating my wardrobe. But no matter how much I busied myself with work, it wasn't enough to take my mind off of Dante Fine-As-All-Hell Sullivan. So instead of blowing his phone up, I thought it better to go to his office and surprise him with a picnic lunch. It was a beautiful Thursday afternoon for it with the rain finally letting up after days of a heavy downpour. I packed the basket with one hell of a spread: fried chicken, spiral ham slices, potato salad, buttered rolls, cold slaw, crinkled season fries, and Hershey's Chocolate Cheesecake for dessert. I couldn't wait to see the look on Dante's gorgeous face when he saw all the food. It's like my mama always told me: the way to a man's heart is through his stomach.

When I entered the eight-story, red-brick building, I was mesmerized by its beauty. The marble flooring, the solid oak tables, and plush lobby chairs. I made my way up to the receptionist desk, armed with enough food to feed a small village. This brown-skinned chick who looked to be in her early twenties was sitting behind the black-and-white marble desk. Her hair was long and straight down her back. She had split ends and it was obvious to me that she was frying it with a flat-iron. I could see the bumps on her forehead behind caked-on makeup. She gawked at me with a kind of grimace expression on her flawed face, looking at me like I'd just crawled from under a rock.

"Can I help you?"

It's "may I help you," dumb bitch. Read a book, why don't you?

Her gold-plated name tag read *Lakrecia Courland* in black emblazoned letters.

Shit, with all those blackheads on her forehead, she warranted being called *Lacreature*.

"Good afternoon, Lakrecia. How are you? My name is Tangela Michaels." I gave her a false last name. "I'm here to see Mr. Sullivan."

"Do you have an appointment?"

"I don't. He did some pro-bono work for me, and I thought I would come by and surprise him with lunch."

This bitch twisted her top lip up slightly. Not even five minutes in the building and she was already starting to piss me off. I wanted to jump behind that desk and rip out the rest of her damn split ends. The picnic basket was heavy and was starting to put a strain on my arms with all the food inside, so I plopped it on the end of the receptionist desk. The ripe odor of eggs from the potato salad began to waft through the lobby. Just as she was about to call Dante, he entered the lobby with a woman who had pound cake-yellow skin, a head of thick curls, and brown eyes. Lakrecia gave me this sinister look like I was in for it.

"Here's Mr. and *Mrs.* Sullivan now," Petri Dish Face emphasized.

A cold, stoic expression formed on Dante's mug when he saw me standing at the receptionist desk. I had to quickly pull an excuse out of my ass to get out of there.

"Sorry. I think I have the wrong building." I grabbed the picnic basket of food and hauled ass before they could make their way to where I was standing. I was beyond pissed.

Once I put some distance between me and Dante's law office, I noticed a homeless bum sitting on the corner with a piece of white cardboard that read, *Homeless vet, please help.* He looked like he hadn't seen a decent meal or soup and water for days.

I set the basket of food next to him and said, "You look like you could use this. There's some fried chicken in there, some potato salad, some pie; help yourself."

When I got to my SUV, I locked myself inside and could do nothing but scream as loud as any angry black woman could, banging balled-up fists against the steering wheel. I wanted to hit Dante, rip his guts out with my newly manicured bare hands, but he wasn't there, so I had to take my anger out on something. I screamed until I felt myself going hoarse. I slapped myself until the left side of my face started to go numb. I had allowed this man to make a fool out of me, to use me like I was some cheap piece of Frenchtown ass.

"You're just like all the rest of these niggas out here. It's that kind of shit that makes us want to date white men." I was not *the* woman, but the *other* woman. I swore that I would never be any man's mistress. My eyes were hot with betrayal but cold with revenge.

Dante had phoned me several times the next day, but I refused to answer my phone.

"Now your ass knows how it feels."

He would leave messages, expressing his *deepest* apologies, but I wasn't trying to hear nothing this deceiver had to say.

In one message, he said, *"I want to see you. Call me back at this private number. Let's have dinner."*

Even though I missed him and his deep-dick long strokes, anger had gotten the best of me. "No one makes a fool out of me, goddamn it."

I thought about Dante's last message, and a plan started to brew in my head. I had decided to give Dante a call three days after I saw him at his office with his wife. The phone rang twice before he answered.

"Hello?"

"Come over to my place."

"Tangela, is that you?"

"I want to see you, baby. All is forgiven. Come over here and fuck me."

I didn't say another word and ended the call. I changed into some sexy lingerie, something to get his dick hard, and poured us two glasses of red wine. I took a sip before setting both glasses on the coffee table. Twenty minutes after I had gotten off the phone with Dante, my doorbell rang. I checked my hair and tits in the mirror that hung above my scarlet-red leather sofa.

"Right. On. Time." When I answered, Dante was breathing heavy like he had run to my house. "Good evening."

"Hey," Dante said, his eyes scanning over my bountiful breasts pushed into a black, lace brassiere. "I'm glad you called."

"Come on in."

Dante couldn't keep his hungry eyes off my titties. I led him into the dimly lit living room. We made ourselves comfortable. I handed him his glass of wine.

"I want to explain about—"

"Shhh." I pressed my index finger against his lips. "Let's make a toast. To forgiveness."

We clinked our glasses together. I watched Dante as he drank.

"I'm truly sorry about—"

Dante started to shake profusely.

"Oh, this would be you having a seizure."

Spit began to run from his mouth, trickling down his chin. Dante gawked at me with the realization that he had been poisoned.

I grabbed him hard at the chin. "Did you really think that I was going to let you make a fool out of me, that I was going to let you what…hit this and simply go back to your diamonds and pearls lifestyle with the wife? If your lawyer brain thought for a second that I would just become another notch on your bedpost, you were sadly mistaken."

Dante grabbed at his chest like he wanted to reach in and rip his heart out.

"Now this right here would be you going into cardiac arrest." I looked into his brown eyes, glazed over with tears as the cyanide worked its magic. "You see, Dante, I'm not one of these club hoochies whose legs you think are easy to spread like peanut butter. You should know that this is all your fault. Had you been straightforward with me from jump, you wouldn't be sitting here on my sofa, dying right now." I watched the last speck of life leave his body as the poison did Dante in. His body fell still, lifeless finally. I pried his lids open to see if he was gone. "Yep, dead as a door nail."

I went to my bedroom and got dressed, cloaking myself in a pair of Fendi shades and a black Michael Kors trench. I plucked a pair of black Chanel gloves out of one of the dresser drawers and slid them over my hands. "Might as well commit murder in style."

I had to move Dante's Beamer out of the driveway and under my garage. He parked next to my Escalade. I searched his body for his car keys, which were in one of the front pockets of his khakis. My neighbors Charmaine and her husband, Jamaal, were in Cancun for the weekend and weren't due back until Tuesday, so I didn't have to worry about them seeing anything. I let the door of the garage up and parked Dante's vanilla-scented car in the garage. With all the junk I had stored under it, I was surprised there was room. I quickly let down the garage door, grabbed two large trash bags, some rope, and sprinted upstairs to the living room where I'd left Dante's dead body.

"Good thing I didn't go with my initial idea to stab your ass. All that blood would have ruined my rug."

I shook one of the garbage bags open and eased it over Dante's head. I crossed his arms over his chest. I took another bag and worked it over his legs, up to his waist. I then took some rope and tied his legs first and then the upper part of his body.

"That oughta do it, nice and tight."

I pulled the coffee table back to avoid any accidents while trying to get Dante's body to the garage. I dragged him by his legs off the sofa. His head made a loud thud when it hit the floor. The heels of my black Jimmy Choos clattered as I pulled Dante across the living room. I was pouring with sweat when I got to the garage. It took all the strength I had to work the heavier part of Dante into the trunk of his car first.

"Damn, you heavy."

Surprisingly, he slid in easily, but his long legs were another matter. The bottom half of him hung out across the trunk. I pushed and stuffed as hard as I could, but with the strong elastic of the plastic, his beanstalks were not budging.

"Okay, Tangela, think, bitch, think." I looked around the garage to see what I could find. "Damn, it's hot out here."

I noticed a sledgehammer that was sitting in one of the corners. I figured the plumber from last week must have left it behind.

"Perfect."

I dragged the heavy instrument across the garage floor. I lifted it over my head and brought the steel end of the hammer down on Dante's knees as hard as my little muscles would allow. I heard one of his kneecaps snap like a tree limb to the blow. I lifted the sledgehammer again and, with a second mighty wallop, came down on Dante's other leg. I stuffed his broken limbs in with the rest of him and shut the trunk.

I headed back to the main part of the house where I made sure there wasn't a thing out of place as I wiped away any prints. I took Dante's glass of wine and poured it down the kitchen sink before I scrubbed it with bleach. As much as I didn't want to get rid of my gloves, I threw them in the fireplace and burned them.

"It's just material things."

I sipped the rest of my wine when I heard a cell phone ring. It wasn't mine, but Dante's. I searched everywhere until I found it hunched down in one of the sofa cushions. I studied the flat-screen on his iPhone. *Tarisha*, it read.

"It's probably your wife wondering where your cheatin' ass is at." I tossed the phone in the fire with my gloves and watched it burn. "I want nothing less than respect."

34

KASHAWN

When I got the news that Bree had been arrested, I jumped up out of bed and got dressed. Ma and Yvonne were sitting in the kitchen, running their mouths about Bree, I was sure.

"Kashawn, what's the matter?"

I was about out of breath, sprinting down the stairs. "It's Bree. She's been arrested."

"For what?" Ma and Yvonne asked simultaneously.

"Murder."

"Oh, Lord. I'm going with you. Let me get my purse."

"Me, too," said Yvonne.

"It's late. You all don't need to—"

"I'm going. End of discussion," Ma said.

I grabbed the car keys off of one of the end tables in the living room and drove as fast as the Escalade could take me.

On my way to the police station, I kept racking my brain, wondering what Bree had gotten herself into. My heart was still beating triple time from her telling me that she had been arrested for killing somebody. I knew, without a doubt, that there must have been some mistake. I wanted to say that Bree didn't have a killing bone in her body, but honestly, I didn't really know what Bree was capable of doing. When Ma and I got to the police station, all I wanted to do was see Bree, to know that she was all right.

Ma, Yvonne, and I waited patiently in the lobby of the Tallahassee

Police Department. I sat rocking on my elbows on my thighs, staring quietly down at my black Dearform slippers that Ma got me as a Christmas gift last year.

"I've always thought you could do better, cousin."

"Yvonne, seriously, not now."

"You see what she does? She's nothing but trouble."

"Don't start. I'm nowhere near in the mood for a lecture right now."

"The day I laid my eyes on Bree, I knew she wasn't any good," Ma said.

I let loose a long sigh like it was a fart I had been forced to hold in. "Ma."

"If it isn't one thing, it's another with her, bringing all these shysty people into your lives. She used Deanthony and she's using you, baby."

"Ma, can you do me a favor?"

"Anything, son, what is it?"

"Will you please shut up?"

Ma gawked at me with her hair done up in jumbo, pink rollers, like I had asked her a dirty question. "What did you say to me?"

"I love you, but I need you to…sit here right now and be quiet."

"That's not what you said to me. What did you say to me?"

The fat, blond cop stared at us annoyed.

"Why do you have to make everything about you? Not everything is about you."

"You can be real coldhearted sometimes, you know that?"

"Says the woman who's lied to me for thirty years of my life."

"What are you talking about, Kashawn?"

"It's so convenient for you, isn't it?"

"What did I do this time?"

"You throw stuff like this out there and then when someone calls you on things, you back off like you're so innocent, like you didn't do anything."

"Fine. I'll hush my mouth then."

"Why didn't you ever tell me that Edrick wasn't my real daddy?"

"Is that why you're acting like a fool up in this place?"

"Thirty. Thirty years, Ma, you had me believing that this man I loved and looked up to was my father and you never opened your mouth."

"Edrick was the only father you needed to know."

"Oh, so that's my fault?"

"You need to hush about this."

"No. I want to know the truth. Who is our real father?"

Ma paused, like she was searching for something to say. "Yvonne, baby, can you go get me a soda? I'm thirsty." Ma reached inside her purse and pulled out a few dollars and handed it to Yvonne. "Get whatever you want."

"The reason why I didn't tell you boys who your real father is, is because for thirty years, I've tried to put it all behind me, hoping, praying that, as your mother, this day would never come."

"What are you talking about?"

"When I was nineteen…" Ma got up and started pacing the lobby of the police station. "When I was nineteen, I was raped."

"What?"

"It was by one of my mama's boyfriend's. Willie Patterson was his name, some stray she pulled out of some juke joint. Mama always left me home alone with Willie when she went off to work. He was a drunk and quickly took a shine to me. I was washing and putting up clothes when he came into my room. That night, I was surprised that the man could barely stand. He stormed in, calling me a tease, telling me that I was nothing but a tramp. I told him that he was a drunkard, that he should go sleep off the gin. That's when he slapped me, telling me that he hated women who sassed him, saying that…I needed to be taught a lesson, so he threw me on the bed and undid his pants.

"Stop," I said. I couldn't hear anymore. "What did Grandma do?"

"When I told her that Willie raped me, she didn't believe me, accusing me of coming in between her and him, saying that, 'He wouldn't do that. He's a good man.' She told me to never talk about it again, so I didn't."

"Until you found out you were…"

"Until I found out that I was pregnant with you boys, yes. When I told Mama, she called me a tramp and kicked me out of the house and tossed every strip of clothing I had out onto the street. I'll never forget what she said: 'A trash bag for trash.'"

"My God, Ma."

"Luckily, I had some money saved up and stayed at a motel for a week until your Aunt Gertie took me in and fed me. That Dutch apple cheesecake that's your favorite?"

"Yes."

"Ms. Gertie, bless the dead, taught me how to make it."

"Did you ever go to my real father and tell him you were pregnant?"

"No. He has no clue that he has children in this world, and, as far as I'm concerned, I don't want that rapist bastard to know about my boys."

"I never asked you this, but how did you meet Daddy, the man who adopted me and Deanthony?"

"I was walking out of the grocery store when I almost tripped over something. It was your father's wallet. I called him and told him that I found it. He came to Ms. Gertie's to pick it up. Your father was so handsome, Kashawn. He was a proud man, like his brother. I cut him a piece of apple cheesecake that day, and he told me that a woman who makes cheesecake this good, has to be his wife, and the rest was history."

"How did Daddy react when you told him you were pregnant?"

"I didn't go into details about what happened to me. Edrick said it didn't matter, and that he wanted to raise you boys as his own. I knew then that your father was nothing but God-sent."

I wrapped my arms warmly around Ma. "I'm sorry."

"For what, baby?"

"For everything."

"I tried to find the right time to tell you about him, but I discovered there's no such thing."

Yvonne returned with two cold cans of grape soda.

"Look, I know y'all are upset about what Bree has done, but she has really gotten me through a lot of crazy...excuse my language, and the past few weeks have been hard for both of us."

"I know, baby."

"What I'm saying is, I don't care what Bree did in the past. We all got a past, and sometimes it's nothing pretty. Not us, you, or anybody has a right to judge her. Especially me."

"What do you mean?" Yvonne asked.

I took a deep sigh as I leaned back into my chair. "I cheated on Bree with Tangela."

"Oh, Lord. Kashawn," Ma said with an air of disappointment in her tone.

"I'm no angel and I haven't been the perfect husband. I want to change that. I want to be the husband that Bree married by first telling her the truth. I love her and nothing and nobody is going to change that. I don't care what she's done. There are people out here who have done worse things than she could ever do. I'm tired of everyone pointing fingers like she assassinated somebody. I haven't done right by her and that stops now. I'm going to be the husband she needs me to be, Ma. If I didn't love Bree, I wouldn't be here."

Ma began to caress the side of my face with her hand. "Have I told you how proud I am of you?"

I let loose a grin. "Yes…but I never get tired of hearing it." I rested my hand softly on top of Mama's.

"I'm sorry, baby, and you're right. There needs to be a change, because at the end of the day, family is all you have, and Bree needs that more than ever right now if she's going to get through this."

As we waited, Deanthony blew in through the double glass doors of the police station. Needless to say, the man who slept with my wife was the last man I wanted to see.

"What are you doing here?"

"Don't be mad, baby. I called him," Ma said.

"He doesn't need to be here. I don't need him here."

"He's your brother, Kashawn. Your twin brother."

"Is it true?" Deanthony asked. "She got arrested for killing some-body?"

"We're trying to find out what's going on," Ma said.

"Speaking of which." I walked back up to the front desk to find out what was taking them so long. "Excuse me." The blond, porky-faced cop looked up at me annoyingly from a stack of papers she had sprawled out in front of her. "Can you tell me what's going on with my wife? Her name is Bree Parker. She was brought in like an hour ago."

Katherine McGhee, her silver-plated name tag read. "They may not have processed her yet. Let me find out."

"Thank you."

Katherine picked up the phone and pressed a number. I waited anxiously to get word on Bree. I could barely hear what she was saying due to the plate glass that separated us. "No, they haven't processed her yet. She's in holding."

"Can we see her?"

"She's only allowed one visitor at a time."

I walked back over to Ma and Deanthony to tell them what was up. "They've already processed her. They said she's only allowed one visitor."

"Go on in, baby. Give Bree our love."

I sauntered back up to the help desk and gave Katherine, the pie-faced cop, my name. She tapped on the keyboard with her plump fingers. The light from the flat-screen Dell reflected in the lenses of her wire-frame glasses. She slid a laminated visitor pass under the dip cut in the plate glass and buzzed me in. I pinned the name tag on the breast pocket of my pajama shirt before I walked through the heavy, steel door. I walked down a cold corridor where the walls were lined with photos of cops past, men and women smiling big in their uniforms, followed by plaques of those in recognition for their lengthy years of loyal service upholding the law. To the right of me was a long desk where three male cops sat. They gave me a sinister glare as if they were ready to tear into my black ass if I made any sudden moves. One of the men, a brother, who had to be like seven feet tall, chest like a bird, arms like sledgehammers, told me that I had to be searched for weapons. He told me to spread my legs and hold my arms out to my side. He patted me down, running his hands along the sides of my arms and thighs, careful not to graze my balls. This man looked at me like he wanted to rip my head off. I was trying to think of the last time I was patted down by a cop. Fucking never.

"What's in your front pocket?"

"Oh, they're just my car keys."

"Place them in the bowl," he said. He walked back behind the desk. "Walk down the hall, make a right, take the elevator to the fourth floor, level E." He sounded like he ate bullets like they were Fig Newtons. "You got thirty minutes."

The hall smelled sickly of bleach. I took the elevator to level E and sat in front of more plate glass. I looked about, but all I could see were jail cells and female cellmates prancing around in orange jumpsuits and white, plastic sandals. I saw Bree before she saw me. I knocked on the glass to get her attention. She ran toward me, crying when she made me out. We pressed our hands up to the glass as we picked up the phones and placed them up to our ears.

"Baby, are you all right? How are you doing?"

"I've never been so glad to see you, Kashawn."

"Baby, what happened?"

"I just wanted to talk to her, that's all."

"Talk to who, Bree?"

"Katiesha. I swear I found her like that. I didn't kill her."

I exhaled breath that I had been holding in ever since Bree called me.

Bree looked awful, like she had been up all night.

"What happened?"

"I went to Risqué to look for Katiesha. She wasn't there, so I went to her crib. I knocked on the door and there was no answer. I saw blood coming from under the door, so I went in and there she was, dead on the chair. My hand to God, baby, that's what happened."

"Okay, I'm going to get you out of here."

"Kashawn, you believe me, don't you?"

I searched Bree's eyes and knew right then that she was telling the truth.

35

TANGELA

As soon as I strolled into Top Flight, all eyes were on me, men zeroing in on my ass like they were heat-seeking missiles. I wasn't doing cute. I was doing drop-dead gorgeous with my leopard-print skirt, black blouse, and candy apple-red, fuck-me pumps. A girl can work up a sexual appetite when plotting to steal her best friend's man. I was in need of some serious unwinding. I thought to go home and soak in a warm bubble bath with a nice glass of red wine by my side, but I was in the mood to mingle. I was tired of being around chatty chicks at the salon all day, running my fingers through somebody's nasty hair. I loved my boss, but, damn, sometimes she got on my last nerve. If she wasn't complaining about one thing, she was nagging me about another. By the time six o'clock came, I was good and ready to take my ass home. I had Leandra in my ear, and Bree, who had been blowing up my phone. I was supposed to hook up with her at Risqué, but that only would have gone against my plan to fuck her life up. I was in no mood for the latest in Bree drama. I needed some me time every now and then. I was sick of being her damn shoulder to cry on.

I thought about going to Grown Folk's Night at The Moon, but decided I wanted to flip the script a little bit. I was over the same old, same old. The trolls in pastel pimp suits and snakeskin dress shoes, pushing and rubbing up against me, trying to holla, blowing their boozy, pungent breath in my face. Young dick was what this pussy needed.

I saddled up to the end of the bar where I could still feel ravenous eyes ripping off my clothes. This shirtless, dark-chocolate brother wandered over to where I was sitting. He looked like he had a smidgen of East Indian in him.

"How are you tonight?" he asked.

I felt myself starting to droll to his muscular arms in the white tank top, oiled skin glistening under the club's red and blue strobe lights. He set a small white napkin in front of me.

"What can I get you to drink?" He had to be about six-three, looking like he should be playing professional ball instead of slinging drinks in a bar. He had pretty, pearl-white teeth as he flirted. He looked to be in his early twenties. Twenty-two, twenty-three, maybe.

"I'll have a watermelon martini."

"Wow, I haven't made one of those in a while."

I smiled. "Do you know how to make it?"

"I think I can manage." He smiled.

"I trust you."

I watched him mix the drink, adding the right amount of alcohol and watermelon schnapps, finishing it off with a cherry as a sweet afterthought. He set the martini in front of me.

"Tell me what you think."

Oh, trust, I will.

I took a sip. "This is actually one of the better watermelon martinis I've had."

"I aim to please." The fine bartender smiled. "I have all night to make it better for you." If flirting was an art form, this man was a regular Basquiat. "My name's Amir." He extended his hand to greet mine.

"Tangela." My hand intertwined with his. His palm felt warm and damp from slinging drinks.

"That's a pretty name," Amir said.

"Yeah, my mama told me that any name that begins with a vowel, you can stick any letter in the front of it and it will make sense, so she said she always liked the name Angela, but my aunt took the name for her daughter, so Ma went a step further, stuck a 'T' in front of it, hence the name Tangela."

"Well, it's definitely a name you will never find on a key chain."

I started laughing. "This is true." Little did Amir know he was already scoring major points with me. Ten for making me laugh and ten more for looking like sex on a platter.

"You have a pretty smile."

"Now see, you keep that up, and you will be surprised where flattery will get you."

Amir wiped the bar with a white hand towel. His smile alone was already making my lavender Victoria's Secret panties wet. I took a sip from my watermelon martini to cool myself down.

"Amir, that's an interesting name. Where are you from?"

"Originally from Hollywood, Florida, but my father is Pakistani and my mother is black. They moved to Florida when I was five. I moved up here to study law at Florida A & M University."

Just as I was losing myself in Amir's cinnamon-brown eyes, three loud-ass hoochies strolled up at the other end of the bar.

"Hello, bartender," one of them yelled.

"Barkeep," hollered another, the three of them laughing like three ugly hyenas.

"We are in need of some libations down here."

They were three of the most trifling skanks I had ever laid my eyes on. Humph, ladies was the last thing that came to mind looking at these hood rats.

"What Dumpster did they slither out of?"

One of them had weave that had all the colors of the rainbow.

All three of them wore skin-tight pencil dresses. There was only one store in Tallahassee that sold those hooker ensembles they were dressed in: Diamondaire's over on South Adams Street where Church's Chicken used to be. Street walker couture, I call it.

"I'll be back. Let me go take care of these ladies," Amir said.

"Hurry back," I said before taking a sip of my fruity martini.

I felt like poor Amir was about to wander into a den of man-hungry lionesses. One of the hoochies was plump, wearing a short blond wig and bronze lipstick. Who the hell wears bronze lipstick? Obviously this heifer. Who in the world told her she was cute? The other one reminded me of Halle Berry from that movie *B.A.P.S* with this synthetic monstrosity on her head. She was wearing white lipstick, looking like she had just bit into a powdered dough-nut. Of course, they were the loudest bitches in the club. Once the DJ put on Nicky da B, you couldn't hold them back from hitting the dance floor. They were out there, shaking their asses so hard, I thought something was going to drop out. They thought they looked cute, but came off looking like corny-ass skanks. I couldn't keep my eyes off Amir, his coffee bean-brown skin glistening under white strobe lights. I could tell he had dick for days. He noticed that I was running low and made his way back down to my end of the bar.

"You want another one?"

"Absolutely."

Amir took my empty glass and started making me another water-melon martini.

"I'm glad you came out of that unscathed."

"Who? Oh, them? It's cool. They come here just about every weekend. I'm used to them."

"Yes, but why would you ever want to get used to…that?" I studied them with pity on my face.

"You're a funny lady, Tangela."

"Are they your type?"

"Not really, no. I'm more into someone from the human species."

"Yeah, I could tell they weren't your type."

Amir finished off my watermelon with a cherry and set it in front of me. He grinned, showing those pretty white teeth. "And what type do you think I'm into? Girls are cool, but I like a woman, you feel me? A lady who has herself together. Someone like you." Damn, Amir was laying it on thick. Peanut butter, crunchy style.

I let loose a flirtatious laugh. "What makes you think I have it together?"

"I could tell how you slinked in here. You're a woman who knows what she wants and, what you don't have, you're not scared to get out here and take it. Am I right?"

I traced the rim of my martini glass with my finger. "True. True."

"Yeah, see. That's what's up. I know these things."

"Look, brother, I'm not going to lie. You're a good-looking man."

"Thank you."

"But you ought to be on the cover of magazines instead of working in this shit hole-in-the-wall."

"Well, thank you, I'm flattered."

"What exactly is your type?" I asked.

"Someone with brains."

"That's me."

"A lady who knows what she wants."

"That's me."

"And someone who likes to live a little on the wild side."

"Oh, that is most definitely me right there."

"A lady who knows who she is."

"Um, hello, here I am." I pointed at myself. "Look no further."

"You're funny. I haven't stopped laughing since you walked in here."

"That's a good sign then."

Amir stood in front of me, drying some glasses. "Of what?"

"That it's likely that I might take you home tonight and fuck your brains out."

Amir chuckled. "Damn, ma, you don't pull any punches, do you?"

"Sorry. Was that too forward?"

"It's like you said. A lady who knows what she wants."

"And that's me."

"And, yeah, my going home with you is pretty likely."

"Well, let's do this then. What time do you get off?"

"In about forty-five minutes."

"Good. Let's get out of here," I said.

"The bartender who's here to relieve me just walked in," Amir said.

My pussy was dripping to the thought of Amir between my chunky, chocolate thighs. It felt good, knowing that I didn't have to compete with Bree. Back in the day, she already would have had someone like Amir cornered, deep-throating him in the supply closet. I wouldn't have stood a chance. I didn't want to drink too much. I didn't want Amir to think that I was some drunk-ass lush before the night even started. I was ready to leave. The club was getting thick and DJ Master Blaster's techno was taking a toll on my nerves. The shit that was going on in the club was the last thing I was thinking about, being that my libido was going into four-wheel overdrive. If I didn't get some dick soon, my pussy was going to shrivel up and fall out. I'd always believed that a pussy can't survive without a steady diet of dick. I loved Kashawn, but I got tired of holding out, hoping for a booty call from his Bree-whipped ass. And I loved my vibrator, but nothing beat the real thing, and tonight, some real dick was exactly what I was going to get.

36

TANGELA

The club was thick with bodies filling every corner of the dance floor to the point where you could barely move. Amir made his way toward me through the crowd of people dancing, drinking, and smoking. He was wearing a black tank top and black jeans.

"You ready to go?" he asked.

"Lead the way."

Amir took my hand into his, leading me past the schools of people toward the exit.

"Hey, where are you going?" one of the hood rats asked, tugging at Amir's arm. They rolled their eyes, mean-mugging me when they saw that he had made his choice for tonight of who he wanted to be with. They were hating on me hard. If they had heat ray vision, they would have burned a hole clean through me.

"My wife and I have to get home. I think we left the iron on," Amir joked.

"You married?" the one with the bronze lipstick asked loudly, hooking her hand on her side.

"Happily," he said, gripping my hand.

I snickered at the element of surprise that ran across their faces like the cheap, Walmart makeup that caked their ugly mugs. As we walked hand in hand out of the club, I glanced over my left shoulder at the thirsty bitches and winked. They sucked their teeth and sneered.

All is not always fair, girls, I thought.

"So you want to follow me back to my place?" I asked.

"Girl, I would follow you anywhere. I'm parked over here in the black Mountaineer."

"This is me right here."

"I'll be right behind you."

I pushed my SUV as fast as I could back to my house, careful not to get stopped by the cops. They're always out, looking to catch drunk drivers. By the time I was done with Amir, I would have him speaking in tongues once I threw this pussy down on him. He pulled up behind me in my driveway.

"This is nice."

I tucked my clutch under my arm as we made our way to the front door. "It isn't much, but this little box of sanity is mine."

"So what kind of work do you do, if you don't mind my asking?"

Amir's question forced me to pull a lie out of my ass that would impress him. "I own my own salon over on South Monroe. Slick Cuts." I pressed a key into the gold-plated lock and opened the door.

"I know it. My sister goes there to get her hair done. That's a pretty high-end salon."

"You didn't know. It's only the best hair salon in Tallahassee."

As soon as we stepped in, Amir felt on my booty. I threw my clutch on the sofa and turned around to face him. This brother wasted no time pulling me into those massive muscle-bound arms of his, grabbing me like I was some prize he won. I wanted to be controlled tonight, taken over. We started kissing. Amir shoved his tongue into my mouth, but I didn't give a damn. I ran my hand down to his crotch where the biggest bulge tented those tight black jeans. I began fighting with his belt, pulling it loose. I had problems with the clasp. Amir undid his jeans without any effort and unzipped. The imprint of his dick stretched the tight, white cotton of his drawers. I yanked the black denim down around his firm thighs.

Fuck yeah.

"Damn, Tangela," he moaned as I traced his dick with my fingers.

A spot of sticky pre-cum soaked through the cotton. I used my tongue to lap it up. This was about to be some straight-up, freak-nasty shit. I had teased his young ass enough. I hooked my fingers over the elastic waistband of his underwear and pulled until Amir's dick popped free from its cotton cocoon as if it had been held prisoner, aching to be released. It was nine inches, maybe ten, from what I could tell. Amir's dick was circumcised with a single pencil-thick vein running along the top of the shaft. The crown of his piece was a caramel-sweet hue with a teardrop piss slit. His Brazil nut-size balls hung like earrings.

Damn, I thought.

A brother this fine, I don't know why I was surprised by his endowment. I looked up at Amir as I started licking the tip of his dick, as I roped my juicy, cherry-red lips around the fat tip. I gently started to suck him, taking inch after Mandingo inch as I slid down his battering ram. I played with his balls, caressing them with two middle fingers. I pictured Kashawn's face in the place of Amir's as I slurped on his dick. I devoured him until I had his entire dick in my mouth, the tip of it banging against my tonsils.

"You keep on, and I'm gonna nut."

I slowly pulled off his dick that was dripping wet with spit. He had another thing coming if he thought he was going to nut without satisfying my hungry pussy.

I got up off my knees. "Let's continue this in my bedroom."

With his dick hanging limp but hard over the waistband of his drawers, I led Amir up the stairs to my bedroom. You could have set your watch in the time it took for us to get out of our clothes. Amir couldn't cut his eyes away from my breasts. I probably was the finest bitch that had ever stood in front of him. We were both butt-booty naked. His dick was throbbing like it was breathing. As we made out, I could feel Amir's dick pressing hot and erect against my thighs. Amir moved down to my breasts, tongue-tickling my nipples, sucking them past his lips. I pulled this gorgeous half-black, half-Pakistani man onto the bed with me, his dick mashing against the pink lips of my pussy. Amir kept at my breasts, sucking crazy like he was trying to suck milk out of my breasts. I rolled on top of him. He moaned when I slid his dick in easy. He held onto my ass like handlebars as I rode his dick as if it was a Harley-Davidson between my robust thighs. I worked him steady, his dick stretching my sugar walls.

"Shit, girl," he moaned under his breath.

Amir felt good as hell inside me. Before I could blink, he rolled me over, switching positions. He took my legs and pinned them atop his shoulders.

"Fuck yeah, baby. Tear it up, deep-dick this pussy."

That night, Amir fucked me every which way: on my back, on my side, on my hands and knees, laying some Barnum & Bailey, acrobatic kind of fucking on me. The sound of the bed springs echoed throughout the bedroom.

"Damn, this is some good pussy."

It turns me on when men talk dirty. "Take it. This pussy's yours."

I grabbed his ass with both hands, holding onto his double-chocolate, bubble booty tight. Each time I shut my eyes, Kashawn appeared, smiling down at me as he twisted me out. Bree didn't deserve a man as good as him. It should be me. It always should have been me in that big house, sharing his bed, driving expensive cars, covered in furs, drenched in jewels from head to toenail. Amir flipped me over on my stomach, pulling my ass to his dick soaked with my juices. I thought to object when I felt the tip of his dick at my booty hole. I wasn't too experienced in getting fucked up the ass. It wasn't my favorite sexual position, but I didn't mind it so much. A hole was a hole. I fisted the pillows over the slight discomfort that lasted for a few seconds. I was good once Amir slipped his dick in my butt.

The last man who took me from the back was Tyrique. It happened a few nights before Bree and Kashawn's wedding. I never told a soul, not even Bree. Tallahassee is microscopic, and people around here can't hold water. That's why Tyrique was always throwing shade whenever he saw me, thinking that I was going to tell his wife. I didn't find out that he was Kashawn's friend until I saw him standing alongside Kashawn at the altar as the best man. And I was literally sitting behind Ebonya at the wedding. As far as I'm concerned, we both got what we wanted.

"Damn, I'm about to pop."

"Do it. I want to feel your juices inside me."

"Are you on the pill?"

What? Was this man serious?

"Yes."

He pulled my hair as he fucked me, pressing me into my king-sized mattress.

"Ahhhhhhhhhhh, shit!"

Amir let loose. I lay there and took his essence inside me. I clenched my rim, forcing every drop of nut out of that baby arm-thick dick.

"Fuck, Tangela," Amir said, collapsing next to me on his side.

Amir had gone from fine-ass bartender I wanted to fuck, to sweaty gorilla I was ready to kick to the curb. I had better things to do than lie in bed with him all night on cum-stained sheets. It was time for me to pull one of my tricks I did to get rid of one-night *quickies*. I slid naked out of bed and walked toward the door.

"Where are you going?" Amir sweetly pulled my arm, not wanting me to leave. Yeah, this brother was the clingy type. Probably got abandonment issues and I had *zero* fucking time for that.

"I need to check and see if the door is locked downstairs. I'll be back."

Amir lay flat in the middle of the bed, his arms tucked behind his head, his dick lying flaccid against his right thigh. "Hurry back. The way I feel, I can go another round."

I scurried down the carpeted steps to the living room where I dialed my own number, forcing it to ring. I held it in the air to make sure Amir heard it going off. After two minutes, I ran back upstairs where Amir was lying under the covers. The white sheets juxtaposed against his chocolate-chocolate skin.

"Is everything okay?"

"Not really. It's my girl, Bree. She's on her way over. She and her husband just had another one of their drag-out fights."

An expression of disappointment formed on Amir's chiseled face. "She's coming over now?"

I started to get dressed, slipping one leg and then the other back into my dress. Amir wouldn't budge at first. He took me by the hand and pulled me back into bed, forcing his tongue into my mouth. I went with it if it meant getting him the hell up out of my house, but then he started feeling up my titties, attempting to coax me back into round two of sex.

"Babe, I really can't. She says she's only ten minutes away." Amir gave me this puppy dog look in an attempt to soften my heart. "How about this right here: how about I cook you dinner sometime? I can make the hell out of some lasagna. It'll be nice."

Amir's frown turned upside down. "I love lasagna. It's a date. When?"

I grabbed his shirt off the floor and handed it to him. "I'll call you."

Amir took his tank top and put it on. "You don't have my number."

I searched the room until I saw a Post-It pad and pen on the nightstand. "What's your number, baby?" I wrote it down as he read it off, stepping one firm leg at a time back into his underwear and jeans. I walked Amir to the door, my marble floor cold beneath my feet.

"Call me tomorrow," he said.

"When's the best time?" I put on a front like I gave a damn.

"I don't go in until five tomorrow, so any time before that is cool."

"Sounds good." Amir leaned in to give me one last kiss. There was no tongue this time, but a light peck on the lips. "Have a good night," he said. "Be safe."

"You, too, baby. I'll give you a call tomorrow." I waved goodbye as I slowly shut the door. "Yeah, I'll call you all right. Be sure to sit your ass by the phone until I do." I laughed.

37

KASHAWN

"Good morning, baby," Ma said as she walked into the kitchen, dressed in a white-and-red-rose-printed robe, her salt-and-pepper hair done up in big pink and turquoise rollers under a nylon purple scarf.

"Good morning, Ma." I was sitting at the kitchen table, picking over a bowl of soggy Raisin Bran with my spoon.

"Coffee smells good," she said.

"I just made some fresh."

Ma got a cup from the cabinet above the microwave and poured herself a cup. "How did you sleep last night?" She pulled a chair out and sat down next to me.

"Not too good. I tossed and turned all night. If anything, I've only been able to close my eyes two to three hours at a time and when I do manage to go to sleep, I keep having this same nightmare."

"About Bree?"

"I'm standing at the end of this long, dark hall at the jail, and at the other end is Bree with her arms outstretched, reaching out to me. I start running toward her, but the faster I run, the further away from Bree I move. I run and run, never drawing closer. She's crying and hollering my name, but I can't hear her. There's no sound coming out of her mouth. Just when I think I'm getting to her, the bars of her jail cell slam closed and I wake up drenched in sweat."

"Baby, don't worry. Bree will get through this. She knows she's not alone, that she has you and that she has family."

"Thank you, Mama, but how can I not worry? I'm frustrated because I feel helpless at this point."

"Have you talked to Kent Crump? What did he say?"

"He told me that the cops found Bree's fingerprints on the door-knob of the house."

"Lord, Jesus," Ma sighed. "Did she tell you what happened?"

"She said she was going over to just talk to Katiesha about what happened here at the house that night."

"Do you believe her?"

"I know that what someone says they're going to do and what ends up happening are two different things, but, yeah, I believe her. Ma, you should have seen Bree. I took one look in her eyes and knew she wasn't lying. She was scared to death, and there isn't too much she's afraid of. I don't think she did it. I don't think she killed Katiesha. Look at the neighborhood Katiesha lived in."

"That's true. I'm always seeing on the news about someone getting shot and killed on Pepper Drive."

"That's what I know, and Kent told me that the girl was on drugs and was a stripper, so with her track record, anybody could have killed her. Maybe it was a boyfriend or some pusher she did wrong." I pushed the bowl of soggy cereal away from me. My stomach was in too many knots to eat.

Ma rested her hand on mine and said, "You just have to keep your head up and pray to the good Lord that Bree will get through this mess, baby."

"Ma, do you believe she's innocent?"

"Kashawn, it's not about what I believe."

"She didn't kill Katiesha."

"No, I don't think she did it. It sounds like she was in the wrong place at the wrong time. I know that things have been rough for you two, and I haven't made it any easier with my talking bad about her. When I get in front of her today, I want to apologize for the way I've been acting. I want to make it up to the both of you."

"Good morning, y'all." Yvonne walked in, wearing one of those one-size-fits-all T-shirts with a teddy bear on the front and purple sweats. Her round, fat face was covered in this light-green goop.

"Good morning, ba—. Girl, what in the world is that mess all over your face?"

"It's called a guacamole mask. It's supposed to clean all the dirt and bacteria out of your pores."

"On you, it's an improvement. I think you should walk around with that goop on your face for the rest of your life," I said jokingly.

"Oh, you got jokes. That's good, I like that. Let me call Steve Harvey, tell him we got the next king of comedy right here in Tallahassee."

"Y'all stop."

Yvonne rummaged through my refrigerator like it was her house. She and Ma were spending the night, being that Ma couldn't bring herself to sleep at her house without Uncle Ray-Ray. I told her that she could stay as long as she wanted. That invitation wasn't extended to Yvonne the moocher, though. A big three-bedroom house and she's scared to stay in it. If she got herself a man, she wouldn't be scared of nothing. Instead, she wanted to be all up in everyone's business because she had none of her own.

"Kashawn, you don't mind if I go with you today to the arraignment hearing, do you?"

"Of course not, baby," Ma said. "Bree needs to know that we're here for her, that we're family, and family sticks together no matter what."

Yvonne turned to me as if she needed to get an official okay from me to be in the courtroom.

"Yes, you can come."

"I know we have our differences and whatnot, but I want to squash all that and be there for you. For Bree, too."

"Thank you, Yvonne. I appreciate that."

"Is Deanthony coming?" Yvonne asked.

"I hope not," I said.

"I want y'all to stop this, Kashawn," Ma said. "He's your brother and I want you to make things right between the two of you. It breaks my heart to see the two of you at odds with one another. With the loss of Ray-Ray, I have realized that life is too short for mess."

"We wouldn't be at odds if he hadn't have slept with my wife."

"And that's the elephant in the room you two need to get from under. If it takes you two fist-fighting it out to get past this, then do what you have to do, but I'm tired of all this mess, so fix it." Ma finished the rest of her coffee and placed the cup in the kitchen sink. I got up, walked over to her and gave her a kiss on the cheek. "What's that for?"

"I love you."

"Child, tell me something I don't know." She laughed. "Now y'all, come on. We have to get dressed. Bree's going to wonder where we at if she doesn't see us in the courtroom."

I picked up the phone and dialed Deanthony's number. It rang twice before he picked up.

38

MAMA LIZ

Nineteen. That's how old I was when my mama kicked me out
of the house after finding out that I was pregnant. I don't
know how she found out, but she did. Seeing how small
Tallahassee is, anyone could have said something.

"Every time I try to have something, you get in the middle. He
never would have done anything to you if you hadn't have been
shaking your tail in front of him. I told you what would happen if
you kept acting fast." Mama flung everything I owned out in the
front yard. "So if you're grown enough to open your legs, then you
old enough to live out here on your own."

Everyone in the neighborhood was looking and staring as I
scooped my clothes off the ground out of the dirt. Mama threw a
black garbage bag at me. "Here, a trash bag for trash."

I didn't shed a tear. I wasn't going to give her the satis-damn-
faction of her seeing that she had gotten to me. I threw my garbage
bag of clothes over my shoulder and walked down the street I was
born and raised on, leaving behind everything and everybody that
I knew. I struggled to hold back tears, but the harder I tried, the
harder they came.

My plan was to tell her nothing until I moved out with a place of
my own. I was working as a maid at the time, so I used the money
from my check and got a room at the El Camino Motel that was
known as the place whores took their tricks. With the little money

I was pulling in cleaning white people's houses, it was the only thing I could afford at the time. I was pregnant, pretty much homeless, and barely hanging on. I paid up for a week until I could get something stable. I thought about going to Willie Patterson to tell him that I was pregnant, but decided that my babies were better off not knowing that they were conceived through rape. They didn't need a drunk for a daddy. I figured I wasn't the only girl he had done this to.

I told Mrs. Cozart, this white lady I was working for, that I was available to put in more hours. Her fish belly-white behind was all too eager to work me to the bone, tacking on extra work like washing all ten of her windows in her big, ugly house, to polishing her silverware and cleaning out her stove and refrigerator every other week. Mrs. Cozart paid me a dollar extra if I stayed overtime to wash and fold her and her nasty husband's dirty drawers. Mr. Cozart was a lawyer, who was always getting fresh with me. He would sneak off to the laundry room where I would wash clothes, and start hugging and kissing on me.

"Come on, now," he would say. "Give me some of that brown sugar."

Twice a week I would have to claw that white fool off me. Mrs. Cozart didn't have a clue, or maybe she did and didn't give a damn. It was too bad I couldn't get paid extra for Mr. Cozart pinching and grabbing all over me. I took every penny, nickel, and dime I earned working for them and stashed it away for my babies.

I dreamt of fish the week before I found out I was pregnant. They took my blood and told me what I had already known. I thought about getting an abortion, but when the doctor said that I was pregnant with twins, I knew it was a blessing from God.

I thought I would end up like Mama, a spinster, until I met Edrick.

A day didn't go by that I didn't think about him, especially now with his brother Ray-Ray gone. I was glad that Edrick went first because I don't think he would have been able to handle Ray-Ray dying. I wished Edrick were here. He would know exactly what to do in a time like this. I didn't think any of this mess with Kashawn would have been happening if Edrick was around. My Edrick had an answer for everything. It hasn't been easy holdin' all us together, but I did the best I could do.

The first time I met Edrick, I didn't meet him. Not in person anyway. I was coming out of IGA when I nearly tripped over a brown leather wallet that was on the ground in the parking lot. I looked inside for an I.D. I remember his wallet was fat with all these business cards stuffed inside it. It barely closed. Along with his driver's license, Edrick had about five hundred dollars in one-hundred-dollar bills. He looked like a vacuum cleaner salesman on his driver's license. I thought about taking it to the police station, but it was way on the other side of town. After working twelve hours on my hands and knees for the Cozarts, I was dead tired, so I held on to his wallet until I got back to the motel.

I was walking from work one hot June day when I saw a sign outside of this house over on Saxton Street that read, *Room for Rent.* This old, lightskinned lady, Ms. Gertie, was renting out the room. She told me that it was her son's, who was helping starving children over in Africa. When I told her that I was pregnant, her face softened. She even waived first month's rent. I moved out of that whore-infested motel as fast as my feet could take me. I told Ms. Gertie that my mama had kicked me out of the house, that I didn't have anybody but my babies. She treated me so nice, cooking and washing my clothes like I was her daughter.

"It ain't safe for a young girl like you to be out here on your own without a husband."

She had an old-fashioned way of thinking, like Mama. One thing about Ms. Gertie was that she was some kind of nosey. Getting all up in my business, asking me about my family, if I knew where my daddy was. All I remembered about him was that he left my mama when she was a few years younger than me. I was three. I remembered him being tall and real black, like he had been double-dipped in molasses. He used to pick me up and give me big kisses on my cheek. The last time I heard his name, Mama said that he was killed, shot in the chest in a juke joint over some mess about a woman. Mama was dressed all in black with a big church hat. I wiped away tears that streaked her face. I remembered after that, men were in and out of her life. They would buy me candy, take me to the playground, trying to win my attention, all of them trying to win a role at playing my daddy. Once they drained Mama dry, none of them stuck around long enough for nothing. I swore that I would never end up like her: alone and bitter as hell.

The same day I found Edrick's wallet, I looked him up in the phone book. I knew he must have been going crazy, looking for his wallet. There were about twelve E. Parker's in the phone book, so I called every single one listed. After about the eighth call, I had finally reached him.

"Hello, is this Edrick Parker?"

"Yes it is," he'd said.

I had breathed a sigh of relief. I had told him my name and that I'd found his wallet.

"Thank God. Where did you find it?"

"I was coming out of IGA yesterday and nearly tripped over it."

"I was turning my car and office upside down, looking for it. My whole life is in that wallet," Edrick went on.

"Surely not your whole life," I'd said, fingering through the thick stack of business cards.

"I was about to get on the phone and cancel everything before you called, Liz."

"Well, I know how it can be when you lose something, especially when your whole life depends on it. I was going to turn it in down at the police station, but they probably would have taken forever and a day to let you know that someone had turned it in. You can come over and get it. I live on 1412 Saxon Street."

"I can stop by tomorrow after work to get it."

"I should be here 'round four if that's good for you."

"Sounds good," he'd said. Edrick sounded older and debonair on the phone. I couldn't wait to meet him, match his voice to a body.

I had thought about Edrick all that day he was supposed to come by and pick his wallet up. Ms. Gertie was off running errands, so I had the house to myself. He'd come by a little after five, pulling into Ms. Gertie's narrow driveway in a shiny green Gran Torino. He was dressed to a T in a black suit and black wingtips. I had wondered what it was he did for a living, being so dressed up. He looked to be about in his late twenties, early thirties. Turned out, Edrick was thirty-two.

I had checked myself in one of the wicker mirrors Ms. Gertie had hanging in the living room. The whole house, even my room, was filled with wicker furniture. I had put on a little lipstick, some blush, nothing special. I'd waited for him to ring the doorbell. I'd prayed he wasn't crazy. Didn't sound on the phone like he was. When I'd heard the bell ring, I'd answered. Edrick had stood behind the screen door, fixing his tie. I could smell his English Musk cologne before he had even walked in the door.

"Are you Liz?" he'd asked.

"I am, and you must be Edrick Parker."

"Yes."

"Come on in," I'd said as I held the screen door open for him. Lord have mercy. This man was good-looking. He looked like a preacher in his suit. He towered over me like he was seven feet tall, with dark-chocolate skin and deep-brown eyes. "Did you have a problem finding the house?"

"Well, I'm from here, so I know Tallahassee like the back of my hand."

"You, too?" I had given a flirtatious smile.

"You from Tallahassee?"

"Born and raised."

"Well, ain't this somethin', small world."

"Small town."

The smell of Dutch apple cheesecake Ms. Gertie had made filled the house. I couldn't bake to save my soul. I'd tried to make a sweet potato pie once and it had come out all runny. I'd tried again and ended up burning the pies. That was the last time I'd tried my hand at baking anything.

"Oh, let me get you your wallet." I had put it in one of the end table drawers for safe keeping. "Everything's in there."

"It's fine, Liz. I trust you."

Edrick had the most beautiful smile I had ever seen on a black man. He could have blinded me, his teeth were so white. Mama always told me to never trust a man who had teeth that white. It meant they had something to hide.

"Something smells good," Edrick had said.

"I just made an apple cinnamon cheesecake," I'd lied. "You want a slice?"

"I shouldn't, but I can't pass up a smell like that." Edrick had undone one of the buttons on the jacket of his pricey-looking suit.

"Sit down, I'll cut you a slice."

I had gone to the kitchen, plucked a small pie saucer out of the cabinet above the counter, and cut him a big slice. I knew a man his size always had an appetite, and being that he was the size of a refrigerator, he didn't look as if he missed any meals. I had set the large piece of apple cinnamon cheesecake in front of him.

"Let me get you a fork. I got some coffee, fresh brewed."

Edrick wasn't one of these shy kinds of men who tried to come off like he didn't want to be greedy.

"So how is it?" I'd asked. I acted like *I* was the one who had slaved away all morning long, making the dessert.

"This is my first time trying apple cinnamon cheesecake, but this is the kind of thing I could marry a woman over."

My heart skipped a few beats when he'd mentioned marriage. "So what kind of work you do?"

"I own Parker & Son Auto Parts over on South Adams."

"I know it. I go by there every day on my way to work. I wouldn't have pegged you as a businessman."

"What did you think I did?"

"With that suit, I thought you were a preacher."

"Well, I am a church-going man, but no preacher," he'd said. "So what about you, Ms. Liz? What kind of work do you do?"

"I'm a housekeeper, working for this well-to-do-family out in Ox Bottom Manor."

"It's good work, honest work," Edrick had said as he cut a piece of the cheesecake away with his fork. "So since you found my wallet, you should let me take you to dinner sometime, maybe go see a picture."

The last man who ever took me out anywhere was Henry, who took me to a chicken fight.

"All right then," I'd said.

"So I'll pick you up Friday night, 'bout eight."

"I'll be ready."

We had spent the rest of the evening talking. I was surprised to find that we had so much in common. Being that we were both from Tallahassee, I wondered why we had never run into each other. I was counting down the days until Friday. I was rummaging through my closet, trying to find something to wear, but they were all clothes I wore to work mostly, nothing good enough to go out in. I was going to dip into the money I was saving up for me and the babies until Ms. Gertie came into my room with the prettiest black dress I had ever laid my eyes on.

"I don't know, Ms. Gertie. This is too pretty to wear out. I don't want to get it dirty."

"I've put on a few pounds, so I can't fit into it, but it's perfect for you, baby. A few months from now, you won't be able to get into it."

We both had grinned. I had gone to the bathroom to try it on and Ms. Gertie was right. It was a little tight in some places, but it was perfect for my date with Edrick. I didn't want to bore him, but make sure that he would never forget me. I looked at myself in the full-body mirror, rubbing my hand over the small bump that was forming.

"Are you going to tell Edrick about you being with child?"

"Yeah, but I want to see how things go first."

"Can't nobody blame you for that. Hold on. I got some black shoes that will go real good with this dress."

I had wanted to go to Terri's to get my hair done, but didn't have the money, so I had done a quick at-home, hot-curler job. By the time I was done, it had looked like I had spent an arm and a leg on my hair. The night of our first date, I had been a mess of nerves. I had drunk some ginger ale to calm the butterflies in my stomach. I couldn't stay out of the mirror. If Edrick hadn't noticed how good I looked, then he was blind as a damn bat. I had jumped when I heard the doorbell ring.

"Child, you a mess, calm down," Ms. Gertie had said as she answered the door.

Edrick was dressed to the nines in a black suit and burgundy wing-tips this time, armed with two bouquets of red roses. "You must be Ms. Gertie."

She held the screen door open for Edrick to walk in. "I am."

"These are for you."

"Well, goodness. How nice."

"And these...are for you, sweet lady."

No one had ever given me flowers before. I was swooning that night. We had gone out on about four dates after, one being a Sunday afternoon picnic in Myers Park. I had made fried chicken, potato salad, cold slaw, and for dessert: apple cinnamon cheesecake.

"Can you do me a favor?"

"What?"

"Close your eyes."

"What?"

"Close your eyes for me. I have a surprise."

I had done what he wanted and had shut my eyes.

"No peeking."

"Oh, Lord, what is it, Edrick?"

"Now you can open them."

When I did, Edrick had held a ring in his hand. I had gasped.

"Remember when I told you that if you kept cooking like that, I would have to marry you?"

"Oh, Lord."

"So will you? Will you marry me, Liz? Will you be Mrs. Elizabeth Parker?"

Before I could give Edrick an answer, I knew that I had to come clean with him about me first. "There's something I need to tell you." He'd looked at me like a big question mark had formed on his handsome face. "Before I met you, I was in a relationship with a man. And I got...pregnant. I will under—"

Edrick had rested his finger against my lips to stop me from saying another word. "That don't matter. I love you and I want to marry you. Babies or no babies."

I had looked at Edrick. "I don't deserve a man as good as you."

"You deserve that and a whole lot more. I want to give you everything."

"Then yes. Yes, I will marry you, Edrick Parker." He'd slipped the ring on my finger, which was a perfect fit.

Ms. Gertie and I had cried happy when Edrick and I gave her the news. I went to Mama to tell her how good I was doing, that I met a good man and we were getting married, but she wouldn't even come to the door. I told her that we were going to have a small ceremony downtown at the courthouse, that she was invited if she wanted to come. I prayed that she would, but I had my doubts.

The day of the wedding, I had worn this eggshell-white dress that Ms. Gertie had given me to wear. She'd done my hair up in a tight beehive with tendrils of curls flowing down on both sides of my face. Even my fingernails were painted white. I couldn't believe that I was going to be somebody's wife, that I would have a husband. Mama never did come. I tried a few more times to talk to her, and each time, she wouldn't so much as come to the door, but sit there in her recliner, watching her game shows. After that, I was done trying. I loved Mama, but I was through. I had a husband and two babies on the way.

Edrick bought a house on the north side of town in Apalachee Ridge Estates. It was a damn sight better than the roach motel I had stayed in eight months before. I was sad to have to leave Ms. Gertie, but told her that I would come and visit her twice a week. Edrick was doing real good with the stores and decided to open up a second one on the side of town we lived on. That same year, he bought me a car, a black Monte Carlo with white leather seats.

I was crazy about that car, being that it was my first one. I didn't know how to drive. Edrick would take me out on the weekends on an old dirt road in Woodville and teach me.

Edrick gave me everything I needed for both me and the boys. I decorated one of the rooms all in blue. We filled it with more toys than you could shake a stick at. I quit my job after Edrick proposed. I was glad to finally get away from that ole nasty Mr. Cozart. I used my last check from them to get Ms. Gertie something nice, thanking her for all she had done for me. I got her a gold necklace with a birthstone heart. She had cried when I gave it to her.

By the ninth month, I was so big, it's a wonder I could fit through my front door. Edrick thought that me being as big as a tractor was cute, but I'd told him, "We'll see how you feel when you have the ass the size of a cement mixer and have to run to the bathroom every two minutes." I hated when he rubbed my belly like it was some kind of crystal ball. I was past ready for Kashawn and Deanthony to come out of me.

At 1:16 a.m. on a Tuesday morning, July ninth, my water broke. The new bed sheets I bought were soaked. I just about had to push Edrick's snoring behind out of the bed to get him to wake up.

"Baby, wake up."

He grunted awake like a big ole hog.

"Get up, my water just broke."

He jumped up, bat-shit crazy. I was calmer than he was. On the way to Tallahassee Memorial, I thought I was going to give birth to my babies right there in the car. After ten hours in labor, I gave birth to Deanthony first and Kashawn came two minutes later on July tenth, 11:15, Wednesday morning. I'd always liked the names Anthony and Shawn, but wanted something I knew that no one else would have, so I slapped a "D" in front of Anthony and a "K" in front of Shawn and there it was: Kashawn and Deanthony. Edrick kept taking pictures from every angle of me and the twins until I had to tell him to stop. Giving birth to Kashawn and Deanthony was the second-best thing that had happened to me, next to marrying Edrick.

A year had passed and things couldn't have been better. The second store was doing better than Edrick had hoped. So much so that Edrick and I started to look for a new house, a three-bedroom for us and the boys. Kashawn and Deanthony were one year old and growing fast. It was the day of our one-year anniversary when Edrick and I met. I had slaved in the kitchen all day, making Edrick's favorite dishes: roast beef with carrots and red potatoes, field peas, yellow seasoned rice, and crackling corn bread, with Dutch apple cinnamon cheesecake for dessert. The house smelled so good, I had to chase the neighborhood dogs off with a broom when they came sniffing around the house for something to eat. I had been grinning ear to ear all that day, thinking of that first time Edrick had shown up on Ms. Gertie's doorstep in that navy suit, sweat glistening like Vaseline on his face. I was so captured by how handsome he was, I had forgotten about his wallet.

I was sitting at the kitchen table, shucking some field peas and watching my soaps on the small TV that sat in a corner on the kitchen counter, laughing as I thought about what Mama had always told me about never trusting men whose teeth are too white. As I had run my fingers through the bowl of peas and about to rinse them, the doorbell had rung. I had checked the corn bread in the oven that still was not done yet. I had figured it was Nadine's little girl, Lynette, going door to door, selling Girl Scout cookies. She knew I was good for two boxes of Thin Mints. I had wiped my hands dry on the yellow apron I had tied around my waist as I'd walked toward the door. Two white police officers were standing on my porch in front of me.

"Good afternoon, ma'am. Are you Mrs. Edrick Parker?"

"Yes, I am," I'd said, looking at the officers questionably.

"Ma'am, can we come in?"

"What's wrong?"

They'd had a look to them like they wanted to be anywhere but standing in front of me that day. They'd told me that Edrick had been in a car accident, a head-on collision with a semi. They'd gone on about how apparently Edrick was driving on the wrong side of the road, that they'd found an open bottle of Vodka in the front seat of his Cadillac. The news of my husband's death had numbed me.

"We're deeply sorry," they'd said in unison.

I didn't scream, but kept it together until they'd left. I'd gone to the bedroom and shut the door. I had grabbed the first thing that I could get my hands on, which was a lamp that was sitting on the nightstand next to Edrick's side of the bed. I had taken it and thrown it at the mirror above the dresser. Glass had shattered to the floor. I could hear Kashawn and Deanthony crying in the next room. When I was done, the room was a mess, broken glass everywhere. My feet were bleeding from stepping in it, blood staining the carpet. I had looked down at my feet and felt that it was a pain I deserved for turning a blind eye to Edrick's drinking, for not seeing the signs: him passed out in front of the TV with a bottle of gin at the foot of the sofa. I could smell booze on his breath in the middle of the afternoon, but I didn't want to be one of those nagging wives who was always on her husband about this and that and the other.

They'd told me at Strong & Jones Funeral Home that Edrick's face was so badly disfigured, they recommended a closed-casket funeral. Ms. Gertie had come to the house and stayed a few weeks to help me with the boys. She was my rock at the funeral. Without her, I don't think I would have been able to keep it together. People who were friends of Edrick and loyal customers of the store had come up to me to offer their condolences. Some of them I had met at different gatherings like cookouts, dinners, and church functions.

The first time I had ever laid eyes on Ray-Ray, he was kneeling at the head of Edrick's casket, crying harder than I had ever seen a man cry.

"Look at Ray up there, makin' a fool outta himself," I had heard Edrick's busybody Aunt Millie say, who likes to talk mess about everybody.

It had taken everything in me to keep from hauling back and slapping the old bitch in the mouth. What kind of Christian are you to talk about your own nephew at his brother's funeral? One of the ushers had escorted Ray through the rear of the church like they were embarrassed by his grieving.

"Ms. Gertie, watch the boys for me."

As I had gotten up to go see how Ray-Ray was doing, I'd heard Millie say, "Where does she think she's going?" That heifer was glad that I was in the Lord's house.

Ray-Ray was leaning against an oak tree, his arm propped against the trunk.

"Hey, Ray, you doin' all right?"

He had turned his six-two, 320-something-pound frame to face me, his round, fat face streaked with tears. I had never felt so sorry for anyone that day as I felt for Ray-Ray. I had pulled my handkerchief from the sleeve of my black dress and handed it to him.

"We didn't talk for five years," he'd said. "I fell into a bad crowd, started drinking too much. Ed was there when nobody else gave a damn."

"So what happened between y'all?"

"He washed his hands of me after I stole from him."

Edrick had spoken once or twice about Ray-Ray. Never much in detail, only that Ray-Ray didn't come around much.

"Ed put up with a lot of my shit and I never got a chance to pay him back, to say that I'm sorry."

"He knows. He's looking down on you, and he knows." He was this giant of a man who towered over me as I'd consoled him.

Ray-Ray started coming around the house more. He was so good with the boys, and I was more than happy to have him around, seeing as how they'd lost the only daddy they knew. We were the only family he'd had. Ray-Ray stayed in a one-bedroom place over on Saxton Street by himself. I'd told him he could move in with us if he didn't drink.

"I haven't had so much as a sip of anything for a year," he'd told me.

The boys were smiling ear to ear when I'd told them that their uncle Ray-Ray would be staying with us. There was nothing he didn't do for me and the boys.

39

KASHAWN

My heart was racing and my palms were drenched with sweat as Ma, Yvonne, and I rode the elevator to the fourth floor of the Leon County Courthouse. I was dressed in a charcoal-black Bill Blass suit, Ma in a white silk blouse and black skirt, while Yvonne sported black dress pants and a red, sleeveless blouse. We looked like we were on our way to church and I wished that was the case. Once we reached the fourth floor, I spotted Deanthony sitting on one of the benches, wearing a white dress shirt and navy blue slacks. It was uncanny how identical we were—at least on the outside anyway.

"Hey, Ma," he said, wrapping his arms around our mother.

"How you doin', baby?"

"What's up, D," Yvonne said.

"What's up, cousin? Don't think I've ever seen you look this good."

"I'll take that as a compliment," she said.

"You just got here?" I asked.

"Yeah, about ten minutes ago."

"Well, I appreciate you coming."

"Thanks for calling to let me know what's up."

"Ma, why don't y'all go on in," I said. "I need to talk to Deanthony." Ma looked at me, unsure as to what I was going to say or do. "It's all right, Ma. Everything's fine."

Ma looked at me and then Deanthony before she went hesitantly with Yvonne to the courtroom where Bree was to be arraigned.

"How's your lip?"

"Shit. It's not like I didn't deserve it."

"Well, you give about as much as you get," I said, pointing to the shiner over my right eye.

"Look, bro, I've given a lot of thought to that day at the homecoming party, and just all this crazy shit that has gone down since I've been back."

"You don't need to apologize. I had no business coming at you like that."

"Bro, you had every right. Hell, I would have done the same thing if I was in your shoes. Look, you asked me why I came back to Tally and why I left like I did." Deanthony sat down on the bench, looking as if he was ready to unload something that had been riding his back way too long. "I felt all my life that I've lived in your shadow. We're identical twins, yeah, but Ma, I felt, always treated you like royalty. You're the one who got straight A's in school, who got the new car for getting into Florida A&M, while I always got the hand-me-downs, the crumbs, if anything at all. I got the belt across my ass while you got treated to ice cream."

"You know Ma loves us both equally."

"You could do no wrong in her eyes, but all Mama saw in me was wrong. And straight up, I started hating you for that. That's why I left. I didn't want that hate to eat away at me. Kashawn, I needed to find my own way, figure out what kind of man I wanted to be instead of this thug Ma always saw me as. I split to Los Angeles to see if I could make the acting thing work. The truth is, after a few bit parts here and there, I fell on hard times. I didn't want to come back here just so you and Ma could say that y'all told me so. I really wanted to make things work in Cali."

"D, what do you mean you fell on hard times?"

"I met some people at this party a producer was throwing. There was booze and drugs everywhere, mountains of coke, weed, booze, you name it. I was so fucked up that I couldn't remember anything. I found out a week later that there was this sex tape."

"What the fuck?"

"Yeah, I said the same thing when I saw the tape."

"And you don't remember any of that going down?"

"I swear on our daddy's grave that I don't. I had to pay a pretty penny to get all the copies of the tape and get the video pulled off of YouTube."

"Damn, D."

"So I came back home to get my life back on track."

"So are you clean now?"

"Three months clean, knock on wood."

"I wish you would have called me. I could have helped you."

"What, clean up another one of my messes?"

"D, we're brothers. That's what brothers do instead of running away."

Yvonne caught our attention when she whispered at us to come to the courtroom. "The judge is about to come in."

"Well, I'm glad you're home."

"Right now, let's keep this between me and you. I'm not ready for Ma to know what's really going on."

"And she won't."

Deanthony threw his arm around my neck as we walked like brothers toward the courtroom entrance.

40

BREE

was so tired and my back was screaming for some well-deserved relief after the beat down the lumpy mattress had given it, not to mention my upset stomach from the pig shit they were trying to pass off as food in the jail. I told that dyke cop that I had a sensitive stomach, that I couldn't eat just anything.

"What does this look like to you," she'd said, "The Radisson? You eat what we give you, Princess, and if you don't like it, you have two choices: starve and…starve."

I swear they stuck me with the biggest mega bitch ever. I only hoped I wouldn't shit my jumpsuit from the moldy-ass bread I had to force myself to eat. If I wasn't on the toilet shitting half the night, I was tossing and turning. I swore that if I got bedbugs in my coochie, I was going to sue the balls off the city, county, and state for every penny their asses was worth.

Don't even get me started on this bitch they put in the cell next to me who paces the floor saying, "She wouldn't stop crying…she wouldn't stop crying…she wouldn't stop crying."

I asked Iron Titties what her problem was.

"She drowned her five-month-old in scalding hot water because the baby wouldn't stop crying. They say she's crazy, but I think it's an act. Between you and me, Princess, I hope they fry the baby-killing bitch."

The females in the jail would yell at her to shut the fuck up, but she would only get louder with all of her crazy talk. She paced until she got tired and finally fell off to sleep.

I hadn't been able to stop replaying the events of that night in my head. I had been having nightmares about Katiesha, finding her lying dead like that with her head split open, all that blood. "I should have stayed home that night," I kept telling myself. "I never should have opened the door." I didn't like Katiesha, couldn't stand her, but, damn, ole girl didn't deserve to go out like that.

It was a good thing Tangela didn't show up that night or both of us would have been locked up. I would be lying if I said I wasn't scared shitless about the outcome of this whole thing. I told everybody and their grandmama what had happened that night, including Kent, who hadn't done much of nothing but jot shit down on his yellow pad. He'd told me the cops found my prints on the door and on the vodka bottle.

"I don't care what they found," I'd told him. "I didn't kill Katiesha." He had asked me what my relationship was with her. "She and I danced at Risqué together, that's it. It's no secret that we didn't like each other. You can ask anybody at the club."

"I did, and they said there was no love lost between you two girls, especially a Ms. Nakia Wilder, who didn't mince words about Katiesha and Ms. Ursula Reynolds not liking you. If the prosecution gets ahold of her, and they will, she will be a witness for them. I understand that your brother-in-law was in the room when you attacked Katiesha Foster."

"Yeah, so?"

"The prosecution will be calling him to the stand, as well as the officers that arrived on the scene."

I hated how he sat there, looking at me over his glasses like I was something he needed to scrape off the bottom of his six-hundred-dollar wingtips. I set his uppity-ass straight quick.

"I know you think I'm shit, but you can blow it out of your ass. No, I didn't like Katiesha, and I tried to beat her ass down when I caught her in bed with Kashawn, but I didn't kill her. I don't know how many times and how many people I have to scream it to."

"It doesn't matter, Bree, how I feel about you. Kashawn has been a friend of mine for many years, and he hired me to represent you. I'm going to do that to the best of my ability," he said. "The evidence they have stacked against you is insurmountable, but first we need to try and get you bail."

"You have to get me the hell out of here. I can't do time for something I didn't do." It felt like what I was telling Kent was going into one ear and out the other. I didn't have much faith in this ambulance chaser.

"Rise and shine, Princess. It's time for your arraignment."

Speak of the devil.

I finger-combed my hair, considering I didn't have any tools to groom myself proper. I got one shower a week, and the rest of the time, I had to go around smelling funky. I hated the idea of looking at somebody in their face with stink breath. Iron Titties cuffed my wrists and ankles and escorted me to the courtroom. Kent was sitting at a large oak table with papers strewn out on it. He didn't bother to look up at me. He didn't look too confident. He was dressed to the teeth in a black suit with pecan-brown wingtips. There weren't many people in the courtroom. I thought it would look something like *Law & Order* or some shit, but no. I was so happy to see Kashawn behind Kent. And next to him were Mama Liz, Yvonne, and Deanthony, whom I was a little knocked on my ass to see. I was embarrassed for Kashawn to see how I looked. Instead of the beautiful woman he'd married, I looked like I had been dragged through a ditch of shit. My hair was a rat's nest and orange was not my color.

I didn't care what Mama Liz and Yvonne thought of me. I was done licking their booties. Kashawn stood up when he saw me. Our eyes met. I hadn't seen him since the night they'd brought me into the jail. I walked over to my husband, wrapped my arms around him, and hugged him as tight as any human being could. I glared at Deanthony over Kashawn's shoulder, who cut me a soft smile.

"Hey, baby girl, how are you holding up?" Tears welled up and poured, and Kashawn smeared every streak away with his thumb. "I love you."

"I love you more." The strong scent of Irish Spring shower gel permeated from every part of his body. "I'm sorry, baby. I'm sorry for everything. Please forgive me."

"Already have, Bree, already have."

"Hey, baby. How are you holding up?" Mama Liz asked.

"I'm just trying to keep my head clear. It's not easy, though."

"We're here for you," Yvonne said, placing her hand warmly on my shoulder.

"I've been a horrible wife to you. If I don't get out of this—"

"Don't talk like that," Kashawn interrupted.

"In case things don't come out in our favor, I want you to move on with your life. Forget about me. Your mama is right. I'm no good. I've never been any good."

"Baby, I owe you an apology for how I've treated you," Mama said. "I admit that I didn't give you a fair chance."

"Neither of us did," Yvonne chimed in. "Instead of welcoming you with open arms, I gave you a hard time and I'm sorry."

"I'm sorry, too," said Mama. "We all have a past. Life is too short to allow ourselves to be knocked around by it. We know this is asking a lot, but can we start over, daughter-in-law?"

"Can you give *us* another chance?" Yvonne asked.

I took them both into my arms, letting them know that all was forgiven. "There's nothing I love more than starting clean slates." We all began to cry like it was a teary reunion.

"Bree, we need to take our seats," Kent said.

Minutes later a black woman in a black robe, with her hair tied up in a bun, entered the courtroom. She looked to be about in her early thirties, give or take. This woman looked like money, from tip to tail. I was so nervous, I thought my heart was going to burst out of my chest like that thing from the movie *Alien*.

"All rise," the bailiff said, "for the honorable Shonticia Flowers."

Shonticia? Anyone with a name like that has to be from the hood. Everyone in the courtroom stood up like she was the Queen of Sheba. She didn't look up once at me. She shuffled papers around on that big bench she sat behind. I figured it was my record she was looking at, shocked by the Christmas list of shit I'd done since I was fifteen. The prosecuting lawyer was a white lady with long, thick blond hair. This bitch looked like she didn't have any mercy. I looked at ole girl and knew she was going to filet a bitch. The court clerk read off what I was accused of. It stung to hear my name being read off with murder attached to it. The sound of it made me shake in my ugly, white plastic flip-flops.

"How does the defendant plead?" the judge asked. She still didn't look at me, but kept her head down at whatever she was looking at.

"Not guilty, Your Honor," Kent said.

Good answer, I thought.

The prosecutor started going on about how I was a flight risk, when I'd never been on a plane in my life, telling Shonticia that I'd been in trouble since I was eighteen and whatnot. She did and said everything Kent told me she would say, about how I had previous run-ins with Katiesha.

"Your Honor, Mrs. Parker is the wife of a prominent doctor in the community and is not a flight risk."

Kent and the other lawyer were arguing back and forth like two cats scraping for a rat. Shonticia beat her gavel until they shut up.

"Bail is set at one million dollars."

"Thank you, Jesus," I heard Mama Liz cry out.

My heart bottomed out when I heard how much the bail was. I turned to Kashawn and hugged him.

"I can post it. Bree, baby, you're coming home."

"I love you," I said.

As Iron Titties walked me out of the courtroom, Kashawn, Deanthony, Mama Liz, and Yvonne hugged. I was happy as shit that I didn't have to spend another night on that lumpy mattress, or be kept up all night with diarrhea and having to listen to baby-killing Claudine's crazy ass. If I had to spend another second in that jail, I was going to pull out what was left of my hair extensions.

41

TANGELA

"What the fuck!"

I nearly choked on the mouth wad of barbecue chicken sandwich when I saw Katiesha's and Bree's faces splashed across my
flat-screen HDTV. I grabbed the remote off the coffee table to
turn it up. I was officially knocked on my ass when it was reported
that Bree had been charged with Katiesha's murder. It was obvious
that if they had arrested Bree, then the cops didn't find my prints
on anything. Bree, murder? No-fucking-way. Home girl was capable
of a lot of things, including fucking her husband's brother, but killing somebody? I didn't even want to think about what she must
have been going through, hell, what my baby, Kashawn must have
been going through. I needed to get down to the jail. I had to get
my story straight first, though, in case the cops got a hankering to
come sniffing around here to ask me questions. I was home all
night and didn't leave my house. I turned in early because I had
an early day at the j-o-b. Yeah, that's what's up.

Bree must have come by Katiesha's crib after I'd left when she
didn't find Katiesha at Risqué. With Bree finally out of the picture,
this shit could be a blessing in disguise. It opened up all kinds of
opportunities for me and Kashawn. He must be devastated. He was
going to need support, a shoulder to cry on. It's funny sometimes
how shit just falls into your lap. I went to my bedroom closet to
find something sleek and fierce to wear. I took out this royal-blue

pencil dress with a peek-a-boo keyhole in the middle that showed off the perfect bit of skin without it looking too hoochie. I pulled a black-and-white shoe box off the shelf above the rack of clothes and got out the pair of fuchsia, eight-inch pumps I'd been dying to break in. I was giving plus-size supermodel realness.

A celebrity's donkey booty didn't hold a candle to these double-chocolate cakes. As an added bonus, I sprayed on a little Estee Lauder between my breasts before checking my hair and makeup in the mirror one last time.

"Kashawn Parker, I'm about to show you what you've been missing."

I'd never had a problem getting a man. Finding a *good* man is where the problem comes in. Give these brothers out here a taste, next thing you know, they want to play house with a bitch. But I didn't play that. I cut them off at the knees when they start tripping.

I'd come a long way since my bookish, nerdy girl days in high school. Amazing what Proactiv and a little makeup will do. After graduation, I couldn't wait to get that damn barbed wire cut off my teeth. Boys back in the day wouldn't so much as fart in my direction. Now I had to beat them off with an ugly stick. There isn't a man yet that has been able to resist my curves, not even Kashawn. I bet he still thinks of that night I sucked his dick, the night I went down on him when Bree was off in Atlanta, probably fucking every man that made a pass at her slutty ass.

"Where the hell is my earring?" I was rummaging through the jewelry box Mama had given me last year on my twenty-fifth birthday. "Oh, shit. No, no, no, please, God no!" I dumped out the contents of the jewelry box on my dresser, checking every earring, necklace, and brooch. Shit, it must have fallen out of my ear at Katiesha's house.

Fuck, what if the cops found it? That shit would link me to knowing Katiesha. I couldn't go back to that house now. Cops were probably swarming like flies around that place, fucking crime scene tape everywhere. If I went around the cops, asking questions, it could put suspicion on me. They would have tracked me down by now had they found something.

Okay, girl. Keep it together. Calm down. There's way too much heat right now with this whole mess with Bree and Katiesha. First thing's first. Time to go play the concerned best friend.

42

TANGELA

My mood soured when I pulled in front of Kashawn's house to find Deanthony's SUV parked outside behind Kashawn's. Damn twins even drove the same car. It was all good, though. I wasn't going to trip. I would get Deanthony's punk ass together if he tried to come for me. I checked in the rearview mirror to see if I had any lipstick on my teeth and made sure my titties were nice and secure in my Michael Kors original. I got out and walked up to the front door. Just as I was about to ring the doorbell with my red, manicured finger, Deanthony answered. Needless to say, he was the last nigga I wanted to see.

"What the hell are you doing here?"

"This is my brother's house. Unlike you, I don't need an invitation."

"Tangela?" Kashawn asked.

What the fuck!

"Bree! Oh, my God." I slipped past Deanthony and wrapped my arms around Bree, giving her a hard hug like I hadn't seen her in months. Kashawn, Mama Liz, and Yvonne were all sitting in the living room. "Girl, what happened? I just saw you on the news. Are you all right?"

"Oh, Lord, I'm on the news?"

"Yeah, it's all over the TV."

"Oh, God, there's going to be news people all in front of the house."

Christmas has come early. I am living for this shit.

"I doubt that." Deanthony grinned. "These people don't give a damn 'bout no black stripper who lived in the hood being bodied."

"Baby, don't worry about all that. I'll protect you." I thought I was going to throw up my chicken sandwich when I saw D wrap his arms lovingly around Bree.

"All of us are just glad to have you home, baby," Mama Liz said. The one woman next to me who couldn't stand to breathe the same air as Bree, now, all of a sudden, was her biggest supporter? Bitch, please!

"So, Tangela, where are you going all dressed up?" Yvonne asked.

I turned to face her like she had just slashed me across the back with an ice pick.

"Yeah. A little too early for the club, ain't it?" Deanthony asked.

Fuck was this, Twenty Questions? Why was everyone sweating me? These people don't feed, fuck, or finance me. Where I go and what I do, was no one's business but mine. I had no nerves left for Deanthony and would cut his ashy ass to the white meat in due time.

I had to think of something quick, being that I couldn't come right out and say, *"Oh, I'm just here to seduce Kashawn."*

"I was invited to a party that one of the girls from the salon was throwing. I was on my way over there until I had to hear about my best friend being arrested for this craziness. How come no one picked up the phone and called me?"

"Sorry, Tangela," Kashawn said in his sexy-ass voice. "So much has been going on, I forgot to call you."

Deanthony started flapping his gums again. "All of us have been busy with Bree being accused of murder."

"Deanthony, hush," Mama Liz said, cutting his dumb-ass a grimace like he had just called her out of her name.

"I tried to call you to let you know about what's been up and about the arraignment, but I couldn't get you," Yvonne said.

"Bree, I'm so sorry, girl. I should have been there."

"It's all good, girl. You're here now and that's all that matters."
I felt dry heaves coming up as she rubbed affectionately on the
back side of Kashawn's hand. "Somebody must have gotten there
before me."

"Before where?" Kashawn asked.

"To Katiesha's house."

"Baby girl, it doesn't matter. All that matters is that your friends
and family are here to support you."

"Kashawn, look, baby, I love you, but I could be facing death row.
If not, then life in prison." Bree looked around the living room at
all of us. "I don't think I can survive that."

"Bree's got a point," Deanthony said, like somebody gave a damn
what he thought. "What other explanation could it be?"

Ain't nobody ask you nothin', Sherlock-fucking-Holmes.

"D, chill, you're scaring Bree," Kashawn said.

"No, he's right," Bree said. "The cops, the judge, that prosecutor,
they don't care if I rot in prison. To them, I'm just another hood
rat. That judge didn't look at me once the whole time I was in the
courthouse. I could get the lethal injection and she couldn't even
take the time to look up to see who was standing up there in front
of her uppity-ass."

"Baby, try to calm down," Kashawn said.

"You ain't never lied," Yvonne added.

"I gotta get proof."

"What?" I said.

"What are you talking about, get proof?" Kashawn asked.

"I have to prove that I didn't kill Katiesha."

"Bree, what are you saying?" Kashawn asked.

"How do you plan on doing that?" I asked.

"The only way is to find the person who did it, who actually had
reason to kill Katiesha."

"Bree, you're not serious," Kashawn said.

"Baby, what are you talking about doing?" Mama Liz asked.

"I gotta go back to Pepper Drive, talk to people, and ask if they saw anybody that night."

"Girl, are you crazy?" I asked.

"No, she's not, because she's not going back to that neighborhood," Kashawn argued.

"Kashawn, I—"

"No!" Everyone quieted down when Kashawn yelled, "Do you know how dangerous that neighborhood is?"

"I know more than anybody sitting in here how dangerous it is."

"Bree, you need to let Kent handle this. Girl, listen to Kashawn. Going to Pepper Drive is only going to make matters worse," I said.

"And what if I go to court and a jury finds me guilty, Tangela, what then?"

"I would rather we take our chances in court with a jury, than for you to go back to that neighborhood and risk you ending up like Katiesha," Kashawn said.

"Somebody saw something that night. Somebody was at Katiesha's house before I got there. Somebody had to have seen someone enter and leave her house."

"Even if someone did see something, what do you think they're going to do? March to the cops and say, 'Hey, I saw that stripper get killed the other night'?" I asked.

"Tangela's right," said Kashawn. "People who live in places like Pepper Drive don't like strangers snooping around, asking questions."

"I hear they got a gang in that neighborhood," Yvonne said.

"More than one, from what I'm told," I said, attempting to discourage her from going back to Katiesha's house.

"Y'all are not the ones who could be facing death row. I am. My freedom is on the line, not yours."

"Okay, so you go back there and start asking people questions about that night and somebody says they saw someone. Your chances of getting them to go to the cops and telling them what or who they saw is slim at best," Kashawn said.

"I gotta do something. I can't sit around and wait for them to build a case against me."

The last thing I needed was for Bree to go poking her ass around, asking a bunch of damn questions. I knew that look in her light-brown eyes all too well. It meant that once she got an idea in that stubborn head of hers to do something, there was no stopping her. And with murder being her case, she was going to keep on digging until some shit came to the surface. I knew then that I would have to get to that house before her. If Bree found something to tie me to being there the night I killed Katiesha, she would no doubt snitch on me to the cops if it meant keeping her ass out of prison.

"Bree, let Kent handle this. He's the best criminal lawyer in North Florida. Let him do his job. This is what he's getting paid to do." Kashawn took Bree's right hand into his. "I want you to promise me that you won't do anything crazy." Bree glanced at Kashawn, speechless. "Baby, I'm serious. I don't know what I'll do if something happened to you."

"Kashawn is right," I said. "It's too dangerous and I don't want to think about what the cops will do to you if you went back to Katiesha's."

"Throw you back in jail, that's what they would do," said Mama Liz.

"Okay, fine, I won't go back."

"Or to Katiesha's house," Kashawn said.

"I won't go back to the house."

Bree was the kind who would say one thing and do another. There was no way I could risk her finding out what really happened that night, and I damn sho' wasn't going to go to jail for her ass. I would do whatever I had to do to keep Bree off my ass. Damn! None of this would be happening if she hadn't gotten so damn greedy. Trust, I'd take her ass out just like I took out Katiesha. Bree and Deanthony. Fuck a friendship.

43

DEANTHONY

was about to fall asleep when I heard my phone ring. I thought to let it ring, figuring that it was Tangela. She was the last bitch I wanted to talk to. I clicked on the nightstand light and studied the number. It was Bree.

"Hello."

"Hey, I need you to come pick me up."

"What? Pick you up from where?"

"My house."

"Why, what's up?" I said, straining my eyes against the lamp's light.

"I want you to take me to Pepper Drive."

"Bree, you told Kashawn that you weren't going back there, and I agree with him. It's too dangerous."

"I have never known you to run away from trouble, but run straight into it. What the fuck happened to you?"

"You should know where trouble gets you when you go looking for that shit."

"Deanthony, are you going to give me a lecture or help me? Either way, I'm going and I'm going tonight."

"What about Kashawn?"

"He'll understand."

"No the hell he won't."

"I want to go back there, see if maybe the cops left something behind."

"Like what?"

"Hell, I don't know. Maybe there was something they forgot."

"Kashawn would have my ass if I let something happen to you."

"Just let me worry about him. Are you coming or not?"

"Give me ten minutes," I told her.

"Don't come to the house. Pull up at the front gates. I don't want you to wake up Kashawn."

I got out of bed and dressed, slipping into a pair of jeans, a wife-beater, and boots. "What the fuck am I doing?" I quietly reached inside the nightstand and fished out the semiautomatic Kashawn had bought to protect the house. It felt cold against my stomach when I stuffed it in the waistband of my jeans. I hoped that I wouldn't have to use it, but if I had to, shit, I had to. Place like Pepper Drive, I wasn't about to roll up in that shit with a damn plastic butter knife.

When I reached the gates of Ox Bottom Manor where Bree said to meet her, she was standing outside, wearing jeans and a *Menace II Society* T-shirt, something that fit the mood of what we were about to do.

"Hey," she said as she climbed into my whip.

"You know this shit is crazy, right? Did Kashawn wake up?"

"Hell no. You know how he snores."

"What if he wakes up and finds out you done dipped?"

"Not a chance. I ground up three sleeping pills and put them in his soda at dinner. He's out of it."

"Bree, this is crazy."

"I called you because, despite everything, I knew I could count on you. Don't make me regret it."

"If you find any proof to show that you didn't kill Katiesha, then I'm down."

"I know someone had to have seen something. You don't live in a neighborhood like that and not see shit."

"What were you doing there that night by yourself anyway, knowing how dangerous it would be?"

"Tangela said she would go with me that night to go find Katiesha."

"Tangela?"

"She was supposed to meet me at Risqué, but she never showed up. I tried calling her, but her damn phone kept going to voicemail. So when she didn't show, I was like, fuck it, I'll go at it by myself."

"You should have called me. I would have gone in with you."

"People need to stop treating me like I'm some fragile china doll. I might live in a nice house, but I grew up on streets just like this."

"So did Tangela ever tell you why she didn't show up at Risqué that night?"

"With all this shit that's been happening, I never thought to ask her why she was a no-show. I didn't really need her. Katiesha wasn't working that night anyway."

"Did you call Tangela after you left the club?"

"No, I was too busy trying to get up out of that cesspool. I went to Katiesha's after that. Her Cutlass was in the yard and the light in the front room was on, so I knew she was home, probably getting high or some shit, knowing her. Why you got this concern for Tangela suddenly?"

"I'm just trying to piece all this shit together."

When we got to Pepper Drive, it was dark as fuck. The bulbs in the streetlights had been busted out. The one streetlight that was working wasn't worth a damn.

"I can't believe you rolled up in this shit by yourself," Bree said.

"What, you scared or something?"

"Never that, baby boy. I got this right here." Bree pulled the burner out of her waistband to show me what was up.

"Where the fuck did you get a piece from?"

"I wasn't going to come up out here with a box of damn Girl Scout cookies."

"Girl, give me that before you hurt somebody." Bree hesitantly handed me the burner. I pushed the gun down into the waist of my jeans. *Crazy-ass black women,* I thought.

I drove slowly around the neighborhood until Bree pointed out Katiesha's crib.

"Stop, that's it, that brick house right there with the white swing on the porch." A string of yellow crime tape ran around the perimeter of the house.

"Hold up, let me get somewhere out the way." I parked between some bushes. Nobody would see my whip with how dark it was.

"You got a flashlight?" Bree asked.

The back side of my hand grazed against her knee when I opened the glove box. "It's one somewhere in…hold up." I felt on the floor behind the passenger seat. "Here it is," I said, showing Bree the black heavy-duty flashlight. She grabbed it out of my hand like that shit was the key to the city.

"Let's do this."

After we got out, I locked the doors. Like my ride being locked in that neighborhood mattered. It was a little past three in the morning and other than a few cars whooshing by on one of the main streets, it was quiet as hell. My hand rested on the gun like it was my dick. Bree ducked under the crime scene tape like it wasn't nothing.

"Slow up. You can't be bopping around here like you're at a playground. This ain't Chuck E. Cheese." There was crime scene tape everywhere. Bree stepped up on the porch. She jiggled the handle of the front door, but it was locked. "Come on," I said, "Let's check around back." The back sliding-glass door was locked, too. Any other time, I would have busted it out, but I didn't want to risk bringing attention to ourselves.

"There has to be a window or something open," Bree said. She went around the right side of the house to try one of the windows there. She tried lifting it. "Damn, shit is jammed."

"Here, move," I demanded.

"Be careful." Bree stepped out of the way behind me, flashing the light on my hands. The window gave.

"I'll go in first to check it out."

"Hurry up."

I checked the hallways and kitchen. I saw in the living room where there was all this blood on the sofa, floor, and some on the walls. "Damn, what the hell did they do to her?" The house reeked of death.

"Deanthony, come help me up."

"Oh, my bad."

Bree reached in with her arms through the window. With all her weight, she was heavy as hell. "Hurry up, pull me in."

I worked to pull her big breasts and ass into the window. Bree stumbled in on her knees in the hall as I worked her through.

"Let's get this over with," she said, like this was all my idea. "Let's start in the living room."

"Place is a mess. I doubt we'll find anything in here."

"I've watched enough *First 48* to know that they always leave something behind. Look for something, anything out of the ordinary."

"I'll start in her bedroom," I said.

"Come back out here when you're done."

"Yes, Your Highness."

Pearls and necklaces hung around one of the bedposts of the big king-sized bed that sat against the wall. Posters of Drake, Jay-Z, and Young Jeezy were thumbtacked on the blue-painted walls. There were dirty clothes everywhere. This picture of Katiesha in a bikini with a pink feather boa wrapped around her neck sat in the frame of the dresser mirror. I recognized one of the girls in the picture. Josette from Risqué. The other girls I think I'd seen once or twice at the club. As I walked around, my feet kicked something on the floor. I picked it up and opened it to a page that was bookmarked with a pink Post-It strip. There were a number of things listed:

*Check-into-rehab

*pay-off-debts

*down-payment-on-car

*plane-ticket-to-New York

*presents-for-the-girls

The bottom of the page was torn off after the last thing listed. "Bree, I got something."

"What did you find?" She came into Kateisha's room.

"It looks like some kind of to-do list." I showed it to her.

"She couldn't afford any of this on a stripper salary when she had a thousand-dollar-a-day drug habit."

"The first one says *check into rehab*, so maybe she was going to check herself in to get clean."

"It says 'plane ticket to New York' on here," Bree said.

I was looking around, being nosey, when lights from a car flashed through the bedroom window. Bree and I ducked. A whip pulled into the driveway.

"Who in the hell? That's Tangela's ride," Bree said after peeping out. We sneaked out of the room and hid around the hall. "How the hell does she know Katiesha?"

I fucking knew it. I knew that Tangela had something to do with Katiesha's death. That bitch was trying to do everything she could to keep Bree from coming here. We held still as we heard her pick the lock to the front door. She burned a flashlight through the house. I knew she was up to something. Tangela was feeling between the cushions of the sofa, flipping them over.

"What is she looking for?" Bree whispered over my shoulder.

Tangela took the cushions and threw them across the room. "Fuck!"

"We need to go."

"Fuck that. I want to know what she's doing here."

"We need to go now, come on." I pushed Bree back through the window and I climbed out after her. As we moved to get back to my SUV, a blunt force struck me. The last thing I heard was Bree screaming.

44

BREE

The floor was blurry when I woke up. My throat felt dry and salty. My feet and one of my hands were asleep and my shoulder hurt like hell. It felt like it was broken. There was something holding my wrists together. When I tried to pull at my binds, my skin went with it. My ankles were held together by duct tape. My neck popped when I raised my head up. My sight was coming in clear. Deanthony was sitting quiet next to me, knocked out. I noticed a line of blood that had run down the back of his neck, staining his T-shirt. I could tell he was still alive from his chest constricting from his breathing. It smelled like wet and rot wherever we were.

"D," I called out to him, but he wouldn't open his eyes. "Deanthony, wake up."

"Don't worry about him."

I heard a voice coming from behind one of the cement poles where we were being held, but I couldn't see who it was or where that familiar voice was coming from. "Who is that?" He wouldn't answer but gave this devilish laugh. "Who the fuck is out there?" I hollered. My heart beat like a drum in my chest. This figure slowly started to make his way out of the shadows, into the sliver of light. "Blue?"

"Hey, Hot-Pink."

"What is this?" I asked, working to break free of the duct tape that held my ankles together.

Blue looked sleazy as ever in dark-blue baggy shorts that knocked against his knees and a black wife beater. A thick gold chain with a marijuana leaf charm hung around his sweaty neck. "Hush, girl. I'll be the one askin' the questions," he said. I jerked away as he caressed my cheek. "B, I gotta tell ya, when I saw you at the club the other night, it brought back a whole lotta memories. I remember the first night you went up on stage. I could tell you were scared shitless, but you did a damn thang. You had them fools droolin', eatin' outta ya hands like you were the Pied Piper of black men. Was makin' me money, hand over fist for a long time. Pullin' in, what, a grand, sometimes two, a night?"

"I told you. I'm done with that life. I'm married now."

"Went and married you a doctor, all fancy livin' out there with all them well-to-do white folks?" Blue yanked my head back, fisting a hand full of my hair.

"One thing that hasn't changed about you, Blue."

"And what's that, Hot-Pink?"

"After all these years, your breath still smells like shit." I laughed.

"That's my Bree. Always the comedian, always the funny bitch."

"Invest in some breath mints, nigga."

Before I could take another breath, Blue slapped me hard across the face. The pain was like a thousand and one bumble bees stinging me in the face. I tasted blood pooling in my mouth.

"Fuck you," I said, spitting blood in his face. I felt around with my tongue to see if all my teeth were still attached. They were. Blue licked his lips as blood and spit dripped from the tip of his nose. He wiped me from his face, licking the tips of his fingers like my blood was syrup. "It was you, wasn't it, who killed Katiesha?"

"That lyin' bitch. You know, when Katiesha first came to me, she made a shitload of money. It was nowhere near as good as you, though, baby girl. I told her I was done with her as soon as she started messin' with crack." Blue took the gun Deanthony had in his waistband and started waving it around.

"I knew she was caught up when she started coming to work late, and you know betta than anybody that I can't stand tardy bitches. Kateisha was high all the time, losin' weight and shit, coming to work with sores on her legs, bags and shit under her eyes. The last time I let her go on stage, she fell on her ass. That was the night before you came to see me at the club." Blue straddled me, holding the gun against my face. "I told her to take her ass home, that she didn't have a job until she got herself together. Night before you came was the last time I saw her."

"You're a liar. She was making all that money for you, but when she got messed up, all that stopped, right? So what did you do, come over here, y'all started fighting, you brained her in the head?"

"I got an idea," Blue said.

"There's a first."

"Why don't you leave that bookend nigga and come back to me? All will be forgiven. We can run Risqué together."

"Nigga, you crazy. I would rather eat glass than go back to that shit hole."

"You ain't think it was so bad when yo' ass was on the street, when you didn't have a pot to piss in. Strolled up in my club, lookin' like you weighed about fifteen cents. Now you all high and mighty, walkin' around my club with that nose of yours up in the air."

"Nigga, didn't you get the memo? I *am* better than you. I regret the day I ever met your trifling ass. You ain't shit, and you—"

Blue wrapped his hand around my jaw and squeezed, as if he was trying to stop the insults from tumbling out of my mouth. Deanthony was starting to come to. "You know what, I'm done with you, bitch. I'm sick of your mouth. Maybe this nigga right here will be more cooperative." Blue got up off me.

"Listen to you," I said, "using big words now."

He turned his attention toward Deanthony. "Wake up, pretty boy." Blue slapped Deanthony awake. The bleeding behind Deanthony's head had stopped. I was glad he was alive. It sounded like he was trying to say something. "Rise and shine, hero." Blue snatched the duct tape off Deanthony's mouth. "What's that? Speak up."

"Let her go."

"Why do they always say that shit? You ever notice in movies when the guy is tied up, he always tells the bad guy to let the girl go, like the bad guy actually would?"

"You're fucking crazy."

"This shit here ain't no movie." Blue hauled back and hit Deanthony across the face with the butt of the gun.

"That's enough!" a female voice yelled from the right side of me. "I told you to cut out all that rough shit. I don't want that bastard dead yet." It was Tangela. "Bree, I'm so sorry, girl, about all of this."

"Tangela, what did you do?"

"It all just got out of hand. I didn't plan for it to go down like this."

"What are you talking about?"

"She did it," Deanthony said.

"What?"

"She killed Katiesha."

"Shut the fuck up," Blue warned. He backhanded Deanthony.

"Tangela, what the fuck is he talking about?" I asked.

"It was an accident."

"She was the one who hired Katiesha to fuck Kashawn that night. She wanted to make it look like Kashawn was messing around on you. She figured you would leave if you caught him fucking somebody else," Deanthony said..

"Shut him up," Tangela said. Blue took the roll of tape and went once around Deanthony's head, muffling his mouth.

"What the fuck is he saying?"

"Bitch, do you have any idea how hard it's been to see you walking around here with a man that good on your shoulder? A good man you cheated on, a man you clearly don't deserve."

I couldn't believe this shit.

"He was mine. I saw him first at Roxy's that night."

"Is that what this is about, you holding a five-year grudge because I got Kashawn that night instead of you?"

"He told me he wished he had married me instead of you."

"You're lying."

"Remember what you said to me the day before you took your whorish-ass to Atlantic City? You told me to take care of Kashawn, so I did. He told me that he was embarrassed to be married to a stripper, said he wished he could have married a lady, someone he could respect, a proper doctor's wife and not some trash from the byways of the ghetto."

"All this time, and it was you stabbing me in the back. So you told Katiesha to dope Kashawn up."

"Just enough to put him out, but that bitch ended up putting him in a damn coma."

"Bitch, Kashawn almost died because of you."

"I thank the Lord he didn't. It's been in God's plan all the while for Kashawn and me to be together. You have everything, Bree. You live in a palace, you have cars, a designer wardrobe, and what do you do? You trade in a life any bitch would kill to have for his low-budget thug of a twin brother? What kind of bitch does that?"

"You would be surprised what she's done," Blue said, laughing like a mischievous demon from hell.

"Oh, I doubt that. I've known Bree for a minute. I've learned after all these years not to put anything past this man-stealing bitch."

Hearing all of this, I couldn't help but start laughing.

"What the hell is so funny?" Tangela asked.

"You. I can't believe that you went through all that to get a man who isn't even yours. It's the most pitiful thing I've ever heard," I said.

"That's what someone like me is willing to do for her man, unlike a selfish bitch like you."

"Here's the thing, though. Kashawn isn't your man and he never will be. You know why? Because he loves me."

"Well, once you're out of the picture, baby girl, I will be there to console him during his time of loss and grief. In time, he'll forget that he was ever married to you. We'll get married, I'll move into that mansion of his, and erase any trace of your ass. I'll give him some children. Children you can't give him because you're too busy opening your legs to this piece of shit."

"So why did you kill Katiesha?"

"That crackhead bitch got greedy. I paid her five stacks to help me break you and Kashawn up, to keep her mouth shut about me and what went down. I didn't care what she did with the money. She could have smoked it up on crack, for all I cared, as long as she left town so nothing would come back on me. But no, she got it in her head to blackmail me for more money, saying that she was going to run and tell you everything if I didn't pay her dirty ass another fifteen stacks. I couldn't believe she had the lady-balls to try and shake me down for more cake. When I found out Kashawn was in the hospital from a drug overdose, I knew she had something to do with it."

"How could you do this to me, to Kashawn? You were my best friend. There was nothing I wouldn't have done for you."

"I guess I got tired."

"Tired of what?"

"Tired of seeing you prance around in that nice house, driving a car for every day of the damn week, while I can barely pay my rent."

"You could have said something. I would have helped you."

"Damn, bitch, you still don't get it, do you? I'm not the kind of woman who settles for a piece. I want the whole damn pie with whipped cream on top. I couldn't have done it without your fuck-toy here, who had a hand in helping me carry out *our* plan."

"What?" I said, turning my attention to Deanthony.

"Believe it, Bree. You see what the power of pussy will do to a man. When I convinced him that ending your marriage to Kashawn meant getting you back, he was in this shit to win it. Ain't that right, D?" Tangela ripped the duct tape off his mouth.

"I'ma kill you, you fucking bitch."

"That will be hard for you to do with a broken shoulder."

"What?" Deanthony asked, gasping for breath. When Tangela nodded at Blue, he grabbed a baseball bat that was leaning against the wall of the garage door.

"What are you doing?" I asked.

"Damn, I can't look," Tangela said.

Blue held onto the base of the bat with both hands.

"No, stop! Don't!" I pleaded.

Blue positioned himself, lifted the bat over his head, and took a swing, slamming it into Deanthony's right shoulder.

"AAAAGGGGHHHHHHHH!!!!!"

I had never heard anyone holler in such agonizing pain as Deanthony did. His screams sent my eardrums rattling. I could literally hear the bone in his shoulder shatter. Tangela pushed the tape back over his mouth to drown out his screams.

"That should shut your ass up."

"You bitch! You fucking bitch!" I felt the adhesive of the duct tape starting to wear down from the pulling against the binds.

"I knew he was going to back out of the plan, so I took this to keep him in check." Tangela pulled her iPhone out of the front pocket of her sweatpants. "Now before I show you this, viewer discretion is advised," she joked. Tangela held the phone to my face, showing me a video of Deanthony ass-fucking some man in a motel room. "This is going to give Mama Liz a heart attack when she sees this. I hope so anyway. I sent a copy of the video to her phone an hour ago. It will be a nice surprise to go with her morning coffee."

My wrists were free from the ties of the tape. "So you're scraping the bottom of the barrel, in cahoots with this motherfucker."

"Shut your mouth, bitch," Blue said, behind gritted teeth. One thing Blue was known for was his temper. Back in the day, he damn near beat a pimp to death when the man tried to coax Nakia from under Blue's smelly ass.

"Don't pay any attention to her. She's just trying to get you off your game."

"Tangela will say it was your idea if you get pinched by the cops. I know her. Look what she's done to me and Deanthony." I could tell I was breaking Blue down by pouring the seed of suspicion in his ear like a poisonous elixir.

"Don't listen to her, Blue."

"She'll roll on you if it means she won't get the needle."

Just as Blue came for me, Deanthony tackled him to the floor, knocking the gun out of his hand and sending it skittering across the floor of Katiesha's garage. Before Tangela could react, I lunged at her, punching her in the face until it smudged with blood.

"This is for almost killing Kashawn, and this is for pretending to be my best friend, and, for what it's worth, this is for killing Katiesha, you cold-blooded, murdering bitch." The last punch knocked Tangela unconscious. Just as Blue was about to hit Deanthony, I cold-cocked Blue as hard as I could in the head with the butt of the gun. "Deanthony, are you all right?"

Minutes later, the door of the shack flew open. "Freeze!" a cop yelled. "Ma'am, put down the weapon."

"Don't shoot, that's my wife." Kashawn broke past the cop. I dropped the gun to the floor when he took me into his arms.

"How did you know we were here?" Deanthony asked.

"I heard Bree talking to you on the phone about coming here. I saw her get in your SUV, so I followed y'all and called the police."

"Thank God," I said.

"They have everything Tangela said on tape."

"All this is my fault," said Deanthony. "If I hadn't have gone through with what that crazy bitch was planning, none of this would have happened. It's not worth losing my family over."

Before I could react, Tangela grabbed the gun at my feet and shot Deanthony in the stomach. He collapsed into Kashawn's arms. He held his hand to the growing pool of blood that soaked his shirt. A cop shot Tangela in the leg, sending her crashing to the garage floor.

"Die, motherfucker, die!" She laughed.

"Stay with me," Kashawn pleaded. Deanthony's eyes clamped shut, his body still.

45

KASHAWN

Two Weeks Later

"Hey, you ready to get out of here?"

Deanthony was stuffing shirts and jeans into a small, flower-printed suitcase Ma let me borrow to put his clothes in. "I've *been* ready to go. You know I can't stand hospitals. Where's Ma?"

"At the house, cooking enough food to feed a village."

"Fried chicken?"

"Ham, greens, black-eyed peas, biscuits, and two Dutch apple cheesecakes."

"Damn, here I was getting used to all the weight I was losing, and Ma's going to put it right back on me."

"I'm sure you won't miss the hospital food."

"True. It will be nice to get a decent meal."

"How are we feeling today?" Eboni, the RN, asked, rolling the wheelchair into Deanthony's room.

"Like I just walked off a battlefield, but if I get to take you home with me, I'm sure I will start feeling much better."

"Don't pay any attention to him, Ms. Brooks."

"I haven't yet." Eboni smiled.

"Oh, my brother didn't tell you? I'm allergic to wheelchairs."

"It's hospital procedure. Now sit down."

"I love it when they're feisty." Deanthony sat down in the wheelchair like he was told.

"Remember what Dr. Wilkinson told you about getting plenty of rest. Don't overdo it and don't pull your stitches."

"Yes, Mama," Deanthony teased.

Deanthony didn't speak much as we drove back to the house. "So how are you and Bree doing?" he finally asked.

"We're taking it one day at a time. Things aren't great, but they're good."

"I'm glad, with everything that's happened, y'all have been able to patch things up."

"She wanted to move out, but I recommended we seek counseling instead to help us cope with everything that has gone on to try to get things back on track. Neither one of us is perfect. We all have made mistakes."

"What happened to Tangela?"

"She's laid up with a head wound. The bullet to her leg missed an artery. The police has round-the clock surveillance on her. Next stop: prison."

"I hope they put her ass under the jail," Deanthony said.

"Listen, I was going to wait until after dinner to tell everyone, but Bree and I are going to try and start a family."

Deanthony smiled at the good news. "That's great, man. I say it's about damn time y'all gave me a niece or nephew to spoil."

"Have you decided if you're going to stay here, or make another go at the acting thing in L.A.?"

"I really haven't put much thought into going back to Cali. Right now, I think I'm going to chill in Tallahassee for a while until I decide what to do. I'm done running away. It's time I face my problems head-on."

I could smell the soul food before we even got to the house. Mama didn't even give me a chance to get to the door before she ran out in the driveway, an apron wrapped around her robust waist, her arms outstretched for a hug.

"Hey, Ma."

She wrapped her arms around Deanthony in an embrace that seemed long-awaited. "Thank the good Lord." Ma started crying.

"Come on now. Stop all that crying. This is a time to celebrate."

We all sat down around a table of good-smelling food. I said grace, giving a special blessing to Uncle Ray-Ray and Edrick, the only daddy we knew as far as Deanthony and I were concerned. As the days, weeks, and months came and went, things between Deanthony and I got better. For the first time since Uncle Ray-Ray's passing, we were starting to become a family again.

46

TANGELA

I didn't know what was worse: these damn handcuffs biting into my wrists, or the stench of this cop's bargain-bin cologne. Before a hearing, before being sentenced to death by a jury of my peers, I was going to die by this pig's putrid poodle juice.

"Hey, man, I'm not feeling so good. Can you let a window down?" He kept driving like he either couldn't hear me, or didn't want to. The smell was making my gut turn. "Hey, did you hear me? I need some air back here."

"Shut the fuck up!" he yelled with venom in his tone. He looked at me from the rearview mirror with a grimace of annoyance.

"If I die on your watch, I don't need to tell you whose ass will be in a sling. Come on, sir, please, I need some air."

The cuffs cut into my wrists as he jerked the wheel of the patrol car to the right, pulling off on the side of the road. "I'm about to give your ass something to whine about." He got out, opened the backseat door, grabbed me by the arm and pulled me out like I was a sack of dirty laundry.

"Ow, fuck, that hurts."

"I would be whining too knowing that I was going to spend the rest of my life in prison. If it was up to me, I would round all you niggers up and execute your black asses."

Damn, of all the pigs to end up with, I get some redneck racist motherfucker with a badge and an itchy trigger finger for black people.

"Better yet." He took out his gun and pointed it against my left temple. "I can save the court and the hardworking taxpayers' money, and blow your nigger bitch brains out right here. Bury you in these woods like a dead dog."

My heart was racing like a greyhound after a rabbit knowing that I was about to die by the hands of this Nazi bigot fuck. I had to think of something quick before he pulled the trigger.

"Please don't, I'm sorry." He relaxed the barrel of his gun away from my head. "I'm sorry for insulting you." I made out his name on the piece of rectangular chrome that was pinned on the left side of his chest. *Ofc. Dillon Conner.* "Please let me make it up to you."

"And just what do you have in mind?"

Damn, his breath stank. Like he had drunk a shit and onions milkshake.

"I'm sure we can think of something."

He ran the nose of the gun along my chest, between my breasts. Men and their predictabilities. Forever letting their dicks do the thinking. "So um…is it true what they say about black bitches: blacker the berry, sweeter the juice?" He smiled, exposing a set of butter-yellow teeth.

"Take off these cuffs and you can taste just how sweet my juice really is, baby."

Pig Cop looked up and down the long stretch of road that was lit by the streetlights above us. "Let's go, but if you try anything, I will end your ass right here, and don't think I won't shoot a woman." He took a set of keys from his belt, turned me around and undid the cuffs. The feeling was already starting to rush back to my fingers. With the help of his flashlight, he led the way along a graveled, narrow trail. "It's been a long time since I got some good head. Betcha those juicy lips of yours are gonna feel good around my dick. Bitch, I'm gonna skull-fuck you so hard, your mama's gonna feel it."

The thought of sucking this hick's dick made me sick to my

stomach, but with the odds stacked against me, I had to do what he wanted. Had I known that I would be walking through the boonies in heels, I would have changed into a pair of raggedy-ass sneaks. But then again, I had no plan to get arrested for murder. "Right here is good. This is deep enough," Officer Shit Breath said. He pulled me onto my knees. He towered over me like a giant. He undid the pants of his uniform and took out his dick. To my surprise, it was smaller than what a lady like me was used to. *I'd had cocktail shrimp in my mouth bigger than this*, I thought. "You like that, bitch?"

My first instinct was to laugh, but I held strong. "Damn, baby, it's big."

"Think you can handle it?" he asked.

Sure, if it doesn't take a magnifying glass to find that circus peanut between your legs. Officer Puny Peter stood with his hands on his waist, anxiously waiting to get his knob polished. When I drew in closer about to do the deed, the odor of sweat made my nose twitch in disgust. Not only was his dick small, but it wasn't clean, either. I ran my hands up alongside his legs. "It's all yours, baby," he said. I felt the dense steel of Itty-Bitty Dicky's gun that rested idle in his holster. Just as I was about to put him in my mouth, I went for his piece. Before Shit Breath could react, I had it cocked and pulled the trigger. The sound from the shot echoed through the air. I got off my knees, holding the gun on him. He looked at me with a wide-eyed disbelief that a nigger bitch had gotten over on him. A thick stream of red flowed from his mouth, down the side of his face; the cold earth that was as hard as my heart, drank him in. I unloaded one more shot into him. The last one in his dome. I could have written a book on the shit I hated. Cops and bigots were at the top of my list. I tossed the gun into the bushes before making my way toward the opposite side of wherever the hell I was ready to begin anew.

ABOUT THE AUTHOR

Shane Allison is a Florida native, noted poet and writer. His poems and stories have graced the pages of over a dozen anthologies, and online and literary magazines. When he's not hard at work writing short stories, he's busy working on new novels and collections of poetry.